MW00723743

BISHOP

By Victoria Slatton

Published by:
Light Switch Press
PO Box 272847
Fort Collins, CO 80527

Copyright © 2017

ISBN: 978-1-944255-73-2

Printed in the United States of America

No part of this publication may be reproduced, stored in a retrieval system, or transmitted in any form or by any means – electronic, mechanical, digital photocopy, recording, or any other without the prior permission of the author.

All rights reserved solely by the author. The author guarantees all contents are original and do not infringe upon the legal rights of any other person or work. The views expressed in this book are not necessarily those of the publisher.

For Monte Slatton

"I am hopeful that others who have suffered sexual harassment will not become discouraged by my experience, but instead will find the strength to speak out about this serious problem."

-Anita Hill

May 20, 2016
Julia

To an outsider, the funeral probably would have felt thoroughly conventional, but the event was plagued with a rare balance of anguish and reprieve. The bulk of those in attendance were naive to these dark undertones and merely grappled with the inevitable shock that follows an abrupt departure. However, for the few who appreciated the truth behind the otherwise beloved deceased, bitterness haunted every sweet sentiment expressed about his passing. They carefully crafted the mask of a mourner, but underneath the shallow veneer laid a sense of comfort lingering through the cracks of heartbreak.

Naturally, no one openly expressed this emotional contradiction, but the feeling hung in the air, creating a strange tension for those who understood and internally acknowledged the awkward presence. When the guests spoke of his grand achievements and kind demeanor, those who knew the truth about his character allowed their eye-contact to linger, scanning their companions' face for any small hint of this forbidden knowledge.

Even a man of poor reputation is rarely criticized in death, as recognizing fault in the deceased is a notoriously distasteful taboo. If such shortcomings are acknowledged, they are generally followed with compelled justifications for such weaknesses or praise for his superior qualities which served to righteously mitigate any and all of these said faults. When a man is murdered, any sort of gentle criticism that would have otherwise been tolerable at such a funeral becomes altogether forbidden, as every guest is secretly searching for a small hint of guilt in the words of their fellow participants.

So like every funeral of every murder victim who came before Anthony Bishop, each attendee stood around his grave, playing their role, creating a perfect facade so that the mourners and truth-knowers became altogether indistinguishable. Julia recognized these expectations and discreetly concentrated on contorting her face so that it matched the surrounding grievers. After a year of deception, this proved far easier than she had anticipated before arriving. She suspected that she was not the only one relieved by his passing, and couldn't help but wonder how many others who stood beside her had also fallen victim to his twisted set of manipulations.

Although it had been a week since his death, it wasn't until an hour before his funeral that she had finally worked up the nerve to read his excessively long-winded obituary. As she stood around his grave, consciously mirroring the faces of his genuine mourners, the words still echoed in her head, lingering like an unshakeable nightmare in the brief moments after waking.

...He dedicated his life to civil rights advocacy and has been recognized as one of the most influential experts in his field. Every year he accepted anywhere from 10-15 pro-bono cases, including the infamous "Maryland v. Garcia" which was argued in front of the Supreme Court. The decision led to a drastic change in human trafficking laws, and most attribute his fame in the legal field to the outcome of the case. Those who knew him well described him as a brilliant scholar, a passionate advocate, and a selfless human being with an unyielding commitment towards law and justice. However, his true passion and greatest personal accomplishment came from his time as an educator at Brooktown Law School, where he served as a tenured professor for over 15 years...

This aggrandized depiction had thrown her into a blind fit of pure hostility. Instead of trying to half-heartedly stomach the remainder of the article, she had callously ripped the paper into tiny pieces before thrusting it into the garbage and spitting on the remains. While the obituary was admittedly true on a purely technical level, she had never read such an inaccurate reminiscence. Now it felt so absolute and imperishable.

Anthony Bishop had ruined her life, well almost anyway. As the timeline of their tragedy struck her in a flash, once again she scanned the circle around his grave and wondered how many others also benefitted from his demise. She had fantasized about his death on countless occasions, but watching it at last materialize failed to bring her the well-earned relief she had so longed to indulge in upon hearing of his passing. Instead, she only felt a deep animosity in her inability to rid his memory of public righteousness. Julia turned to leave, continuing her conscious display of outward grief as she made her way back to the parking lot on the opposite end of the graveyard. She had tears in her eyes because they were expected, but they rolled down her cheeks with hollow indifference.

The words of his obituary were still plaguing her senses with deep feelings of injustice when she was abruptly struck by the unbearable realization that Anthony Bishop would have, in fact, loved the twisted dynamic of his own funeral. She could almost feel his continued satisfaction seething through his now lifeless body. How thrilled he would have been to see how even in the throws of his own death, he had somehow managed to maintain control over everyone he had faced in life. Those who knew the truth wouldn't dare speak a word about his faults, and the rest were still entirely star-struck by his alleged life of virtue and celebrated achievements. His passing, which should have released them all from his influence, only served to tighten his hold. They were still all playing his game, and even now she felt the unbreakable force of his authority.

For the first time since his death, she began to cry with undeniable sincerely.

May 13, 2016
Julia

Amidst the final hours of Anthony Bishop's bare existence, Julia observed Daniel with a comforting sense of familiarity as he meticulously fidgeted with the corners of his dark-rimmed glasses. She graciously sanctioned the act as one of the many nervous quirks he had habitually adopted during the ongoing turmoil of law school. The couple stared at each other with agonizing tension as they hastily ordered a five-course dinner and waited for their lavish meal with a shared sense of deep-seated misery. The dread was so enveloping that neither party dared even acknowledge the imposing New York City skyline glowing in the background of what should have been a conventionally flawless scene of envied romance. She entertained a gnawing desire to reach for his hand or rub his neck, any soothing gesture that could possibly alleviate a fraction of his nerves, but her own shameful contrition stopped her from moving to address his blatant discomposure.

"You don't have to do this," she anxiously whispered with forced sincerity. She wasn't even certain of her own intentions in offering him a belated escape, but the feeble gesture, though empty of substance, delivered a modest taste of selfish relief.

"Why else would we come to New York? The entire plan was devised around this trip," he shrugged in a half-hearted effort to dismiss her hesitations. For a brief second, a sign of annoyance flashed across his face as he lowered his gaze to his half-eaten salad.

"To see the city? To take a needed post-graduation vacation? To spend time together?" She prodded, all the while knowing that these overdue suggestions were futile in the face of their inevitable course. Enough factors of their scheme had already been set in motion, and she could feel the components of their plan falling into place like a row of heavy dominos. The window for a graceful retreat had evidently passed long ago.

He nodded as an exhausted, warm smile finally stretched across his handsome face, "I want to do this, Julia."

"Do you really? I mean, I know we talked about it a little, but that was before... well all of this happened. It's ok if we wait before we make it... real. Admittedly it's not the best time."

"I don't want to wait, Julia. How many couples could have survived what we've been through this year? Despite everything, I still love you and want to be with you. Do you know how rare it is to find something that strong?" As he unearthed each justification with a swift nod, his voice, though still weary, seemed to be picking up pieces of his old humble confidence. "There's only one way to go from here, right? Things have to get better."

"Knock on wood." Julia let out a nervous laugh as she lightly pounded her fists on the table. She looked down at the uneaten pasta in front of her and half-mindedly began to twirl it around her plate with her heavy fork. She had barely eaten for days, and the thick sauce drenching the meal suddenly looked too rich, unappetizing.

Daniel shook his head. "I don't need luck. I've made my decision."

She breathed a prolonged sigh of relief and finally met his smile with a humble lift of her head. "For the record, Daniel, you've gone above and beyond what any boyfriend could possibly be expected to do."

He closed his eyes with a satisfied grin and gave a small shrug of his shoulders. "I don't think you fully understand how much I love you. You know I would do anything for you, Julia."

"Including this though? I'm sorry to be this nervous, but I'm having doubts. I know what needs to happen, but I just don't want to force you into it. How do you feel?"

"Really lucky," he said with genuine reassurance. Underneath his nerves was an earnest layer of confidence she felt had been buried in him for months now. It was oddly refreshing to watch his old mannerisms resurface, especially in the face of such dreadful circumstances.

"So… it's real for you then?" She asked with shaky apprehension.

"If it is for you."

"Yes," she answered without pause. "I want this to be real. After this whole thing is over, I want to marry you."

"Well in that case, I'm going to do it," he settled with a small wave of his hand.

"I love you, Daniel."

"I love you too."

With one swift breath and a nervous quiver, he promptly stood and meekly began to clink his empty wine glass with a fork. She felt a fresh wave of guilt wash over her as she watched his chest break out into small convulsions, knowing his ideal proposal would be one without a packed audience and such dire time-constraints. One-by-one the patrons of the opulent restaurant grew silent and turned to face the couple's table with looks of excited curiosity and optimism. Julia watched Daniel's feeble poise grow weak at the overwhelming flood of attention. Even after three years at a rigorous law school with countless hours of forced public speaking, Daniel detested the burden of addressing a crowded room.

"I just want to say," Daniel finally rattled on with an exaggerated level of certainty, "that three years ago I met the most incredible woman in the world. I can't imagine my life without her. We've been through more hardships in these past three years than most people go through in an entire lifetime, but she's handled every struggle with incredible strength and unyielding goodness."

He wiped his soaked forehead with the back of his sleeve before slowly turning towards her, lowering himself onto one knee, and reaching for a small ring nestled in the pocket of his dad's old suit. "Julia," he spoke so quietly now that the she could almost feel the rest of the room lean forward with a new heightened level of anticipation, "I have something to ask you. It's a question I knew I would ask since the first moment I met you. Please, will you marry me?" She wiped tears from her eyes and nodded her head with effortless enthusiasm. A candid smile stretched across her face as she answered with a booming, "Yes! Of course I will!" The restaurant exploded into applause as the young couple melted into a tight embrace before turning to express their gratitude to their newly invested audience.

"So you promise you're not just acting?" Daniel whispered as he swung her around in a display of elation which suddenly felt strangely calculated and stiff. His physical motions were robotic and rehearsed, but a sincere excitement still radiated through his awkwardness in a way that only Julia could subtly grasp.

"No Daniel," she cried softly, wiping her tears with a fresh napkin. "I'm not just acting. I love you so much."

"I love you too. You have no idea how happy I am."

He reached for her again, tightly enveloping her into a new embrace that almost felt distant and dolefully novel. It had been months since he had held her, truly held her like this, the way he used to hold her so naturally before Anthony Bishop had ruined their lives.

As a new waiter approached their table with a fresh round of complimentary champagne, Julia felt herself snap back into the reality of the moment and remember the urgency of their underlying task. "Will you take a picture of us?" she asked with such unexpected force that the young waiter seemed startled for a half second before nodding with a trained smile as he reached for her phone. Without hesitation, he energetically began snapping a number of photos, zooming the lense tightly onto the faces of the newly engaged couple as they admired her modest ring. "Make sure you get the city in the background," Julia commanded with a voice that rang far harsher than she intended.

"You should go ahead and post it on Facebook," Daniel said as he let out a nervous laugh, trying to mask a small hint of panic that was uncontrollably rising in his chest. "I can honestly say that I have never been so eager to document a moment."

"Done," Julia said, as she clicked off her phone and flicked it into her large, leather bag.

"How many pictures did you post today?" Daniel whispered.

"About ten… I think that's enough. Do *you* think that's enough?"

"Yeah I think that's plenty," he agreed with a swift nod, "but now it's time to go."

"Back to D.C. already?"

"Yep, you wouldn't want to miss the surprise engagement party I'm throwing you," Daniel winked as he signed the check and began gathering their things to leave.

"Oh no," she groaned with obvious sarcasm, "now you've ruined the surprise."

"No one will suspect. You're a good actress… you're a good liar."

July 1, 1991
Kaitlyn

"We find the defendant not guilty," a faceless juror announced with an air of striking confidence. The words struck Kaitlyn Tryst like a heavy bullet as the courtroom erupted into uncontrollable chaos. She didn't move, frozen in her own trepidation, barely able to breathe as her conscience suddenly collapsed into a constricting sensation of staggering remorse. *They found him not guilty,* the sinister realization echoed again in her head, *they just found our client not guilty.*

She was sick with painful disbelief as her eyes swept across the loaded room in a panic before settling on the panel of gleeful jurors in the corner. She glared at them through her dismay, allowing her head to spin with raw rage at their innocent expressions of staunchly misplaced self-assurance. If anyone on the panel noticed her heated stare, they paid no mind as they smiled at one another, obviously confident in their misguided decision and possibly even a little pleased by the courtroom's polarizing response.

John Rowland, the newly exonerated defendant, skipped with excitement as he hurdled across the floor towards his family before sweeping his wife into a tender embrace. After their affection had subsided, he turned back towards his team of lawyers and reached to shake the hand of David Roth, the head attorney in his defense who happened to be Kaitlyn's beloved superior. Mr. Roth took Rowland's hand without a flinch of guilt and let a rewarding smile stretch across his face. Both men seemed saturated with heavy relief, the sight of which struck Kaitlyn with a new wave of revulsion as she began to sink into a state of dizzy incomprehension. For a moment she thought Rowland might turn and express his gratitude towards her directly, but to Kaitlyn's relief he was immediately distracted by a reporter, who had somehow made her way into the courtroom, calling his name for an interview.

Rowland was by no means innocent, a fact which Kait had casually assumed from the beginning of his representation. Oddly enough he had never actually admitted his guilt, not even to his team of lawyers who had obviously been sworn to a state of unbreakable confidentiality, but his culpability was clear from the details of the crime. The verdict created a new, unhinged reality for Kait, an intolerable truth. She had helped a guilty man escape the consequences of premeditated murder, and now he would be released back into society without serving a single night of his deserved sentence. She sat in silence, letting this new truth sink in, refusing to show any external hint of satisfaction at Rowland's favorable verdict. The courtroom was still in such chaos that no one seemed to notice as she leaned back to sulk in her uncomfortable padded chair, resting her hands on the smooth bench as she fought back tears.

She met Rowland only two years ago after joining the firm. That was back when she was fresh out of law school and somewhat doe-eyed in her infatuation with the unimpeachable justice of the legal system. To her own surprise, she had inexplicably grown to respect him as a client, despite her efforts to keep him at arm's length. It was hard for her to accept that he was, in fact, a rather charismatic and appealing person, even with the gruesome allegations he had hired her firm to defend. He admittedly wasn't the callous monster one would expect from a man charged with first degree murder, but rather behaved with an odd sophistication Kaitlyn found inexplicably endearing.

At some point during his representation, she had apprehensively acknowledged to herself that her and Rowland had grown to be friends, or had at least found some tangled version of friendship amidst the backdrop of his trial. She told herself it was inevitable and natural to develop a bond with someone she had spent so much time with, and justified their friendly connection by reminding herself that the infallible justice system would eventually run its natural course. Their relationship had therefore formed under the premise that he would be going to prison for the majority of his remaining life. She had never imagined an outcome where he would escape from his charges.

Her role was supposed to be that of an obligatory defender, not an active player in facilitating a devastatingly gross injustice.

"Are you ok, Kaitlyn?" Mr. Roth asked with concern as some of the surrounding commotion slowly began to taper off and disperse.

"I think I need to get out of here," she responded blankly, fanning her face with a loose sheet of paper left behind from the trial. Her sudden inability to compartmentalize her conspicuous distaste for the verdict startled both Roth and Kaitlyn alike. She was notoriously the most steadily professional member of their team and rarely showed emotion out of turn.

"Let's go get a drink," he firmly suggested as he gathered her things and started ushering her towards the private side door of the courtroom.

"You have to answer press questions... you have to walk Rowland out."

"I hate the press," he replied with a tiny snort and brief shake of his head. "Nick can take care of it," he settled as he glanced towards his other partner. Nick nodded back with immediate understanding and promptly got up to follow Rowland out of the room.

She realized Roth probably didn't want others to see her problematic reaction. It wouldn't exactly be appropriate if the press caught a glimpse of Rowland's lawyer engaged in a full-blown meltdown over the successful outcome of his case. With this thought, she consciously assembled her remaining nerve and stood with a single, sharp breath of air. She held out a shaky hand and let Roth guide her out the courtroom. Despite her best judgement, she hastily allowed herself one final look at Rowland before they scuffled out the door. She was met with a shameless smile, one that should never have been worn by a guilty man.

Roth and Kaitlyn rarely entertained extended periods of awkward silences, but their dialogue was inherently sparse as he briskly led Kaitlyn to a considerably desolate and grimy bar several blocks south of the courthouse. Visiting such an establishment was a rarity for Roth who customarily celebrated a major victory like this by entertaining his partners among the comforts of a five-star restaurant in downtown D.C. If the victory was particularly memorable, sometimes he would invite the entire legal team for a celebratory toast of his favorite rare scotch on the roof of their office. Kaitlyn had been invited several times in the past, even when their win failed to meet the standards one would generally consider "particularly memorable," but Roth respectfully understood that every case Kaitlyn worked on was somehow met with an instantaneous heightened significance. He had never had an employee who was so profoundly committed to each detail of her taxing career.

It took Kait a moment to catch her bearings as she surveyed the rundown tables, busted overhead lighting, and few patrons. The scene felt raw and almost dreamlike in conjunction with her current emotional state. After associating Roth with the sophistication of swanky city culture, a bar like this seemed inherently undignified for a man of his statute and complexities. Kaitlyn's face must have implicated her own surprise at this choice, as he apologetically touched her shoulder and gently explained that they were less likely to run into any press or opposing counsel if they chose a lesser known establishment.

Kaitlyn barely listened as she staggered to her seat and stared miserably at the beer Roth swiftly bought and placed in front of her with an awkward half-smile. She worried her pressing guilt would force her to throw it back up, but she nonetheless painfully took a sip in an attempt to appease him. He was sitting across the dark table, eying her with an obvious look of heightened concern. She knew her meltdown had embarrassed him and shame was now burrowing into her conscience, displacing some of the immediate guilt from the trial.

By most accounts, this should have been an immensely gratifying experience. All of her hard work over the past two years had finally been rewarded, and she had won the first major case she had been assigned to at the firm. Not to mention her client, who had paid their firm handsomely for his representation, had won an impossibly difficult case, one that most lawyers would have called ludicrous to even entertain. Regardless, she looked at Mr. Roth, her superior and mentor, in hopeless despondency as she gulped down another difficult sip of beer.

"I don't feel good about this," she finally mumbled through her defeated state.

"I noticed," Roth nodded with an ironic, small chuckle. He seemed calmer today, a sharp deviation from his usual stern demeanor. "It was an unusual case Kaitlyn, I can tell you that much. I'm rarely surprised by verdicts."

"He's guilty."

"Well, to be fair I'm not sure I've ever had an innocent client," he smiled again half-heartedly as he stroked the ends of his tangled beard.

"Yes but... what he did was so much worse than most! He planned someone's death and actually followed through with it!"

"Yes, that is in fact the definition of premeditated murder."

"That's not funny. He's twisted. I've never actually felt guilty for any of this before today, but how can I live with myself? How can you live with yourself? We're responsible for putting a murderer back on the streets."

"Is it really that twisted?" Roth asked thoughtfully as he stroked his beard again in contemplation. He lifted his gaze over her head and nodded discreetly as if he was reflecting on a particularly challenging riddle. "I'm not trying to excuse what he did, but I do see why someone in his position would want Jansen dead."

Three years ago, John Rowland's home had been broken into by Gregory Jansen, a notable psychopath with a long and strenuous history of brutally violent crimes. The police had named him as a suspect in a number of break-ins and several rapes, but were never able to collect enough evidence to bring him to trial.

Michelle Rowland, John Rowland's wife, had walked in on Jansen during an attempted burglary of their home. The details of what exactly ensued remain unclear, but by Rowland's account, he came home to find his wife lying on their kitchen floor, brutally beaten and obviously raped. She spent five miserable weeks in intensive care and almost died from blunt force trauma. The police found Jansen within days of the report, and charged him with ten different counts of violent crimes, enough to put him away for the remainder of his life. They had no physical evidence to tie him to the scene, but unlike in his previous attacks, they finally had an eye-witness to corroborate his pattern of behavior. They took him into custody and waited months for Michelle Rowland to recover to the point that she could identify her attacker.

Unfortunately for everyone, but most of all Rowland, Michelle never fully recovered. With the combination of severe PTSD and brain damage caused by Jansen's attack, she sharply disconnected from most tangible facets of reality. In a lineup, she picked out three different men, none of whom even remotely resembled the true perpetrator. In light of her unstable testimony and inability to properly identify her attacker, the prosecutor assigned to the case determined that she was an unreliable witness, once again making it impossible to tie Jansen to the crime. Ultimately the case was thrown out due to lack of evidence. Two months after his acquittal, Gregory Jansen was found dead.

Naturally, the police immediately suspected John Rowland, the defiant husband who had heroically defended his debilitated wife by murdering her attacker for revenge. They arrested him within days of finding Jansen's body, spurring a wild press hunt for details of the provocative story of vigilante justice with scorned acts of love by the victim's heroic husband.

When Rowland came to Roth's firm and asked for representation, all of the lawyers on staff agreed that accepting the case was the right thing to do, even though they knew a favorable outcome would ultimately prove to be a lost cause. No jury would ever find him innocent, but they could at least argue down some of the charges and provide him with a decent defense. Not once did a single lawyer on the team even entertain the idea of their client walking free.

"I could never kill someone," Kaitlyn said firmly, "even if it was someone like Jansen. He's scum but he's still a human being."

"I think I could," Roth responded casually, carefully watching her reaction as she took another sip of beer.

"You have to be fucking kidding me. I don't believe you... especially not like that."

"What do you mean? By poison? I would argue that's a less painful death than the goodbye most of us will face. From that standpoint, Rowland might have done Jansen a favor."

"That's beside the point. I mean... to plan it out like that. He had so many chances to change his mind."

"That's arguably indicative of how important it was to him. You almost have to admire him for it. He got away with murder. That's a feat some of the most brilliant criminal minds in history haven't been able to pull off. He's an intelligent man. If his motive wasn't so clear, he probably wouldn't have even been indicted."

"That's a sick thing to say," Kaitlyn spat in disbelief. "I can't believe you're justifying this! The man is guilty of murder and now he's free to go. He could kill again."

"Well the victim was guilty of rape and assault, and he would have been free to go if not for Rowland. Jansen could have raped and beaten another woman by now."

"We didn't defend Jansen. We wouldn't have defended Jansen. Surely you see why this is not ok. There have to be some moral absolutes. I just don't see anyway to justify this."

Roth dropped his gaze and let out a long sigh, rubbing the temples of his forehead. "I don't know how to respond to that. I understand why you're upset, but I can also see a situation where I might do the same. I don't know, maybe this job has made me hard. I think this work has that effect on people. Most lawyers I know are pretty ambivalent about the criminals they defend. You'll get there eventually."

"No," Kaitlyn shook her head, "I will never let myself get to that point. You can call me naive and try to condescend your way into my conscience, but I will never allow myself to accept this kind of behavior... or defend it."

Roth looked out the window with a disappointed glance, suddenly feeling the need to justify his line of work. Finally he conceded with a small nod for her to continue.

"I have to get out," she said at last.

He demeanor faltered as his ego felt suddenly pierced by her rejection. "I don't think I've ever seen you this upset. What are you saying, Kaitlyn?"

"I think you already know I have to quit."

"Yes, I was afraid of that," he sighed and hung his head. "I was just hoping you would find a way to stay. Where will you go?"

"Brooktown," she responded. He lifted his eyebrows with a sudden burning interest, and she could immediately see he was impressed, another rarity for Roth's persona. Brooktown was one of the best law schools in the country and teaching positions at the institution were highly coveted and immensely competitive to obtain.

"I'm impressed... not that you're undeserving, but how?"

"My best friend from law school worked for Anthony Bishop. He got me an interview. I wasn't really taking it seriously, but after today I think this is the right decision."

"Oh yes, I forgot Bishop teaches there now. I've always wanted to meet him. I hear he's one of the most brilliant legal minds of our time." Roth smiled and gave a small nod, "Will you miss the firm at all?"

Kaitlyn shook her head. "Honestly no, but I will miss working for you and I have enjoyed my time here. I'm very grateful for all that you did. You really took a chance on me and I-"

He held up his hand to cut her off. "You don't have to explain Kait. You don't owe me anything. This job is not for everyone. I'm just sad because I'm losing a good employee, that's all. You're quite brilliant."

Despite her best efforts, she blushed at the compliment and allowed herself to enjoy a modest burst of pride. "It's weird to hear an endorsement like that from you."

He sighed. "I know I can be tough on you all, but I've always found that pushing people requires a bit of tough love," he responded sheepishly. "I will miss you Kaitlyn, I really will. Just know if you ever need anything, I'm here."

March 9, 2009
Gabriella

While she was trekking through the harsh Mexican countryside, Gabriella had foolishly envisioned the border as an unforgiving war zone. She had sulked in her own anxiety throughout her travels with the anticipation that their crossing would involve a series of intricate obstacles around watchtowers, guard dogs, and men with rifles waiting to strike intruders like herself. Instead, when they arrived at the humble boundary that separated the United States from Mexico, they were met with a rather anticlimactic scene of vast desolation. The landscape was undisturbed, almost peaceful, amidst an unbounded desert backdrop that closely reminded her of home.

The only barrier to freedom was a single concrete wall on the other side of a fiercely winding river. She had spent twelve days and six thousand dollars at the chance to make the strenuous trip from Guatemala to Mexico, making their arrival feel surreal as she gaped at the emblematic wall ahead. She let herself enjoy a brief sigh of relief, wiping tears from her eyes as she admired the wild scenery. It was simple, but it was America. Although she was still remarkably intimidated at the thought of entering the States, for the first time since leaving home she felt a renewed sense of confidence in her brash decision to run away.

"Do you see that tiny 'X' on the wall?" Samuel asked, pointing towards a small crack in the concrete marked with a faded squiggle of black spray paint. He was casually smoking a cigarette, as he had often done throughout their trip, and if he had any hint of nervousness about crossing the border, it was impossible to detect through his cool demeanor. He rarely spoke to the girls he was transporting, and when he did it was usually to say something cruel or needlessly degrading. Gabriella had grown to hate his callous disposition, but she still followed him with blind optimism in hopes of finally obtaining her coveted freedom.

"I think so," she replied timidly as she narrowed her eyes to focus on the small, discolored marking.

"Underneath that 'X' is a tunnel that leads to the other side of the wall. Sometimes guards patrol a long way past the border, so we'll have to walk three miles back to the main road once we cross over. That's where we'll find my guy with a truck."

"Ok," she nodded, mimicking his composure. She clenched her jaw and gave her head a little shake in an attempt to collect her nerves. Regardless, her legs continued to rattle uncontrollably beneath her and she could almost hear the increased speed of her own heartbeat.

"We can't all five go together," he continued absentmindedly, "that many people will be too easy to spot. I'll go first and the rest of you follow one by one. Be sure to keep at least ten yards in between each other at all times. Try and stay low in the brush."

"Are they watching us?" Gabriella shuddered with a paranoid glance over her shoulder. Suddenly the openness of her surroundings felt more vulnerable than serene.

"It's hard to tell, but probably not. They rarely patrol this far off the main road," he answered with a short mumble. She could sense him quickly losing his patience, but as she stared at the savage water she couldn't help but entertain a compulsion to delay their departure for just a few moments longer.

"That river looks deep."

"It's not."

"It looks strong."

"It is. Keep your footing and be careful not to fall. If you do, the current will drag you away. If you hit the rapids about half a mile down the way, you're dead."

Gabriella meekly peered back at the other three girls in their ragged convoy and conjured her face into a nervous smile. They were all much younger than she and obviously rattled at the sight of the gushing water ahead. She watched their pale faces stricken with unhinged fear as they gaped at the trial they would soon face, and reminded herself that she had to keep her composure or none of the party would make it over alive. Therefore, lacking any viable alternative or comforting solution, Gabriella took a deep breath and nodded back at Samuel. "Ok, go ahead. We'll follow like you say."

Until she ran away, Gabriella had spent the majority of her life with her paternal grandparents and uncle in the outskirts of Chinautla. Before that, she had a few tattered memories of living with her father in the slums of Guatemala City until he was abruptly sent to prison when she was five. Most of the impressions she had from the time with her father felt too distant and dreamlike to distinguish true memories from the comforting fantasies she told herself on some of the most unbearable days with her grandmother. In spite of herself, she childishly invented a world where he would serve his time and heroically rescue her from the habitual abuse.

Once, when she was feeling particularly daring, she shyly asked her uncle if she could visit her father in prison. He laughed at her request with a dismissive wave of his chubby hand and answered, "No one in this family is going to visit a dirty mara leader." His sharp response struck her with a bitter sense of heartache and guilt, confirming her worst suspicions that her father was not only in a gang, but one of the dreaded branch leaders who notoriously terrorized the most vulnerable poor souls in their neighborhood. After this disheartening realization, she consciously suppressed any further curiosities about his affairs. A life without a father was preferable to a relationship with a shameful mara leader.

Oddly enough, her mother's past had never exactly been a mystery to Gabriella as her abuela callously indulged everyday in reminding Gabriella that her mother had been a dirty whore, a disgraceful slut from the dirtiest slum of the city. "You're a filthy woman, just like your mother," her abuela would customarily yell with a hint of satisfaction seeping through her heartless accusations. "She should have taken you with her when she ran away, but just like a whore she left her child for another to raise."

"Where did she go?" Gabriella once prodded, desperately longing for any modest crumb of information, no matter how appalling the truth. Though she knew her father rarely spoke of her mother, one of his many taboo subjects, she had an obscure memory of him mentioning in passing that she had fled to America after Gabriella's birth. In a strained recall of her past, plagued by years of biased reconstruction, she could vaguely make out an image of him describing her trip to America with a hopeless sense of longing percolating through his tone. Naturally, when she pressed for more information he immediately shut down, returning to his usual quiet state of disinterest. However, the ordeal was so admittedly dim in her memory that she could have imagined the entire scene altogether.

"How should I know where she went?" Her abuela spat. "She didn't want you because you're a useless piece of trash just like her. You share her ungodly troll face and her pathetic excuse for work-ethic. That's why she was too lazy for any job apart from whoring." Gabriella's blood boiled at these accusations, but she stubbornly held her tongue, knowing that no argument was worth the inevitable beating she would suffer if she dared to dispute these allegations, even if she suspected an inherent bias in her grandmother's retelling of events.

After her father vanished into the harsh, unorganized depths of the Guatemalan prison system, her grandparents were flagrantly upfront in expressing their disinterest of taking her in. Although they eventually agreed that they had no choice but to take on the heavy burden her parents had so irresponsibly left for them to carry, they made it clear that her room and board would come with an unforgiving weight of responsibilities. From the moment she arrived, she worked all day for her family, cooking, cleaning, and tending to the family store. None of her work was ever acknowledged, and if she dared to ask for a break, her abuela would promptly beat her with a long piece of cord or plastic until she could barely stand. Although she was rarely physically harmed by her grandfather or uncle, they remained utterly indifferent to these blatantly abhorrent punishments and turned a blind-eye to any fresh bruises and scars.

There were a number of memorably harsh disciplines throughout her childhood, but the most unforgettable and lowest day came when she casually went to fetch water from the spigot in their backyard, a mindless chore she had easily completed hundreds of times. In a sudden burst of unprecedented mindless and clumsy delivery, she stumbled on the uneven steps of the doorway and watched in pure horror as the pail she was carrying tilted to the side, allowing a portion of its contents to spill onto the kitchen floor. Gabriella immediately turned to her grandmother with a desperate plea for mercy, and watched her abuela's face grow red with fury as she spat on the ground in disgust and started towards Gabriella in a fit of obvious rage.

Ignoring Gabriella's cries for help and pathetic whimpers, her grandmother grabbed the pail from Gabriella's hands and dragged her outside, cursing God for plaguing her such an ungrateful and worthless devil of a grandchild. She shook with anger as she poured the remaining water on Gabriella's head, and turned to grab the jumper cables attached to their family's beat up car in the driveway. The last thing Gabriella remembered was the screeching sound of her own pitiful voice as she cried over and over again, "Please, I'm sorry! Please, don't!" Her grandmother, unmoved by and uncaring of Gabriella's pleas, thrusted the wires towards her and laughed as unbearable electric currents shot through Gabriella's powerless body.

She sank to her knees as her jaw clenched tight and her body started to convulse with piercing shock and pain. Her grandmother let her go on like this for a few seconds, laughing at her spasms with a wicked turn of her head before she pulled the wires back and allowed Gabriella to go limp and fall to the ground. As Gabriella crawled from the puddle of water and mud, shaking and gasping for air, her grandmother looked down at her with a heartless smile. "That's what happens when you waste good water, you wretched girl."

Gabriella lived with five cousins, none of whom were subjected to the same tortures. Her grandparents and uncle justified this by proclaiming Gabriella a lost cause, unworthy of the same comforts as the other children in the house. When her cousins went to school, Gabriella asked if she could join. Her grandmother laughed at this request, a deep and sadistic roar which brought tears to Gabriella's eyes. "We all know you'll grow up to be a whore anyway," her grandmother finally countered, chuckling at such a ridiculous notion. "You're too stupid for school, and what good is an education for a whore anyway? You have your mother's blood inside of you. I wouldn't dare waste the good teacher's time on a piece of trash like you."

Sometimes Gabriella would boldly indulge in fantasies about running away, allowing glimpses of hope to momentarily surface as she humored notions of reuniting with her parents and finding some version of relief. In in the end, she would quickly banish these thoughts within moments and suppress her longing. As an uneducated, unwanted woman who grew up in poverty, she understood with bitter resolution that she had nowhere else to go. For years she lived in this hopeless existence, repeating each day in a torturous routine, until the day she was incidentally offered a dangerous way out.

It was an unbearably hot day when Gabriella's neighbor carefully approached the fence which separated their two adjacent properties. Gabriella had been hanging laundry, oblivious to the fact that for days she had been carefully watched by the eyes across the yard. She had seen her neighbor several times from afar, usually rocking in a chair from a porch that overlooked Gabriella's lawn. She was a stout woman, with unkempt hair and deep leathery wrinkles that could only have been formed from a harsh life in the sun. Years ago, she had thrown Gabriella a chocolate bar with a sincere smile and wave of her hand. Gabriella had been shocked by this gesture, and stared at it for a while in a state of sad bewilderment before hastily thrusting it back over the fence with a paranoid shake of her head. No piece of chocolate was worth the beating she would receive if her grandmother found the evidence.

"Child, come here," her neighbor whispered through the fence, startling Gabriella who had been deeply absorbed in her work. She stared in horror at her neighbor's outstretched hand, beckoning for her to come closer, before shaking her head and turning back to the pile of laundry before her.

"I said come here!" the old woman spat again as she hit the rickety fence with her fist, making a small thud Gabriella feared her grandmother might hear from the kitchen. Gabriella shyly turned her head to ensure her grandmother wasn't watching from the window before she begrudgingly complied. "I'm not allowed to talk to you," she responded nervously, fiddling her thumbs to avoid eye contact.

"You look just like Enevelia, just like your beautiful mother."

Gabriella gasped and looked up with a renewed force of interest, "You knew my mother?"

"Oh yes, from the time she first started seeing your father. She was a sweet girl, a kind friend to an old woman like me. I'm Christina, by the way."

"I... I don't think you have the right girl. My mother wasn't nice."

"You're Gabriella Rodriguez. You have your father's name and your mother's eyes. I know who you are, sweet girl."

Gabriella's jaw dropped again in amazement, but she snapped back to her surroundings. This conversation alone would have deadly repercussions if her grandmother peered out the window and saw their interaction. Once her abuela caught her talking to a neighbor boy who asked if she could come play. Her abuela was so furious that she beat Gabriella with a cattle whip until her back was purple and raw.

"I really have to go."

"Listen child, do you know what Facebook is? It's a horribly annoying American website, but it connects people from all different places. Your mama has a profile! I found her online and told her where you are. She's been looking for you."

"My mother has a computer?"

"I'm not sure, but she checks that website everyday. I know she has an apartment though, one in America with a bed waiting for you."

"She told you that?"

"She told me all sorts of things, my love."

"I have to go."

"Child! Listen to me! I've seen your bruises, and I've heard screams from that house. I know what's going on, but until now I couldn't help you. Your mama will send money to get you out. I know a man who can take you to her! Take it and run before that horrible woman kills you."

"I have to go," Gabriella said again, looking back over her shoulder as she turned to run into her house.

"Child!" Christina yelled, but Gabrialla had already rushed through the door.

It was difficult to suppress the seeds of hope her conversation with Christina had sparked, but Gabriella slowly let months pass in silence and readjusted her focus on her daily routines. The tale Christina told about her mother was just that, a tale. It was either a ghastly mistake or a cruel lie, neither of which would give her a tangible chance at freedom. If her mother had been looking for her, she would have known. She had abandoned the idea of finding her parents long ago, periodically reminding herself that such a childish mirage was not worth the heartache of entertaining. Besides, Christina was an ancient woman, probably already half-demented with age.

Gabriella mulled over these justifications for the thousandth time as she swept the floor of their family store, one of her many tedious daily chores. The store was a cramped, modest front with only five tiny aisles packed with canned food and various household essentials. Her uncle had once mentioned in passing that he had built the store from the ground up with Gabriella's father. Naturally, this all came before her father had shamefully run off to join a dirty gang, but the story nevertheless brought Gabriella an odd sense of attachment to the rickety structure. She often surveyed the walls, studying each nail and hook with meticulous concentration, as she envisioned her father building the flimsy store. She allowed herself another intense survey of the hand-crafted shelves, imagining her father amidst the aisles, when her grandmother hissed at her from the doorway, startling Gabriella from her daydream.

"Come outside, stupid girl," her grandmother said impatiently. Gabriella obediently complied, carefully placing the broom in the corner and wiping her hands on her tattered apron as she exited the store into the harsh afternoon heat.

She was met with the sight of three considerably large and intimidating men, one of which was casually holding a handgun at his side as he paced back and forth around the entrance of the store. Each of their arms were broad and muscular, darkened from the sunlight and cluttered with tattoos. Although she couldn't read or write, she recognized the number "13" written across one of the man's forearms, and she gulped with the realization that they belonged to the MS-13 gang, a brutal group which dominated and terrorized the surrounding villages. Although they were notoriously vile and unruly in their reign of her neighborhood, Gabriella had rarely seen a member like this up close. Sometimes she watched them mingle with one another from a secure distance, but had managed to avoid any immediate interaction.

She knew her grandmother paid them each month in exchange for "protection," a practice she often cursed as she collected the large sum of money at the end of each month. Such a practice was notoriously common for most business owners in the area, a custom they almost ironically referred to as "paying rent." Although her family had never missed a payment, she had heard tragic stories of other owners who had been harassed or tortured because of a delay in getting their owed money to the gangs.

"This is my rent now," her grandmother said to the men as she nodded towards her granddaughter. Gabriella shook her head in confusion as she tried to make sense of the encounter, watching the men carefully as they looked her up and down.

"She's a baby," one scoffed and shook his head. "She barely has hips."

"She does! You just can't see them through her skirt. You can touch her if you want. She's practically a woman. I think she's close to thirteen now." Her grandmother spat back as she grabbed Gabriella's arm and thrust her towards the men with a solid, single push.

"I have a woman," the man spoke again, "what I need is your rent. You know the rules. If you do business in this neighborhood, either pay up or close your doors by Wednesday."

A second man took a step forward and held up his hand to the first. He moved towards Gabriella with a curious sweep of his eyes, and casually placed his palm under her chin as he examined her face. She trembled at his touch, suddenly feeling dizzy amidst the dry heat. "I like her," he said at last, "I'd take her for rent, but not just once a month. I get her whenever I want."

"Fine," her abuela shrugged, "it doesn't matter to me. She was born to be a whore anyway, just like her mother."

"We'll consider it," the first man said again with finality, giving the second man a warning glance. "I'm not saying yes until I think this over. A store like this costs money to protect, a fucking baby doesn't pay rent."

The second man smiled and released Gabriella from his soft grip. "We'll be back in four days," he said to her grandmother with a devilish smile, "have her ready for us by then."

Although Gabriella had spent many nights fantasizing about running away, she had never really considered her options until that moment. As the men retreated to their vehicle, loading into their truck and driving away without another harsh word, she suddenly realized that she had no choice but to finally run away. Even if Christina was lying, she would take any chance she could to avoid becoming the whore her grandmother had always foreseen. That night, she would sneak out of her house and cautiously knock on Christina's door. She would tell Christina that she needed to run, and pray her mother was still willing to pay her way to escape. The thought of such a departure was already making her feel sick with hopeless anticipation, but her options were growing too grim to bear.

As she stood at the border, the painful past that had catapulted her to this point seemed too distant to fully grasp. Regardless, she reminded herself once more of her grandmother's fate for her if she had stayed, as she grappled with the idea of finally crossing the border ahead.

"I'm going," Samuel announced with a quick flick of his cigarette as he headed towards the river without any noticeable hesitation or particular concern. Gabriella watched as he carefully crept to the water's edge and slowly waded across the river with his hands outstretched for balance. Even with his weight and experience, the task of crossing looked like an impossible challenge to face. She peered back at the other girls, forced a smile to cross her face, and with a small nod said, "Count to twenty and then follow me, ok? Don't let me get out of sight, but don't follow too closely. This is the last step until we reach America."

"Ok," squeaked Luna, the smallest of the group. Isabella and Ariana also gave small nods to show their reluctant solidarity. Gabriella gave them one last kind look before forcing her feet to move forward in the same path Samuel had taken towards the water's edge. She finally reached the bank and lowered herself into the freezing stream, delicately working to find her footing amidst the rocks that lined the bottom. One step at a time, she gradually made her way across the harsh, rushing current, barely able to breathe with each new step. More than once she almost lost her balance, but stubbornly kept moving forward until she somehow made it to the other opposite, welcoming shore. Samuel was impatiently waiting for her near the wall, crouched under the painted "x" beneath the a pile of tangled brush.

"The tunnel is there. Go and wait on the other side. Remember to stay low."

"What if one of the girls needs my help in crossing?"

"Don't fucking ask questions. Just go!"

She took a single deep breath and reluctantly complied, crawling through the small opening and dragging herself along the narrow path below. It was pitch black below the surface and she barely had room to move. It smelled moldy and rotten, and the rough dirt scraped her exposed, tender skin. Everytime she felt a pang of fear or the urge to retreat, the promise of finally making it to American soil kept her moving forward. The minutes felt like hours as she forced herself along the way, but at last she saw the opening and pulled herself from the tunnel with a sweet rush of satisfying relief. She let herself lay flat on the rough terrain in an exhausted state of delight, running her fingers through American dirt like a child. Tears of joy streamed down her face as she surveyed the foreign country, and enjoyed a brief moment of pride in her own unexpected show of bravery.

After a few additional minutes, Isabella and Ariana appeared from the small opening as well. She met them with a smile, but was immediately struck by the horror strewn across both of their faces. Ariana was softly crying and burrowed her head into her hands as she fell to the ground in a state of raw agony.

"What happened?" Gabriella choked, shaking Isabella's shoulders in a panic. "Tell me what happened to Luna!" Isabella just looked at the ground in despair, too shocked to muster any explanation.

When she saw Samuel crawling through the opening, she instinctively ran to him for answers. "She didn't make it," he said harshly, holding up his hand before she had time to ask. He immediately stood to brush off his faded jeans before scanning the area for border patrol.

"Are you sure?" Gabriella cried, "Should we go back?"

"No," he shook his head, "we're going forward."

"But..."

"What is she to you? You need to just shut up. I'm the only one with any consequences for losing her." He closed his eyes and gave his head a little shake, grumbling something to himself about the inconvenience. "Look, if we're late, I'm in deep shit. We have to keep moving forward."

Gabriella took a deep breath and tried to compose herself. They had come too far to stop moving forward now. She turned to the other two girls with a sad nod of her head, "He's right, we have to go. There's nothing we can do for her now."

"We're going because I say so," Samuel snapped as he slapped Gabriella across the face with a swift flick of his hand. "You don't tell them to go forward, I do!"

"Ok," she nodded as fresh tears sprung to her eyes, her face still stinging from the hit.

"Good, now follow me as you did before. Keep me in sight but stay at a distance." He turned with a grunt and took off without any further instruction. The girls began to follow him one by one, this time with Gabriella last in line. They continued this way for hours, and for a while she worried they might be lost. They were deep in the desert, with no distinct landmarks nearby to help her catch her bearings. Eventually though, in the distance she began to make out a truck like the one Samuel described as belonging to his friend. Her heart skipped a beat at the welcomed sight. This was the truck Samuel said would take her to her mother who, according to Christina, was waiting patiently in El Paso for her arrival.

When she came upon the group at last, Isabella and Ariana were already on the ground sipping water from new cantines. She gave a grateful nod towards Samuel who was shaking hands with the men she assumed to be the friends he had described. One was a short, older man with faded tattoos stretched along his swollen arms. The other was taller than Samuel and carried himself with a rigid demeanor. He eyed the girls with an animalistic excitement, making Gabriella grow weary in her relief. Ignoring these instincts, she reminded herself that their journey was almost over, and suddenly felt the childish urge to embrace the three men out of genuine gratitude.

"We made it," she breathed with heavy satisfaction. "Thank you so much, Samuel."

"This one talks too much already," the shorter man from the truck said with an annoyed glance in her direction. "Tell her to shut up and sit down with the others." Gabriella, embarrassed by this mistake, gave a swift nod in his direction and did as she was told. The shorter man, satisfied by her compliance, turned back towards Samuel and continued, "I was promised four and you brought me three. I will not accept an incomplete order."

"You want me to fucking take them back?" Samuel asked with a roll of his eyes. "These things happen. It's a dangerous trip. If you want a refund, go see the boss."

In an instant, the taller man pulled out a gun from the back of his pants and pointed it towards Samuel, causing the three girls to gasp and grab onto each other through tears of panic. "How about this boss?" The man threatened pushing the gun deep into Samuel's chest as he spat on the ground in disgust.

Samuel put up his hands in a frightened defense, "Whoa, whoa, whoa. You don't want to do that. You'll never do business with him again."

The taller man mulled this over for a few second, darting his glare back and forth from the girls to Samuel. Finally he nodded his head and reluctantly stuffed the gun back into the back of his pants, "I'll take the three then, but next trip I want an extra for free."

"Done," Samuel nodded.

"Alright," the shorter man said turning to three girls still shaking on the ground in a confused panic, "I'm Roberto and that's Eddie. We're taking you to Virginia. You'll be riding in the back."

"Is that near El Paso?" Gabriella fumbled, turning towards Samuel for an explanation.

Samuel shrugged with a small, distant hint of sympathy in his eyes. "No," he said at last, "there was a change of plans. The price went up. You three are going to Virginia now to pay off the debt."

"But... you said six thousand for the trip. Christina paid you to get me to El Paso."

Samuel laughed, "Christina didn't pay me, I paid her. She sold you. Now, get in the truck. I don't want to hear any more questions until we get to Virginia. It's time to get out of here."

AUGUST 1, 2015
Julia

Days before starting her final year of law school, Julia dashed up the towering steps of Brooktown to meet her soon-to-be professor, Anthony Bishop. For the past three months, she had been locked away as a summer associate in a large firm across the city, and her schedule had been so demanding she hardly had time to even acknowledge the distinct yearning she felt throughout the summer to return to Brooktown and its treasured familiarities. As she sped through the prestigious school grounds, she was absorbed by an instinctive of belonging in a way that nearly brought joyous tears to her eyes. She must have passed these buildings a thousand times, but after a stint of absence from the historic campus, she found herself marveling at the gothic architecture and pristine school grounds like she had on her first day at Brooktown.

Julia was early for their afternoon appointment, but raced across campus anyway in a state of uncontrollable excitement. She cursed the unforgiving August heat as she felt a trickle of sweat run down her neck and settle beneath her black, cotton dress. She had spent the past hour meticulously curating her look, carefully picking out a polished outfit she felt displayed a sense of impeccable professionalism for her casual meeting with Professor Bishop. Now, as she felt her red curly hair begin to frizz at the ends and her dress wrinkle amidst the heat, she regretted her decision in opting for a more fashionable look rather than something more practical.

Each semester she had tried for a spot in one of Anthony Bishop's famous seminars, but immediately after registration opened, like every other cycle during her time at Brooktown, all of his classes had filled up within minutes. No matter how she scrambled at the beginning of each semester, she had never been able to successfully secure one of the legendary spots in the limited number of courses he directed. However, after two anxious days of being placed on the disappointingly long wait list, her name had inexplicably appeared as first in line for an extra space. When an additional seat was uncommonly added to the roster, she received an email from the registrar informing her that she had officially been selected to become one of Anthony Bishop's students.

Bishop was Brooktown's star professor and resident celebrity. Most of his fame was due to his work in civil rights after he wrote a series of books calling for reform of human trafficking laws, but that was only a crumb of success on his long list of accomplishments. He had argued in front of the Supreme Court, he had once juggled a caseload far too large for most lawyers, and he even served on President Clinton's legal counsel for a short period during the nineties. He still took on one or two cases a year, but he had given up most of his other work to focus on teaching. When asked why he switched to academics, he always answered that he had never found anything he was more passionate about than his students at Brooktown.

When Julia arrived outside his office, she shyly knocked on his half-opened door. "I'm sorry I'm early," she announced meekly peering into the room, still out of breath from hustling up the stairs. She could feel sweat sticking to her forehead, but couldn't tell if it was still from the heat or a symptom of her nerves.

He looked up at her with an earnest smile. "Better early than late, I suppose. Please, take a seat." He pointed to a dark leather chair across from his desk which Julia immediately settled into and looked up at him with an nervous hush. She had seen Bishop many times around campus, but had never actually made it to such a close proximity. It felt surreal to finally be in front of a figure she had so adamantly admired for years, even before arriving at Brooktown. He was older, with dark grey hair and green eyes hidden behind thick tortoiseshell glasses. He was almost inherently intimidating as he held himself with an unshakeable air of confidence, but his docile smile somehow softened his demeanor. Julia had heard other students comment that he was handsome, but it occurred to her that this was likely due to his enigmatic attitude rather than the realities of his physical appearance.

She watched as he slowly poured a large cup of coffee, which filled the room with a rich and appetizing aroma, from a thermos he casually pulled from beneath his desk. He eyed her gently as he added three cups of sugar, and lazily took a few sips before he seemed to fully give her his attention.

"I'm Julia Harrison," she broke the silence with an awkward chortle.

"I'm aware," he nodded with a hint of condescension in a voice that made her cheeks flush with embarrassment. "I'm Anthony Bishop."

"I'm aware," she echoed, fidgeting under his hard stare.

"What can I do for you, Miss Harrison?"

"Well I'm scheduled to start your class tomorrow," she began. He tilted back in his chair nodded for her to continue as he took another sip of his coffee. "I... well I just wanted to make sure it wasn't a mistake." She found herself almost involuntarily glancing around his office with an awestruck air of girlish excitement. Even upon minor examination, she suspected every picture and piece of decor had a fabulously elaborate story she would have died for the opportunity to uncover. Her eyes were drawn to pictures of him with various celebrities and politicians lining the top shelf behind him. For half a second he caught her gaping at a row of frames with Bishop and several former U.S. Presidents, until she sharply turned back to Bishop with an embarrassed jerk. Out of habit and nerves, she began mindlessly picking at the ends of her auburn curls, softly avoiding direct eye contact as he quietly shook his head and let out a small chuckle.

"Why would it be a mistake?"

"Well honestly, I registered for classes a few minutes late. I was waitlisted for a spot behind ten people, but yesterday my name inexplicably moved the top of the list."

He shrugged, "Did you talk to the registrar?"

"I did... they said you requested a spot for me."

A half-guilty smile crept onto his face as he gently threw up his hands in admission, "Guilty as charged. I did request that they add an extra seat for you in particular."

"But why?" she responded with genuine curiosity, trying to hide her own satisfaction in his confirmation. Because the two had never officially met, it seemed odd that he would go out of his way for her without so much as a proper introduction.

"I like to keep tabs on up-and-coming students I suspect have potential. I hear you're ranked number one in your class. That's quite impressive." She blushed a little at the compliment and let her eyes fall to the floor as he continued. "I saw your name on the waitlist, so naturally I requested that you get a seat. You have a great reputation with the other professors. I had to see for myself."

"Oh, well honestly that wasn't the explanation I was expecting. I had no idea you knew who I was."

"You're pretty well known here, Julia. I simply admire top students and wanted a chance to be your educator."

"Well in that case, thank you so much for doing that. I'm flattered… and a little stunned. I'm really looking forward to your class."

"I'm looking forward to having you," he chuckled. "I'm sure we'll be good friends."

"Welcome to your third year of law school!" Professor Bishop announced brightly the following week with a generous smile. "You are all now on your final step in the arduous journey of entering the one profession universally hated by all in society. Really, you've made a fine choice." A bulk of students let out a unified, nervous laugh as Bishop turned on his power point with a light tap on his keyboard. The words "Constitutional Law" flickered onto the blank screen.

"Who can tell me what the study of this course entails?"

A girl sitting in the front row cautiously raised her hand, and he immediately signaled for her to answer with a nod of his head. "It's the study of Supreme Court cases."

"Interesting!" Bishop responded enthusiastically. "Take no offense to this, but I use the word interesting because your answer wasn't a total failure, which naturally I expect from students on the first day. I can't count the number of times I've heard the response 'It's the study of the Constitution.' However, even though you're technically right, I want to dig a little deeper. Who wants to try again?"

Julia timidly raised her hand, half-hoping he wouldn't see her spiritless gesture, but he abruptly pointed her way with a particularly satisfied expression. "It's the study of our rights guaranteed under the Constitution, interpreted by the Supreme Court," she stated with as much confidence as she could muster.

"That's much closer," Bishop said, beaming at her response. "In truth that's probably the most accurate answer on a purely theoretical level. However, for the sake of complicating an easy definition, here's the answer I want you all to scribble in your notes like the little stenographers law students pretend to be: 'Constitutional law is the body of law which defines the relationship of different entities...'"

The room erupted with the sound of a thousand fingers simultaneously hitting their keyboards and echoed thunderously through the lecture hall. Bishop waited patiently for the frenzy to subside. "Here's the way my course works," he continued, "I'm going to cut you all some slack because, simply by making it to your third year, you have all proved worthy of your place at Brooktown. I know most of the professors here generally employ the socratic method, and unfortunately, I am no exception. However, I like to go easy on my third-years." He looked around the room with a hint of pity in his eyes. "I hated being cold-called as a law student, and I have no intention of imposing unnecessary suffering. If you don't know an answer, just say so and I'll move on. Although, if I feel you are abusing my leniency, my notorious wrath will descend upon you and I will force you to answer every obscure and undesirable question for the remainder of the semester."

Again, everyone let out small laugh in response to this unexpected and calculated rant. Bishop's informal attitude and animated character was a refreshing break from the dull group of professors they had endured throughout the majority of their law school experience. Even on their first day back, they were already feeling burdened with Brooktown's demanding standards. Before his endearing greeting though, everyone had been eager to finally meet Anthony Bishop in person. Just like Julia, they had all scrambled for a coveted spot in his class, as he was notoriously the most popular and well-liked figure on campus. Julia sat in disbelief and smiled up at her new professor, still in shock that she had managed to finally secure a seat.

"Miss Harrison," Bishop called from his podium, "considering you gave us a decent definition earlier, can you acquaint us with your thoughts on the case I assigned as homework last night?"

"Um... I'm not sure what you mean," Julia responded, quickly stirring from her own childish whirlwind of starstruck distraction.

"I mean, will you give us your opinion of this case? It's not a trick question, I just want to know if you think the Court ruled correctly."

"In Dred Scott? Are you asking me if the Supreme Court was correct when it sanctioned slavery?"

"Yes, that's what I'm asking.."

"Um no... I do not think the Court ruled correctly."

"Why's that? Make your argument.."

Julia generally excelled at public debate and class participation, but today Bishop's notable reputation had her feeling a little intimidated and frazzled. "Ok, well, if we're all granted the right of liberty, then under no circumstances can one human being own another." she paused shyly, "I'm sorry, I'm not sure what else to say. I think we can all agree that slavery is inherently wrong. I don't really see how you would argue the other way."

"What if I disagreed? What if I told you I think the Court is right, and that it's fair for one human to own another?"

Julia laughed a little at the irony of a world-renowned civil rights lawyer making a pro-slavery argument, even if it was only to prove a point. "Well, then I would say your opinion is irrelevant in the face of a guaranteed Constitutional right. Also, if that's your disposition, you should probably consider changing fields." The class let out a small, generous giggle in acknowledgement of her witty rebuttal.

"See," Bishop said with amusement as he turned to address his students as a whole. "Was that so bad? My biggest issue with my students is that they are often too intimidated to speak up. In my class I want you all to find your voice. I would rather you give a wrong answer than no answer at all... although I do think it's fair to say that there was really only one correct way to answer that last question."

Julia smiled with relief. Bishop was already her favorite professor.

SEPTEMBER 2, 2015
Daniel

The staggering weight of Daniel's law books seemed proportionate to the heavy depression he had been feeling since his post-summer return to Brooktown. He had never done particularly well in law school, a fact that remained readily apparent to most of his professors and peers. He had foolishly expected a modest improvement by his third year, but so far his classes remained a torturous procession of humiliating experiences like every previous semester. It was a miracle he had survived Brooktown's rigorous standards at all, but to no one's surprise he consistently struggled only to remain at the bottom of his class.

Unlike other phases of academia where he could hide his shortcomings behind his shy demeanor, law school put his incompetence on display by forcing every student to actively participate in the class discussion. As he sat in Professor Bishop's class, a period most of his peers looked forward to with riveting interest, all he could feel was mounting anxiety at the thought of hearing his name being called by his professor from below.

"Daniel Brenner," he heard Bishop's voice echo through the room as if he had somehow read and responded to Daniel's anxious premonition, "can you tell us the facts of this case?" Daniel understood Bishop was trying cut him a break by throwing him a seemingly effortless summarization rather than an in-depth analysis, but even an "easy" task like this seemed impossible to do in the face of his classmate's unyielding judgement. Daniel's heart sank in anticipation as he tried to form a coherent response.

"I-I-I think this case involved a c-c-car search... the officer wanted to search the suspect's car without a warrant, and th-th-the Court ruled that was illegal," he answered miserably as he sank back into his chair in defeat. He looked over at Julia who gave him a reassuring smile, but behind her encouragement he could see a small, uncomfortable suspense. Her skin, which was normally pale and speckled with light brown freckles, had turned red with vicarious embarrassment so that it almost matched her wild auburn curls.

Bishop sighed. "No Daniel, that was the previous case, this one involves an officer who searched a bag that didn't belong to the plaintiff."

"Oh, I'm sorry," Daniel sputtered, trying to make himself invisible as the rest of his classmates nodded sympathetically in his direction. Their pity was almost worse than judgement.

"Miss Harrison," Bishop continued, "Did the plaintiff have standing to sue in this case?"

"No," Julia stated confidently with a light toss of her hair. "The Court ruled that because the bag belonged to the plaintiff's girlfriend and not the plaintiff, his rights were not violated."

"And do you agree with the ruling?"

"No sir, I do not."

"Why is that?"

"The Court essentially narrowed all of our rights based on a technicality."

"Well wouldn't you argue that if something is technically correct, it's a correct ruling?"

"Even if something is technically correct, that doesn't make it right. I think the effects of a decision are far more important than the decision itself."

"Tell that to the Supreme Court Justices, Miss Harrison," Bishop laughed, "I don't think they would appreciate the criticism."

Everyone snickered, and Daniel felt a rush of relief as the attention of his classmates dispersed. Some teachers would have forced Daniel to continue his analysis despite his painful opening, grilling him over every detail of the case until he was either in total psychological disrepair or had absorbed enough class time so that the professor could no longer justify continuing the demeaning charade. For students like Julia, law school was effortless, and maybe even a somewhat pleasantly rewarding experience as she excelled through her courses without a single mishap. For students like Daniel, it was a distasteful form of daily humiliation which served only as a reminder of his own painful ineptitude.

Daniel was diagnosed with an anxiety disorder when he was sixteen. Mrs. Hayes, his high school teacher at the time, noted something was off when Daniel unsuccessfully attempted to give a simple presentation to a modest class of ten people. Halfway through the assignment, he became engulfed by nerves and soon spiraled completely into a breakdown. His head started pounding, his face became coated with sweat, and after a few failed attempts to speak through the tension, he finally ran from the classroom to throw up, unable to finish his speech.

The disgraceful ordeal ended with him hyperventilating in the hallway until Mrs. Hayes found him painfully hunched over in the corner. After patiently waiting for his nerves to unwind, she politely suggested that this level of anxiety wasn't something he should ignore, and recommended that he go in for psychological consultation to evaluate the root of his neurosis. He hesitantly agreed.

The psychiatrist she suggested diagnosed him with social phobia, a generalized anxiety disorder which was borderline incurable at the level he was suffering. His doctor noted that it "really shouldn't be much of a problem" if Daniel could just avoid public speaking and scenarios involving open scrutiny. Although the diagnosis in itself was disheartening, until law school, his doctor's prediction had proved to be shockingly accurate. Apart from a few isolated incidents, his anxiety wasn't an exceptionally pervasive issue as Daniel learned to skillfully dodge situations which inflamed the effects of his disorder, finding it relatively easy to avoid mass attention. He took Xanax when such an occasion was mandatory, but for the most part those incidences were relatively rare.

However, he lost the option of avoiding public speaking when he started law school where constant, open debate was both demanded and often a central component of his final grade. He refused to stay medicated everyday just to survive, forcing himself to endure each embarrassing encounter with raw and unhinged emotion.

He often fantasized about switching careers, but the window for dropping out had long passed. He was close to $200,000 in debt, a burden he had no hope of paying off without an advanced degree. During his second year at Brooktown he considered transferring to a different law school, one that didn't so adamantly employ such a rigid use of the socratic method, but after some preliminary research he found that transferring after his first-year was essentially impossible. He felt stagnant in a path he hadn't even wanted. He couldn't drop out and he couldn't change programs, meaning his only option was to stick to this miserable profession for the majority of his life while he worked to pay off his student loans.

"I think that's it for the day," Professor Bishop announced. "Daniel, can you come see me after class for a moment?"

Once again, Daniel sulked in his own humiliation as the rest of his peers solemnly looked back at him with painful nods of sympathetic encouragement upon their exit. He turned again to Julia who met his gaze with a consoling smile, but even she looked a little nervous on his behalf. He clumsily tried to hide his discomfort with a look of assurance to give her some illusion of strength, but he knew his efforts would be unconvincing given the weight of his pressing dread. He had always been a terrible liar, and Julia was particularly skilled in seeing through his usual facade.

As the remaining students slowly withdrew from the classroom, his anxiety bubbled up and overwhelmed his senses even worse than before. He looked down at his hands which were shaking uncontrollably with adrenaline, and tried to focus on a consistent breathing pattern so he wouldn't start hyperventilating in front of Bishop. *You are in Control. Keep it together Daniel,* he reminded himself in desperation. For a moment he fantasized about Bishop kicking him out of Brooktown for his subpar case analysis. He realized this wasn't realistic, but the thought of being expelled brought him a small, fleeting moment of relief.

"I didn't mean to embarrass you," Bishop stated sincerely after the remaining students had exited the room. Daniel stood to meet him at the bottom of the lecture hall, but Bishop held up a hand for him to wait. Instead, Bishop cautiously climbed the steps towards Daniel and pulled out a nearby seat. He gave a casual smile as he took off his glasses and started cleaning them with the corner of his sleeve. He moved slowly, attentively watching Daniel from the corner of his eye as he nodded for their conversation to begin.

"I-I-I'm so sorry. I know I'm not good at this, but I promise I'm trying. I read the case, I just panicked and got the names mixed up."

"Whoa, whoa," Bishop held up his hand again to cut him off. "I didn't ask you to stay so I could scold you. I just want to talk about your experience so far as a law student. Are you enjoying it?"

The question seemed ludicrous, of course he wasn't enjoying it. He was utterly and hopelessly miserable to be back at Brooktown. "Does anyone?" Daniel finally mumbled, fishing for some reassurance that his bleak sentiments were normal in the face of such dire circumstances. Most of his peers seemed to thrive under pressure, but he suspected at least some of their apparent ease was an act.

"Yes Daniel," Bishop sighed, "some people do."

Daniel oddly sensed that Bishop wasn't intentionally being condescending or cruel, but even with a layer of genuine concern, his words struck Daniel with disappointment as his heart sank in defeat. It was obvious Daniel was racked with anxiety. Even this morning he had examined his face in the mirror only to find that dark circles had appeared under his eyes, his acne had returned for the first time since middle school, and a fresh layer of wrinkles had started forming on top of his brow. He had never been a noticeably attractive person, always too tall and lanky to be considered conventionally handsome, but it was hard to watch his own physical appearance so harshly deteriorate before his eyes. In the past he had felt plain, a look which Daniel had come to appreciate as it assisted him in moving through life unnoticed. However, since starting law school, his body was literally breaking down, making his struggles externally apparent and impossible to conceal.

After spending the greater part of his life in Seattle, Daniel's bleak relocation to D.C. had been a sustained misfortune and a particularly sluggish transition. He had begrudgingly grown to tolerate the city after years of prolonged acclimation, but the mundane habits he had adopted in the area still seemed remarkably dreary compared to his lifestyle back home. He found himself counting the days until he could leave his East Coast prison indefinitely and retreat back to the welcomed familiarities of the Northwest, even if that meant finally joining his family's law firm, something he had fiercely resisted in the past.

Daniel's parents had attended law school in Southern California where they both excelled as notably talented students. They shared a love for land conservation, so after graduation they settled in the Northwest to pursue careers in environmental law. They spent ten years building moderate successes in respective firms, but after balancing their future ambitions, they finally took a leap of faith and bravely started their own practice together, focusing on the legal aspects of the safekeeping and maintenance of natural habitations. Their firm exploded with success and prestige, making his parents two of the most well-established and respected environmental lawyers in the region.

From an early age, Sara, Daniel's older sister, had typically been the more articulate of the two. She naturally developed a profound interest in the legal profession by the time she started elementary school. From her obsession with John Grisham novels to her inexplicable detailed knowledge of Supreme Court procedure, her prospective legal career became an inevitable fixture in their family's set of ambitions. When his parents discussed the future, they always spoke of a time when "Sara would take over the firm," leaving Daniel's career unburdened and exempt from their expectations.

Although their coloring was so similar that they could have been mistaken for twins, both hosting a rare shade of sandy blonde hair and light blue eyes, an additional injustice to the imbalance of their fate was the fact that Daniel's sister was incontestably the more attractive of the two. They had both inherited their mother's notoriously long limbs and skinny torso, but Daniel instinctively moved his body with unpracticed, awkward motions, while Sara carried herself with an elongated confidence that left most people taken with her natural poise.

Daniel never developed a passion for reading like his sister, and instead focused his efforts on studying mathematics and science. Unlike the rest of his family who held boisterous personalities and a shared love for heated debates, he was timid with a mild temperament that was often overlooked and easily dismissed. His role was instinctively in the background of his sister's shadow, but this was a position he quickly and sincerely grew to appreciate. He enjoyed being an observer and understood his place in the family's dynamic. His parents employed blatant favoritism towards his sister, but he always suspected that this was due to their naturally compatible personalities rather than a flaw in his character. The imbalance seemed reasonable in the face of his peculiarities, and he grew to enjoy the freedom of escaping the unwavering expectations and attention Sara often endured.

The most obvious display of favoritism occurred annually in late August. In another somewhat unfortunate twist of fate, Sara's birthday came one week before his own. While every year his parents would throw her a spectacular party, his birthday generally consisted of an intimate family dinner and passed by without much thought. He sometimes heard his parents justify this difference with notion that "Daniel just doesn't like parties," even though he had never actually voiced a position of this nature. Their avoidance to pay him notable attention might have felt troublesome, but he had already accepted these kinds of projections on his behavior. He could have been bitter, but truthfully most of his childhood memories were authentically happy... until the accident, of course.

When Sara turned thirteen, she made a sensational declaration to her family: she would now be using a bicycle as her primary mode of transportation. This decision came with a large stack of research about the incidental impacts of motored vehicles, even those claiming to be environmentally friendly. Her parents acted annoyed with her stubborn, sudden refusal to step foot in a car, but Daniel could see through their artificial disappointment. He strongly suspected that they were both in fact thrilled to watch their daughter grow into a sustained passion which so adamantly matched their own. Every time she gave a self-righteous speech about personal responsibility in protecting their exhausted planet, he knew his parents were deeply satisfied in with her unshakable disposition, even with the accompanying inconvenience.

As a result of her stubborn verdict, she rode her bike everyday without exception, even in the face of extreme weather. She was a talented bicyclist who had studied the laws of cycle traffic and always stayed on designated bike lanes when they were available. Such strenuous efforts suited her rigid personal code and commitment to local regulations, a trait that further hinted at her future career in the legal field. Her mindfulness in personal security and safety knowledge was partly why the accident came as such a genuine shock to everyone who knew her.

It happened on a Saturday afternoon when Sara was biking home from the library. It had been raining with notable force, harsher than the city's usual drizzle. In a fleeting mischance of fate, she passed through a crowded intersection and skid into oncoming traffic. A truck coming from the opposite direction didn't catch sight of her with enough time to stop, and killed her almost instantly in an unfortunately timed and aimless collision. If she had been five seconds slower or faster, she would have survived. Her death was so atrociously random that it took years for Daniel to fully process its effects. He would eventually accept the tragedy and salvage the untouched remains of his former character, but his parents were never the same after that day.

He watched in sorrow as their once infectious personalities grew dim with grief and prolonged depression. In her absence, they both fell into a lifeless cycle of gloom, and withdrew almost as if they were each adopting Daniel's own sheepish demeanor without Sara's balance. He grieved for his sister, but also for the loss of his parents' lively characters and ambitions. He often wondered if they would have been happier if he had been the one on the bike that day instead of Sara. For the rest of his childhood, the whole family lived through a haze of mourning as they carried the burden of losing his sister.

Daniel couldn't stand the thought of leaving his parents in a childless home, so he chose a local college in Seattle where he could live nearby. They told him not to burden his decision with their selfish wishes, but he intuitively sensed their relief when he announced he was staying in the area after graduation. He majored in economics with an emphasis on advanced mathematics, intending to obtain some kind of advanced degree in the field and teach as an undergraduate professor somewhere in Seattle. He wasn't ambitious in the same sense as his parents, but he did well throughout school and was on track to graduate with a nearly perfect GPA.

"You should take the LSAT," a guidance counselor told him during a routine check-in as she looked over his application for a master's program in Seattle. She studied his transcript with an air of excitement, shuffling through the pages with a level of enthusiasm that felt completely foreign to his traditionally humble set of behaviors. He rolled his eyes at her suggestion. He was nine months away from graduating and had his personal timeline set and ready. He was really only seeking advice as a formality before sending off his applications.

"Why? I want to be a professor."

"Well why not keep your options open? With grades like this you could get into somewhere like Harvard or Brooktown Law."

"I don't think I'm even interested in exploring that option. I come from a family of lawyers. Trust me, I'm not the type."

"But you're limiting yourself! Do you know how many students would kill for grades like these?"

"I really don't see that in my future, but if you think it's a good idea I guess there's no harm in taking the test," he sighed. He didn't actually plan on showing up for the exam, but he felt this was the easiest way to avoid disappointing her.

"Exactly! Plus, your scholarship covers the exam fee, so there's really no reason not to. I'll sign you up now," she said, turning back to her computer and asking for bits of his personal information as she typed with unstoppable energy. "I'm printing out your exam ticket. I'm sure you'll do great."

"Thanks," he smiled weakly and stuck the ticket in his pocket. Almost immediately he dismissed the thought entirely, and went back to fantasizing about an advanced degree in quantum physics at Seattle University, a program he had been eyeing since starting undergrad.

The following evening as he sat around the dinner table as usual with his parents, he noticed his mother hiding an oddly mischievous smile in between bites of her spaghetti. Everytime he spoke, she looked at him like a child hiding a delightfully amusing secret as she repeatedly asked if there was anything new going on that they should know about. Obviously, she was fishing for something, but Daniel just shook his head in confusion, repeatedly assuring her that everything in his life was business as usual. "What's going on?" he finally asked with a roll of his eyes after several rounds of this give-and-take. She beamed at him, taking out a slip of paper and sliding it his way across the table. He recognized it immediately as his LSAT ticket. "Oh," he stammered, "how did you find that?"

"It was in your pants pocket, you silly goose. I found it in your laundry. Why didn't you tell us you were considering law school?"

His father's face suddenly lit up as he glanced up from his plate and peered in Daniel's direction. "What? When did this happen?"

"I mean," Daniel fumbled awkwardly, painfully attempting to explain that he had only signed up for the exam to appease his nosey counselor. However, their enthusiastic looks made him hesitant to immediately dismiss this rare display of attention. They sat at the edge of their seats, eagerly waiting for him to continue. The prideful smiles suddenly plastered on his parents' faces were the same ones they had so often given Sara, and he suddenly realized he tragically hadn't glimpsed this side of them since her passing. He selfishly resolved that, for just a moment longer, he would indulge in their happiness. "I just thought I'd take the test and see how I do."

"That's wonderful! Isn't that wonderful?" His mother burst as she turned to grab his father's hand. His father nodded with pride, and for a moment it seemed as though he was holding back tears.

"You know," his mother jumped in again, "it's often those with a knack for mathematics that end up doing well on this test. The misconception is that the LSAT is all about reading comprehension, but really it's about logic. You're so logical, I bet your economics background serves you well."

"I think we're getting a little ahead of ourselves," Daniel interjected with hesitation. "I haven't even taken it yet. I'll probably fail."

"That's ok," his father nodded and put a hand on Daniel's shoulder. "We're just so proud of you for trying. No matter how you score, we'll be happy."

Those words might have been true. It's possible that if Daniel had scored low, his parents would have humbly suppressed their disappointment, and accepted that their timid son was simply not destined to enter their beloved profession. They would have supported him when he took the GRE, congratulated him on his acceptance into a master's program in mathematics, and politely inquired for the remainder of their lives about his career which they would learn to gracefully stomach but never fully understand. Daniel assumed this would have been the case, but he would never be certain as his life changed drastically after the exam.

When the results were released he stared at his number with a surreal sense of distress. He had gotten a 176, an almost perfect score. For a moment he considered hiding the results from his parents, but Daniel had a deeply unconvincing poker face. Even the thought of keeping something like this a secret made him wither with anxiety. He masked his defeat and announced his results at dinner with fraudulent enthusiasm, awaiting the inevitable explosion of unwarranted pride.

Immediately, his parents burst out with delightful squeals and heart-warming tears. His mother opened a bottle of their most expensive champagne while his father dove into stories from his time in law school. "It's the most fascinating program in the world," his father reminisced as he gently swirled his glass around and smiled fondly. "Some of the best years of my life took place at UCLA Law. Do you think that's where you'll go?"

His mother interjected his a playful punch to his father's shoulder, "Now don't pressure him. We loved UCLA and I'm sure he would too, but with a score like this he could go anywhere. He could get into somewhere like Brooktown. Can you imagine a Brooktown education?"

"You're right," his father beamed. "You can go anywhere and do anything. What is it that you want to do?"

"I'm not sure yet," Daniel responded blankly. "This is all happening really fast."

"Well you have plenty of time. You won't even have to apply for another couple of months," his mother suggested. "Maybe we could take a few family trips to visit some of these campuses. That might make your decision easier."

Daniel gave a weak smile and managed a shaky nod of approval. They hadn't taken a family vacation since Sara's death, and the temptation of allowing his parents a few months of happiness was too inviting to suppress. Sara had often talked about her dream schools, repeatedly naming Brooktown as her first choice. He realized this score, these trips, and the prideful expressions on his parents' faces were all meant for her. He was commandeering her dream and stepping into her future as a cheap replacement. "That sounds great," he finally responded, hiding his sweltering anxiety suddenly bubbling inside of him with a practiced, poised grin.

"Well I'm not enjoying myself. I guess I'm not one of those people," Daniel sighed, staring up at Professor Bishop in misery.

"Hey, I'm not criticizing you." Bishop threw up his hands in defense, "I just want to help. I personally hated law school, and I still consider it one of the most trying experiences of my life. In a lot of ways, I thought it was more difficult than my time in practice."

Daniel nodded. He knew this was Bishop's way of trying to help, but he found such an anecdote fundamentally unimaginable. Bishop was infamously brilliant with natural traits Daniel could hardly fathom. Picturing Brooktown's celebrity professor as an intimidated law student seemed somewhat like a preposterous stretch. Even so, Daniel appreciated the soothing gesture, and decided to entertain the illusion. "How did you get through it?"

"Well my first semester was tough, but eventually I adjusted. I was terrified of public speaking when I started, but I'm grateful for my education now. I never could have gone into litigation without the consistent practice."

"You were afraid of public speaking? I-I just can't believe that. You've argued in front of the Supreme Court."

Bishop chuckled as his face lit up with the memory. "Yes, that was actually a pretty nerve-racking experience. I was so scared I started hyperventilating before my argument. For a while I didn't think I could go on, and I almost let my colleague present the case on my behalf."

"Oh... I didn't know that."

"Public speaking is a skill. For some it comes easy, for others it requires a lot of practice. However, it's a skill that *anyone* can master. Trust me, I've seen students who started out far worse than you grow into accomplished speakers by the end of my class."

"Sure... but usually by third year most have it mastered-"

"-Not necessarily," Bishop interjected, "it comes to people at different periods. If you keep trying, I'm sure you'll see vast improvements."

"It's not just the speaking though... I-I-I feel so much anxiety about everything. It's really hard for me to get through my reading."

"I think those feelings are a lot more normal than you think, especially among your fellow classmates. I'm sure many feel the same way but have too much pride to admit it. Tell me, is there anything about law school you do like?"

"I like my girlfriend," Daniel blurted out on an uncontrollable impulse. His face immediately turned red with embarrassment. He knew this wasn't the kind of response Bishop was looking to invoke, even if Julia was undoubtedly the most fulfilling aspect about Daniel's life at Brooktown. "I'm dating Julia Harrison," he finally concluded in a flushed attempt to explain this obvious blunder. For half a second, Daniel spotted a surprising revelation flicker in Bishop's eyes. After two years with Julia, Daniel had grown inescapably accustomed to this type of reaction. She surpassed him in both looks and intelligence, and often when people heard the two were dating, it generally took a moment to reconcile the fact that someone of Julia's status would in-explicably dip to his level.

"That's great," Bishop finally acknowledged a little too enthusiastically, trying to hide his initial surprise.

"I-I'm sorry. I know that's not what you meant, it was just the first thing that came to mind."

"Well honestly, I can see why. Julia seems like a very special person, and I think having a solid social life is really helpful in surviving a place like this," Bishop responded with sincerity. He clearly favored Julia in class, and Daniel couldn't help but feel a small swelling of pride in knowing that Bishop was now enlightened to the nature of their courtship.

"Anyway," Bishop continued, "I just want you to know that I'm here to help you in any way possible. I'm not just saying that to be polite. I think you're a sharp young man, and I don't want you to feel like you're the only one who finds the workload overwhelming. It's a struggle for everyone."

Daniel was taken aback. This was not the conversation he had anticipat-ed. He had half-expected Bishop to encourage him to explore other career options or consider taking a formal break until he could muster some level of an intellectual revolution.

"I'll... I'll do that. I really appreciate this. I'm just a little shocked. This talk wasn't what I was expecting."

Bishop laughed. "I know sometimes professors have harsh reputations, but you'd be surprised by how many of us are actually human once you get past those masks. As for you, you're a good student, but that's not even entire-ly important. Sometimes the people who struggle most in law school are the ones who make the best lawyers."

"I-I-I don't know what to say. That means... just thanks for saying that." He let Bishop's validation generously wash over him, and beamed at his pro-fessor with devout relief and a newfound sense of loyalty.

"Of course," Bishop smiled warmly and put his hand on Daniel's shoul-der. "And take care of Julia. I'm glad you have her. She is a really sweet girl."

Daniel couldn't help but grin. Just the thought of Julia brought him a refreshing sense of comfort.

"I'll see you next class," Bishop said as he gathered his papers to leave. "I'm going to ask you to analyze the issue in 'State v. Maynerd.' Practice your answer and be prepared, that should give you the extra boost of confidence you need to answer correctly in front of the class. Does that sound fair?"

"Absolutely!" It was a small act of kindness, but it meant the world to Daniel. Finally he felt as though things were really were looking up. "Thank you sir," he said as they both made their way to the exit. "I sincerely do feel a lot better."

May 20, 2016
Julia

Julia was leaving the graveyard, tears still rolling down her cheeks, when Detective Weir flagged her down. She immediately recognized him from the day of Bishop's death when he had walked around Brooktown's campus conducting interviews and taking statements. He came to her car window, and his face softened when he saw the state of her disarray. He put on a weak, sympathetic smile as he gently spoke, "Again, I'm so sorry for your loss. I know you were very close with your professor. It's a hard thing to accept."

"His funeral wasn't what I was expecting," Julia cried, trying to hide the depths of her discomfort without avoiding his gaze.

"I know, tragic deaths make goodbyes really difficult. People are still in shock. Plus, he sounded like a pretty incredible person," Weir lightly patted her hand as an awkward attempt at a comforting gesture. "I wanted to talk to you a little about this case though, when you're up to it."

Julia gulped ominously as her heart skipped a beat. She took a few deep breaths to calm herself before continuing. "Are there any leads?" her voice asked with hint of desperation seeping through her fabricated, poised disposition.

"Yes," he answered coldly.

"Oh... Does it have something to do with the death threats he had been getting? I heard they were investigating threats from a few extremists who were angry with his work on gun control." She could feel herself rambling despite her best efforts to stay collected. She studied his face in hopes of uncovering a hint of his underlying intention, but his expression remained blank and unreadable.

"He had a lot of enemies, we're certain of that. He was infamous for his work in left-wing politics. Death threats aren't uncommon in those fields, but they rarely materialize in this form, especially considering whoever killed him must have known him well enough to get onto Brooktown's campus without being noticed. It doesn't seem likely that such an ordeal could be pulled off by some random, angry nutcase."

"I see," she responded miserably. "I just want to know what happened... for closure, you know? He was my favorite professor." The thought of Bishop made her swell with rage, and she began shaking with furious resentment. She prayed he wouldn't notice her body's subtle, uncontrollable outburst.

"Absolutely, I understand. That's a totally natural feeling," Weir agreed. "Knowing someone who was murdered is a very difficult reality to cope with."

"Yeah, I'm just confused how it could have happened. He was a really great man," she stated flatly. She stared at Weir's weathered face, realizing he was probably much younger than his deep wrinkles and greying hair suggested. He spoke with the faded confidence of someone whose profession had become second nature, and she realized with a stroke of panic that the police force would not have assigned such a seasoned officer to a murder case that they weren't taking fairly seriously.

"We're all outraged by it. That's why we're working so hard to uncover the truth. I have no doubt that we will eventually. Secrets like this rarely stay secret forever. That's why I wanted to ask you a few questions."

"What? Why?" her voice cracked a little and she cursed herself for allowing such an exposition of her covert tension.

"It's not a big deal, we just want a full picture of the week leading up to his death. We know you were quite close to him, and unfortunately we don't know a lot of people who were in his inner circle."

"I don't think he had much of an inner circle," she responded honestly. "He was really friendly, but he didn't have a lot of deep relationships."

"Exactly. That's why we're trying to talk to everyone we can who glimpsed his life on a deeper level. As his research assistant, you knew him about as well as anyone. That's why we need to just ask a few questions for context."

"Right now? His funeral was only a few hours ago."

"Oh no, not right away," Weir responded quickly with a wave of his hand. "I'm sure it's been a tremendously heavy day for you. We were wondering if you could just stop by the station tomorrow. It's mostly just routine questions so we know everyone he contacted in the hours leading up to his death. Your information might be more helpful than you even realize right now."

"But I didn't contact him in the hours leading up to his death. The last time we spoke was Thursday, three days before he died. I was in New York the day before graduation, and my friends threw me a surprise party when we got back to D.C.. I was with them all night."

For the first time, Weir eyed her with curious suspicion, and she realized her story must have sounded at least marginally robotic and possibly even rehearsed. "I remember all that," he replied slowly as he watched her squirm a little at his stare. "I got your statement the day of your graduation. I have the timeline all set, but I still want to hear a little more about the week leading up to his murder. I think that conversation would be easier at the station tomorrow, don't you agree?"

"I won't be in custody, right?"

"Of course not, why would you be in custody?."

"I'm so sorry that came out wrong," Julia laughed nervously. "I know I sound defensive. It's the lawyer in me. I was taught you should always ask for a lawyer the moment you start being questioned."

Weir chuckled, "It's not that kind of questioning, Julia. I keep forgetting you're a lawyer. You look so young."

"I am, I'm only 23."

"Well in that case, would you feel more comfortable with a parent present?"

"No, I don't have any parents. Well I have my mom, but she wouldn't come."

"I'm sorry to hear that. Is there anyone else you could bring that would make you feel more comfortable? I suppose you *could* bring a lawyer, but it's really not necessary, especially considering your background. Is there just someone you can trust?"

"No, there's not. I'll go alone. I'll see you tomorrow."

September 5, 2014
Gabriella

Gabriella had been working for five hellish years. She stopped counting the days sometime during her unending stretch of business, but one of the new girls brought a calendar last month which allowed her to calculate exactly how long it had been since Roberto had transported her to Virginia. Time had become an inconsequential and abstract concept, as her days now blended together into one hollow wave of fretful sleep and arbitrary men. She worked in a house in the Virginia countryside, but as far as Gabriella was concerned it could have been a million miles from the rest of civilization. Even stepping outside was a luxury.

Her rate was considerably higher than the other girls in the house. Roberto explained that he set prices based on conventional attraction, and casually noted that she had the shapely body men undoubtedly seemed to favor. He often showed her off to new customers, painfully tugging at her waist-length hair while he vigorously bargained for an inflated price. If they rejected her sizable fee, he would suggest a different girl as consolation. She didn't ask for her physical traits and condemned the uncivil practice of Roberto's bargaining, but that didn't curb the other girls from underhandedly resenting his glaring favoritism. Consequential to this unfortunate imbalance, she had far fewer friends than most in the house. After years of isolation, she sank into a deep loneliness that drove her to insane levels of delusion and detachment. The voices in her head that developed in her solitude had become just another steadily tedious fixture of her tragic life.

The price men paid for her didn't carry much weight with Gabriella anyway. Her income was a meaningless consideration, more of a hypothetical idea than a legitimate wage, as all of her earnings were collected by and remained with Roberto. She used to have childish fantasies about securing enough to stop working and disappear, but she had long given up on such naive delusions. She knew that there was nothing for her on the outside. After spending so many years in the house, instead of dreaming of liberation, she had come to dread the day she would grow too old for her trade.

Gabriella's most traumatizing memories of her years in business collectively accrued throughout the first weeks of her arrival. She had promptly discarded any notions of the future Samuel had promised and bitterly accepted the fact that Christina had sold her just as he claimed. The most difficult aspect of her new reality was stomaching her own stupidity in believing the dubious tale about her mother. She wallowed in bitter regret and relentlessly cursed herself for days.

The lowest blow of the strenuous journey to Virginia came when she learned she would be separated from Ariana and Isabella. Upon entering the state, Roberto explained that the other two would be living in a different home altogether, nearly two hours north of her own. She vehemently pleaded against their disengagement, but within moments of this announcement they were torn from her embrace and placed in a separate truck heading north. She sank to her knees and felt the crushing sense of isolation that flooded her in their absence. Roberto took pity on her heartache, and sympathetically moved to comfort her, holding her through sobs and gently stroking her hair.

"It will all be ok," he said with authentic compassion. "You're so beautiful, I'm going to take care of you." For the first time since their meeting, she noticed the shape of his square jaw and the magnetic pull of his eyes. She sank into his tall, sturdy body with hungry relief, and allowed herself a moment of coveted attention.

They reached her new house after nightfall, nearly three days after she had arrived at the border. It was a drafty, narrow home with covered windows and a crumbling foundation. The inside was poorly lit and smelt of filthy laundry and rotting food. Roberto introduced her to the other five girls who eyed her with judgemental expressions. She met their stares with a frightened smile, and shyly stated her name in a near whisper. Immediately, they burst into giggles at her thick Central American accent, and Roberto snapped his fingers angrily so that they returned to their previous stoic demeanors. He apologized for their immature welcome and explained that they were all from Mexico and unaccustomed to her particular dialect. He went on, explaining that the other girls had been in "business" with him for years now and would learn to welcome her after a little bit of time. Gabriella nodded, even though, at the time, she wasn't sure what exactly his "business" entailed.

He led her to a tiny space in the back of the house, which was uninviting and bare apart from a dusty mattress in the center of the room. He smiled as she settled in, and left her with a reassuring touch of the shoulder. After he closed the door, she curled up on the mattress and bawled in a state of raw loneliness. The memories of those first few hours would burn sharply in her mind for years. She remembered studying the faded wallpaper that lined her room, the dirty smell of the sheets that infiltrated her senses, and the moans she heard from the neighboring corridors when one of the other girls took up another "client."

The home might have been unbearable had it not been for Roberto. With comforting relief, he revealed that she would not have to take any clients to her room like the other girls, and thoughtfully asked how he could help her adjust. He prepared traditional Guatemalan dishes to remind her of home, and bought her new clothes in her favorite colors. He asked about her life with interest, and listened intently as she rambled through stories about her tragic childhood. When she told him that she had never learned how to read or write, he instructed the oldest girl in the house to give her lessons on how to read English, and started bringing her simple books from the library home for her to practice. The other girls were jealous at the special attention and barely spoke to her out of spite, but she became so smitten with his affection that she barely paid them any notice.

Within a month of her arrival, he asked her to be his girlfriend, and she enthusiastically agreed. After that, he started staying in her room nearly every night. At first she hesitated when he asked for sex. Although he graciously agreed to wait, she could sense his frustration and felt him withdraw from the rejection. Reminding herself of his unwavering kindness and genuine endearment, she complied with his request the following evening. The event passed as a surprisingly unremarkable experience, and the act innocently grew into their casual, nightly routine.

She hastily fell in love with him, and became enchanted with the intricate secrecies of his life. He explained that he owned five different houses with six girls in each. She marveled at his empire and didn't think to question his sincere belief in the integrity of his enterprise. Although the act of "working" had once seemed vulgar and profane, his offhand explanations of his business transformed the idea into an elementary transaction. After some time, she grew blindly accustomed to his interpretation.

Eventually he did ask her to take up a client, but not out of impulse or force. He had a bad week in business and asked for one simple favor. The task was an arduous forfeit of her own comfort, but one that seemed proportionate to his unyielding generosity. After some thought, she hesitantly yielded to his request.

She shook with anticipation as she went to meet her first client. He was a short, stocky man who rarely spoke and never looked her in the eye. Roberto quickly negotiated a price, and told him to be gentle with his prized woman as she nervously led him to her room and slowly locked the door. She didn't like the feeling of another man's touch, but endured the discomfort with steadfast resolution. She stared at the ceiling in detached passivity until he finally finished and left without a word. A stab of guilt hit her after the door closed behind him, and for a moment her grandmother's voice screaming "WHORE!" echoed in her head. She turned over and sulked in crushing shame until Roberto came to find her. To her relief, he held her with sincere gratitude and once again showered her with special affection, making the ordeal seem at least somewhat bearable.

The next week he asked her take up just one more client, and then another. They started coming every day, and then every hour. Soon she lost track of the men she had seen, and her days blurred into an immovable rhythm, merging into a single wave of endless patrons between windows of solitude or sleep.

Roberto's curiosity in her steadily dwindled until he eventually stopped looking at her altogether. Although at first she had chased his desire, pathetically trying to grasp at his waning enthusiasm, soon her faith in their relationship faded as her list of clients grew. She never fully overcame the humiliation behind his rejection, but she did eventually grow numb to the heartbreak. She allowed herself to detach with apathetic indifference, and spent the next five years in a state of steady dispassion.

On this day in particular, her first customer was quiet and impassive, traits Gabriella had grown to prefer. He undressed in sobering silence and lifted her skirt without hesitation. She laid back with thorough ambivalence and started the effortless practice of detaching her mind from her tangible surroundings. She considered the outlines forming from the various cracks in her ceiling as her body uneasily stirred with his stiff rhythm. She no longer found the act of sex in itself especially vexing, but she refused to falsely engage or pretend to enjoy it in the way certain men preferred. Sometimes a particularly aggravating client would demand that she moan, but even then it all felt like a mechanical, soulless performance.

When she was with a client her stretches of disengagement usually began by replaying scenes from the book she had read the night before, often envisioning the plot with herself as the heroine. Her one impressive accomplishment since moving into the house was learning how to read and speak virtually flawless English. Not only had she picked up the language in less than a year, she could now comprehend complex and lengthy literature without issue. Her most recent read was "Jane Eyre," which had been too enticing to put down for more than a couple of hours. Instead of savoring the pages slowly, she had negligently devoured the story in only a few days. Now she would likely have to reread it again before she could request a new book from Roberto's weekly trip to the library.

At last she heard her customer finish with an abrupt groan. He haphazardly rolled off of her, and started to dress himself to leave. Without looking up, he listlessly asked for her name.

"Sugar," she responded coldly.

"No, what's your real name?" he mumbled.

"I don't have one," she sighed and laid back on the bed, hoping he would leave quickly so she could read another couple of pages before her next client.

Suddenly there was a large crash from the other end of the house, causing her to stir in unease. She heard a scuffle of bodies and slamming of doors, and cowered as she recognized a scream from the girl whose room was located across from her own. Gabriella heard someone yell "Police!" in a panic, and watched as the man in her room clumsily tried to scurry out her window. He made it halfway through the gravel yard before he was halted by a police van pulling into the alley, blocking his sole means of escape. The entire house was apparently surrounded.

Gabriella watched this alarming encounter with dismay but stayed in bed, frozen with fear. For a brief second she thought this might be one of her nightmares, but as she pinched herself a thick pain shot through her arm. The door to her room burst open and a man appeared with a gun slung across his shoulder. He flashed his badge as if the gesture alone would have any meaning to her, and she shook in horror as he approached her bed.

"How old are you?" he asked in a stern voice.

"I don't know," Gabriella answered timidly as tears began rushing down her face.

The officer's face softened a little. He was a handsome, young man, probably only a few years older than her. His thick blond hair was perfectly gelled into place and his uniform hugged his body in a way that brought a sense of devout authority to his childish demeanor. "I'm sorry, but I don't believe you. Do you have any identification?" He asked.

She shook her head.

"What's your name?"

"Sugar."

"Your real name."

"I don't have one," she instinctively blurted before she immediately recoiled with a small shake of her head, "Gabriella Rodriguez."

"Gabriella, you need to come with me."

"But... you can't take me from here. I don't have anywhere to go. Roberto needs me here."

"I'm sorry," he answered, "but you can't stay here. The owner of this brothel is being arrested, and this house will be condemned. We have a safe place for you to stay until we can take additional steps."

"But... what's going to happen? What steps?"

"All will be explained later."

"Please," Gabriella pleaded, "I'm so scared."

The officer sighed, "You'll go to court to determine if you're guilty of any crimes, and then from there we'll find you a new home before we begin deportation proceedings."

"But... this is my home," she cried. "This is my home!"

September 7, 2015
Kaitlyn

"Mr. Holzen," Kaitlyn called out to her class with an unwavering, stern tone. "Can you tell us the issue of the case?"

"I'd love to," Brian answered with sarcastic enthusiasm. "The issue is whether or not the parents can sue the manufacturer for a design defect."

"No," Kaitlyn sighed, signaling to the rest of the class to interject, "Tell him why he's wrong, class."

"Anyone can always sue anyone," a chorus of students responded robotically in rehearsed unison.

"Exactly," Kaitlyn said. "The issue is never *can* one sue, but rather *should* one sue." Kaitlyn detested teaching Remedies, a subject which was notoriously boring for everyone but held a particularly strong disinterest for third year students who were already prone to disengagement. The subject itself was straightforward enough, but it wasn't an especially compelling course or relevant to her background in criminal law. She found the task of intriguing students with her lecture a tiresome drain, and had grown accustomed to a sea of disinterested faces.

"Right," Brian corrected, "the issue is if the parents can win a lawsuit against the manufacturer of this vacuum cleaner for negligent design... because their son stuck his penis in the vacuum and it got... uh... damaged."

"The vacuum or his penis?" Kaitlyn asked in a stiff professional tone. She was feeling particularly disheartened today, and tried to ignore the few distant giggles from the back row.

"His penis!" Brian answered eagerly, belting out the answer as if it were a gratifying punchline. The entire class let out a small laugh, which only further inflamed Kaitlyn's already sour mood.

"Let's be adults now, class," she said sternly before turning back to Brian. "You're correct. Now, were they successful?"

"Um... I didn't get that far."

"What do you mean?"

"I didn't read the rest of the case... sorry Professor Tryst," Brian mumbled nervously as his eyes fell to the floor. He nervously began tapping his pencil against the surface of his desk in shame. In spite of herself, she relished his discomfort and internally began composing a disparaging speech. The room grew tense as everyone braced for their professor's inevitable outburst. Kaitlyn had stringent expectations and a notoriously rigid temper which readily flared when she uncovered an ill-prepared student.

"I have a question," Julia swooped in, attempting to save Brian from her professor's inevitable fury. Kaitlyn did everything in her power to refrain from rolling her eyes at Julia's overt rescue attempt as she begrudgingly pointed towards Julia to answer.

Kaitlyn didn't much care for Julia. Obviously the girl was bright and habitually prepared, but her classroom commentary had repeatedly undermined Kaitlyn's staunch authority. While most professors found Julia's infallible convictions exceedingly endearing, Kaitlyn was simply annoyed with her student's level of entitlement.

"What's your question, Miss Harrison?" she snapped a little too harshly.

"I was wondering if the financial status of the plaintiff or the marketing strategies of the corporation are ever taken into account in cases like this?" Julia asked cheerfully with a flip of her curly, auburn hair. She had a uniquely staggering beauty that almost distracted from her pronounced intellect. Subconsciously, Kaitlyn had a hard time keeping herself from comparing her own aging appearance to Julia's.

Kaitlyn paused at Julia's question, now partly amused by this deviation. This was a curiously weak argument that could finally pose the long-awaited opportunity to crush her least favorite student in a public debate. "And why is that?" She asked in a voice that came out in a more demeaning tone than she had intended.

"I know it sounds ridiculous that a company should be held liable for a little boy being well... a curious little boy, but it just seems like compensation should be based on the parent's ability to pay for his medical expenses. If a company makes a faulty product and markets it to destitute families, knowing those consumers won't have the resources to sue, I think that company should be subjected to heightened accountability."

Julia paused, allowing the other students to catch up to her muddled logic. Kaitlyn noted this tirade as one of Julia's more obscure tangents, and suspected her rambling was more of a panicked attempt to rescue Brian than anything. Julia often went on rants which laid out frustratingly coptic personal views, but generally the heart of her digressions were somewhat relevant to class discussion. This erratic deviation seemed particularly aimless and somewhat uncharacteristic.

"I... hope that makes sense," Julia concluded nervously after a moment of graceless silence. This was the first time Kaitlyn had ever exposed any hint of shyness or insecurity in Julia's demeanor, and she wasn't about to pass up an opportunity to debate a weak point. Brian's scolding would have to wait.

"So what you're arguing," Kaitlyn mocked, "is that we should give some leeway in the law for people who are taken advantage of by big, bad corporations?"

"I feel like you're insulting me, Professor Tryst, but I do think it's a legitimate point."

Kaitlyn laughed a little too forcefully. "This, class," she began, "is a very naive view of the law and perfect example of someone who is still failing to 'think like a lawyer.' The law is designed to be uniform, predictable, and fair. If you don't understand that, you don't understand the legal theory of remedies, or the law generally."

"Fair? How is that fair?" Julia interjected, "if a company purposefully makes unsafe products anticipating fewer financial consequences, that can't be fair."

"Because we need a uniform standard for *all* companies to follow in *all* cases," Kaitlyn shot back. "Now, it's easy to get wrapped up in the backstory of these plaintiffs and let your emotions overcome reason, but that's not the way to win a suit. Irrational arguments make terrible cases, and irrational people make terrible lawyers."

The room settled into a tense stillness as Kaitlyn finished her glaring speech. For a moment, she feared she might have taken her point too far, but now she refused to back down. She eyed Julia with a derogatory smile, and gave a dismissal shrug at the rest of her students' stunned reactions. Julia's body language didn't show any hint of embarrassment, but her flushed cheeks revealed her true composure. Kaitlyn half expected her to cry, as most students would have at this point in an argument, but Julia somehow held her ground and stared back with equal fury.

"In theory, I understand your point, Professor," Julia stated firmly.

"But you don't agree?"

"No."

"Would you like to elaborate?"

"Not particularly, no. I already laid out my argument so there's not much more to say. I would like to add that human conflict is never black and white, and I personally feel it's actually naive for a legal scholar, such as yourself, to preach such staunch simplicity."

Her fellow students let out a confounded gasp. Julia was notoriously stubborn, but she had never been outright disrespectful. It was acceptable for a professor to routinely make an argument personal, but it was nearly unheard of for a student to do the same.

"Excuse me?" Kaitlyn asked, dramatically accentuating her level of astonishment as she held a hand to her heart. In truth, she found it mildly entertaining to finally see Julia inflamed over an insignificant dispute. However, as Kaitlyn surveyed the room with anticipated satisfaction, to her dismay she noticed a number of students still beaming at Julia, somehow impressed with her refusal to yield. She realized then that Julia was so well-liked by her peers that Kait's attempt to establish her authority through incidental embarrassment had painfully backfired.

"Well Julia, I appreciate your input... even if it's incredibly elementary and off topic. Hopefully you'll learn to detach yourself from these personal feelings before your time at Brooktown has ended. Otherwise the professors here have not done their job of preparing you to enter the field. Now, if we're done here, I'd like to get back to teaching the law."

Julia nodded with an infuriating, triumphant smirk.

"Now... Mr. Holzen," Kaitlyn continued, feeling more perturbed now than before, "I believe we have some unfinished business, don't you? Let's continue with our discussion of your clearly inadequate analysis of the case and your decision to come to my class unprepared."

September 7, 2015
Daniel

"You make it seem so fucking easy," Daniel snorted after Julia explained their assignment for the third time that evening. They sat at his desk with a cluster of books outstretched before them, most marked up with convoluted annotations.

"No, you're just making it more complicated than it has to be. Most of these hangups are in your head. Just reread this paragraph," Julia answered patiently as she coolly pulled her mass of curls into a tight bun at the base of her neck. Daniel sighed and continued to achingly trudge through the material. He had read the case twice already and thought he understood the main concepts until Julia began quizzing him over elementary details of the case. He rubbed his forehead in frustration as he half-heartedly made additional notes in the already cramped margins.

"Hey do you over-achievers want a drink?" Brian called from the other room.

"Dude, it's only six," Julia replied with a playful shake of her head.

"Yes, but I'm getting a jumpstart on my inevitable decent into alcoholism. I'm embracing the lawyer stereotype," Brian announced as he entered Daniel's bedroom with a bottle of whiskey under his arm and three glasses in hand. He was conventionally handsome, tall and still muscular from his days of playing high-school sports.

"How's that working out?" she asked with fictitious concern.

"Wonderful actually, I think this is the upside of our career choice. I can be a raging alcoholic. If anyone protests, I'll just blame it on my demanding job and broken spirit," he shrugged casually, but Daniel cringed at the joke. "Incidentally, maybe the reason why Tryst is such a bitch is because she failed to develop such a healthy outlet. If alcohol keeps me from turning into that bitter old hag, I would dare to say that I'm actually making the better life choice. Can you believe that bitch kicked me out of class today?"

"Don't call her a bitch, Brian," Julia snapped. "Don't get me wrong, I really, really don't like her, but she deserves more respect than that."

"In that case, can you believe that empty-shell-of-a-human-being kicked me out of class today?"

"Ok, well to be fair, you hadn't read the case," Daniel shyly protested. "You know she's prone to pulling stunts like that, especially on third years. She gets frustrated because so many people stop reading."

"You could be a little more supportive," Brian whined, clutching his heart in a phony affront.

Daniel put up his hands in defense, "You're right, I will try to be more encouraging of your academic ambivalence."

"Your support is much appreciated, glad to have you on my side. Speaking of which," Brian said as he turned back to Julia, "I do appreciate you trying to save me today."

"Yeah, well it didn't do much good," she shook her head. "We both just ended up getting humiliated."

"Don't let her do that to you, Julia," Brian said again. "Your point was valid, that bitch just doesn't have a heart."

"Seriously, don't call her a bitch!" Julia grumbled a little more sternly. "I don't like that word, especially not for a professor. She's horrible, but she's not bitch." She looked back at Daniel and softened to a jestful tone. "I can't believe you live with this animal. How did the two of you end up together again?"

"I could ask you the same question." Brian interjected with a half-chuckle which immediately faded when he saw Daniel flinch. Brian caught the subtle discomfort that flared for a moment on his his friend's face, and was immediately hit with a lump of remorse. "I mean, Julia," he continued, struggling to muster a recovery, "I hope you realize that Daniel is clearly settling. I think law school rocked his self-confidence which is why you even have a chance with him."

Daniel breathed a sigh of relief. The fact that Julia was so blatantly out of his league was a delicate topic, one that most of his friends awkwardly avoided with tedious restraint. Even with noble intentions behind their agonizing subtleties, this only proved to reinforce his insecurities. Daniel preferred playful acknowledgement of the imbalance of their relationship over willful evasion.

"Trust me, I know I'm the lucky one," Julia said as she turned to softly kiss Daniel on the cheek. He blushed and gave her a sheepishly admiring grin.

"Well that's just fucking adorable," Brian grunted. "Meanwhile I am starting a long and healthy relationship too with my new best friend, whiskey. I motion that you both take a break from your boring law school endeavors and join me in getting wasted."

"Dude, we have class tomorrow," Daniel stated flatly, knowing full-well this explanation would do little to satisfy Brian. They had been friends for years now and Daniel understood that dodging an invitation to drink would require a much heavier and adamant series of justifications.

"Not until one o'clock in the afternoon, you fucking puritan!" Brian snapped back. "This is the last phase of our student lifestyle. Are you seriously going to waste it on trivial things such as grades?"

"You realize if I say 'yes' that makes me the normal one, right?" Daniel laughed. "We're in law school... grades are basically everything."

"Wrong! You've clearly been brainwashed which is all the more reason for a break. Come on, guys! I encourage you both to embrace the lifestyle and drink! If our professors have the right to subject us to daily humiliation, we have the right to drown our sorrows. Besides, the two of you owe me a favor considering you're leaving me in three days."

"Brian," Julia pleaded, "we've been through this. We're not leaving *you*, we're getting our own place. That's what normal people do after they've been in a relationship for two years."

"I don't care what you call it, it's bullshit. You're abandoning me in my time of need. The least you can do is provide me with a couple of dedicated drinking buddies for the night."

Daniel turned to Julia who shrugged as she closed their law books with relief before pouring herself a generous portion from Brian's heavy bottle. She swirled the dark liquid around a bit before taking a sip with a mischievous smile. Brian beamed victoriously as he reached to pour a glass for both himself and Daniel.

Brian and Daniel met freshman year of college during an introductory economics seminar. Although Daniel, initially hesitant to align with someone of Brian's unyielding energy and bold extroversion, Brian almost immediately took to Daniel's endearingly modest charm. After continually insisting that the two meet up outside of class, Brian quickly won Daniel over and became a vital fixture in his new friend's life. They were an unlikely pair considering the discrepancies in their vastly conflicting personalities, but their characters proved to be more complementary than irreconcilable. Within months they became inseparable.

With his pervasive social anxiety, Daniel rarely surrounded himself with more than one or two intimate friends at a time. Brian, on the other hand, was notoriously approachable and routinely attracted a generous following. He pushed Daniel to abandon his social avoidance and forced him to embrace the blossoming opportunities associated with college life. By the end of Freshman year, for the first time in his life, Daniel had a large group of friends and became a well-known figure around campus.

As their lives integrated, their habits fell into sync. As a dedicated student, Daniel spent nearly every day in the library, so Brian did the same. Although his identity had never been wrapped up in academics, eventually Brian started matching his friend's impressive scores. When their rankings came out towards the end of sophomore year, much to Brian's gratifying shock, they were both on track to graduate in the top 5% of their class. Daniel never understood why Brian thanked him for his placement, and laughed when Brian explained that he couldn't have done it alone. "You're brilliant," Daniel responded, "I really don't have anything to do with it."

Out of impulse and admitted curiosity, they tried adderall together for the first time at the beginning of their junior year while preparing for a notoriously difficult statistics final. Daniel hated the effects immediately and intuitively swore off the drug as an the isolated experiment. Brian shrugged at his friend's aversion and frequently started buying minor amounts of the stimulant. It started out as a trivial habit, a side note of their friendship which Daniel hardly seemed to notice. Brian would pop a pill if he had to pull an all-nighter, which became a typical occurrence as their junior year progressed.

In a sea of overdiagnosed and heavily medicated students, Brian's campus created the ideal atmosphere to downplay his steadily developing addiction as a nonchalant routine. His progressively erratic behavior didn't develop overnight, but rather came in waves of seemingly petty abnormalities. His sleeping habits became increasingly irregular, he stopped eating on an orderly schedule, and he found his prevailing ramblings common and uncontrollable. Daniel subtly noticed these developments and worried with each new swell of outlandish behavior, but every time he gently noted a change, Brian would shrug off his friend's worry as an inconsequential detail.

Halfway through their junior year, Brian's symptoms became unignorable. One day Daniel noticed Brian's hands shaking with abnormal vigor when his friend couldn't unlock the homescreen of his iphone. He watched as Brian's hands clumsily fumbled over the simple pattern on the screen before he hastily clicked off the phone altogether and shoved it into his bag in frustration. "Are you ok?" Daniel asked suspiciously, as he noticed Brian's eyes madly jolting around the room in jittery paranoia. Per usual, Brian just shrugged and laughed off Daniel's concern.

The following day, as the two were walking to the library from Brian's dorm, Daniel noticed Brian's breathing becoming heavy and irregular. In an inexplicable outburst, he watched as his friend fell onto a bench behind him and clutched his heart in an obviously painful exposition. "What the hell, man?" Daniel asked in a panic.

"It's nothing," Brian said between dire gasps for air.

"Should I call an ambulance?"

"No, no... This will pass."

"What are you talking about? You don't know that."

"This has happened... before. I promise... I'm fine."

"What do you mean this has happened before? We need to get help."

"Just... leave... me... alone... for a second."

"Dude, what the hell? What's going on."

After a a few moments of biting anticipation, Brian's breathing started to slow and color rushed back into his face. "See?" he said calmly after his symptoms subsided. "I told you, I'm fine."

"No," Daniel shook his head, "you're not. I think you have a problem. How much adderall are you taking?"

"Dude, I'm fine. Just leave it alone."

Daniel gave him a hard stare and contemplated his friend's response before finally giving a decidedly brisk shake of his head. "No, we need to get you help."

"Mind your own business!" Brian shot back and grabbed his bag to leave.

"Hey! What the hell, man? Where are you going?"

"Don't fucking follow me!" Brian shot back in disgust.

Brian ignored Daniel's calls for four agonizing days. It was their longest stint of silence since meeting freshman year. Daniel's anxiety was constant and thick as he compulsively replayed the sight of his friend clutching his chest over and over again in his head. For the tenth time that day, he dialed Brian's number and was again swiftly forwarded to voicemail. He put his phone down on his desk and absent-mindedly watched the blank screen in a paralyzing state of defeat. He was considering raiding Brian's dorm and demanding an explanation when at last his phone lit up with Brian's number.

"Hello?" he asked after frantically scrambling to answer. He only heard pieces of Brian's inaudible voice through muffled sobs. "Where are you?" Daniel continued without waiting for an added explanation.

"My dorm."

"I'm on my way."

Watching his friend undergo withdrawals proved to be one of the more torturous experiences of Daniel's life. He sat patiently next to Brian's bed, only leaving when it was necessary to restock with food or additional hydrations. Brian trembled uncontrollably and furiously wailed as his body gradually adjusted to the rawness of sobriety. A few times he had adamantly begged for just one more pill, but Daniel would always adamantly shake his head in refusal.

The process dragged with influxes of mild improvements followed by devastating lapses into darkened states. After a week of this painful cycle, eventually Brian's symptoms did subside, and for the first time in months Daniel saw glimpses into the endearing aspects of his friend's former personality. Daniel lightened at this development, marveling at how lively and enjoyable Brian was without his thick pharmaceutical veil.

"Thank you," Brian finally said after nearly a week of Daniel's care. "I'm so sorry, Daniel. I don't know how it got that bad."

"It's ok, Dude. Just... don't touch them again."

"I promise. I don't know what I would have done... I owe you everything. I owe you my life even."

"No you don't-"

"-Daniel," Brian interjected. "Yes I do. I love you."

Daniel smiled at that. Brian wasn't generally one to show affection and his warmth felt particularly rewarding against the backdrop of their painful week. "I love you too," Daniel answered with a small touch of Brian's shoulder.

The dynamic of their relationship powerfully shifted after his recovery. Brian, who had always been the obvious leader of the two, started relying on Daniel to take the lead on major decisions. Their lives tangled and intertwined into a continuous pattern of ongoing and evolving loyalty. Their bond went from intimate to obsessive, so that when Daniel announced he was going to law school, Brian immediately went out and took the LSAT as well.

"Here's to law school. It can kiss my ass," Brian announced to Daniel and Julia as he cheerfully raised his whiskey, lightly clinking glasses with his companions. They both giggled at his enthusiasm as they downed the cheap liquor. After two rounds, all three friends were feeling particularly nice and amiable as they faded into a leisurely state.

"Thank god we're almost done with this bullshit," Brian chuckled as he sat back in his chair and lifted his feet to rest on Daniel's desk. "I'm not going to miss this place at all."

"I'm going to," Julia stated unapologetically. "It's been my home for two years. Honestly, it's the first place I've ever lived that really felt like home at all."

"Well, naturally super-student over here loves Brooktown. What about you, Daniel?"

"No, I won't miss it," he sighed without looking up. "I'm so ready to get out."

"Hey, I'm kind of afraid to ask," Brian abruptly changed the subject, "but why did Bishop keep you after class the other day? I'm curious."

Daniel shrugged, "It's kind of hard to explain. It wasn't a bad meeting, he just wanted to make sure I was doing ok. It's no secret I struggle."

"We all do," Julia said reassuringly, grabbing his hand as a comforting gesture. "It's not an easy program, everyone feels lost."

"Some more than others." Daniel jokingly rolled his eyes at her before turning back to Brian. "Basically, Bishop claims he used to get nervous with public speaking, and thinks law school helped him get past it. Also, apparently he freaked out before his Supreme Court argument."

"That was actually really nice of him to tell you that," Brian added, settling into one of his rare moods of emotional sincerity. "I've been trying to figure Bishop out for a while now. I'm just fascinated with the guy after I found out he was suspended from the bar a couple of years ago."

Julia and Daniel both turned to Brian in shock.

"What?" Julia stammered, "Why? He's so... accomplished."

"Oh is that right, Julia?" Brian mocked. "Is he *dreamy* too?"

"You're disgusting," she replied, "he's like sixty."

"He's like fifty, and you know half the girls in our class are secretly pining after him."

"Maybe we shouldn't gossip about it," Daniel interjected with subtle hesitation. Despite his curiosity, he felt an odd sense of loyalty to Bishop. Participating in a potentially slanderous conversation made him feel uneasy in the face of his professor's recent display of candid sympathy.

"Oh, it's not gossip," Brian said, "I looked it up online already. The Bar Association posts a list of all lawyers they've suspended."

"What for? What did he do?" Julia asked with a surprising level of concern.

"Now this part is gossip because the reason for his suspension wasn't published, but everyone claims he was having sex with one of his clients... Some girl named Melissa."

"Ewwww," Julia sputtered impulsively. "Oh sorry, that came out wrong. He's just so... old."

"Old people have sex too, Julia," Brian jested.

She rolled her eyes, "That's a really lovely image, Brian."

"I'm serious though," he continued in an almost hushed tone, "I've heard it from a few people around campus, and there were some references to it online. Apparently it was a really big scandal a while back, but Brooktown tried to keep it under wraps to protect the 'integrity of the institution' or whatever."

"Are you sure?" Daniel prodded, "I mean, he is a celebrity. People make stuff like that up. This sounds more like a tabloid than a legitimate story."

"That's a fair point actually. You're right, I don't know if it's true. This is all pure speculation and minor internet trolling. It could be fabricated, but why else would he be suspended? Plus he does kind of flirt with Julia, if you haven't noticed."

"Come on, Brian," Daniel snapped. "He does not. She's just a good student so he favors her in class. You're just jealous it's not you."

"That was a joke, Daniel," Brian responded, honestly hurt and a little taken aback by Daniel's reaction. "My point though, is that I can't imagine him committing any other serious offense. He's like Mr. Nobility, or whatever. What else could it be?"

Julia nodded in agreement, "I don't know, but sometimes people can surprise you. I hope it's not true though, I really like him."

"Not you too," Brian snorted, "If I hear one more person compare that bastard to Atticus Finch I'm going to dig up Harper Lee and spit on her for creating such a stupid character."

"Well Atticus ended up racist in the end anyway," Daniel noted, "so that comparison is irrelevant now."

"Unless Bishop was suspended for being a racist!" Brian joked, "Then it would be spot on!"

"I don't think they can suspend someone for being racist," Julia noted sarcastically, "and I highly doubt a man who has dedicated himself to work in civil rights would have been suspended for something to do with that. Jesus, the man is a bleeding heart liberal."

"Isn't most of his work in women's rights though?" Daniel asked. "That's why he does so much with human trafficking."

"Yeah it is," Julia nodded. "What's your point?"

"Nothing, it just seems like he's more passionate about gender issues... he just really likes women," Daniel shrugged.

"What are you saying?" she stared at him blankly, obviously trying not to appear defensive.

"-I don't actually think he's a racist guys," Brian interjected. "It was a joke. I just think it would be ironic. I mean, his suspension is ironic in itself, don't you think?"

"What about that is ironic?" Julia questioned.

"Well, if the rumors about him sleeping with a client are true, and the man's focus is in women's rights, it would just seem a little funny. That's a tad... disrespectful."

"Not necessarily. Believe it or not Brian, you can have sex with a woman without disrespecting her."

"Oh Julia, I know. I heard you both through the wall last night. It sounded like a very respectful encounter."

Julia threw a pillow at him in retaliation. "This is why we're getting our own place, damn it. Let's change the subject anyway," she announced. "This *is* starting to feel too much like gossip."

They steered the conversation into shallow territory, but a strangely restless feeling lingered with Daniel after their deviation. Something about Bishop's suspension inexplicably made his stomach turn.

OCTOBER 3, 2012
Kaitlyn

"Is there any way that we can fire him?" Kaitlyn plead, fully understanding the futile nature behind this solicitation.

"He's tenured, Kait," Dean Herrera responded with an exhausted sigh. "I don't think that's a possibility."

They were situated in Herrera's office which overlooked Brooktown's charming, rustic school grounds. From the large, open windows of the dean's suite she could glimpse the entire campus and survey the students she had grown so passionately fond of as they lingered between classes. Usually this scene would have flooded Kaitlyn with comfort and sentimentality, but today she was spinning with nauseating resentment.

After leaving the firm, she developed a genuine infatuation with the school and her role here as an educator. Despite her reputation of being a particularly sour academic, most of her hardened attitude was a calculated act fueled by her own stubborn convictions. The truth was that she cherished her work and found fulfillment in watching her students evolve through their education. Lately though, her reassuring feelings about Brooktown had been overshadowed with antagonizing indignation. After two decades of purposefully devoting her life to the school, over the course of several months, she had pierced the veneer of the university's integrity and saw the darker side of the prestigious institution. Now the feelings of camaraderie she had once shared with her fellow professors and blind belief that her students were sheltered by the institution's security, seemed tainted with a foreboding sense that something dangerous was lurking under the sparkling surface of Brooktown's pristine reputation.

"I'm telling you, there's something wrong here. I saw the girl at the hearing, I'm positive she's not making this up. I've been a professor for close to twenty years, I've gotten pretty good at sifting through bullshit. She wasn't lying."

"I thought you and Bishop were friends," Herrera asked pointedly. She took off her glasses and rubbed her eyes, obviously drained from the ongoing confrontation. She was older, shrunken with age and stress, but remnants of her youthful energy still lingered beneath her deep wrinkles.

"Does Bishop actually have any friends?" Kaitlyn asked a little too harshly.

"That's a loaded question. I think many people would claim him as friend. Although with his reputation, I think a lot more people would be afraid not to claim him as a friend." Herrera chuckled.

"That's very comforting," Kaitlyn snorted with an exaggerated roll of her eyes. "I'm being serious, have you ever heard him talk about a meaningful relationship outside of his work? He has a lot of enemies too, you know."

Herrera considered that for a moment, before continuing with a dismissive wave of her hand, "Well, maybe it's safe to say that he has more enemies than friends, but it comes with the job. I mean, he gets death threats for his work in civil rights, but those aren't exactly from people I would want as 'friends' either."

"Those aren't the enemies I was talking about, Adrian," Kaitlyn sighed. "I'm sure you've heard rumors about him like I have. Those stories don't spawn from nothing."

"Listen," Herrera said with a stern change of her tone, "all of this is beside the point. He's not the first lawyer to sleep with a client. Hell, he's not even the first one on our staff to do such a thing. There's a reason he's only up for suspension and not disbarment. If we disbarred every lawyer who broke this rule, we'd have a very bare legal profession. I know he made a mistake, but he's also an excellent professor and a celebrity in his field. We're going to need a pretty good reason if we want to take a more drastic step."

"I'm telling you, Adrian, something is off. I saw her. I saw the way... she started shaking when Bishop walked in. She was terrified. There's a lot more to this story than she told that joke-of-an ethics-board we appointed. The way she looked at him, I swear it was like she was expecting him to hurt her."

Whenever a staff member faced disciplinary measures from the bar association, it was Brooktown's policy to conduct its own investigation. Kaitlyn had been one of the five staff members chosen to participate on the temporary ethics board appointed to research the claim. They held a hearing which masqueraded as a platform for both sides to safely share their story, but Melissa Antemie's testimony was promptly dismissed and abandoned moments after she took the stand. Kaitlyn was the only person on the board to advocate for Bishop's expulsion after all of the evidence had been set on the record.

"That's a pretty harsh assumption," Dean Herrera sighed. "Is there something you're not telling me, Kait?"

Kaitlyn hesitated, "I don't know if I can say."

"I won't disclose it to anyone else. I just want the full story. Talk to me as your friend."

"Ok," Kait nodded, "Maybe this was inappropriate, but I talked to Melissa after her hearing. She said a few things that struck me as... odd. She hinted that she was scared of someone."

"Why are you just bringing this up now?"

"She didn't say anything directly incriminating, so it's not like I had anything solid to come forward with, especially against someone with his background. I didn't want to ruin his reputation if it wasn't true."

"Honestly, I think it would take a lot more than that to ruin his reputation. How many people have compared him to Atticus Finch? Even in the face of this scandal, very few would have legitimately questioned his integrity. When the story broke that he was being subject to disciplinary action, I must have received fifty letters defending his honor."

It was true. Even if Kaitlyn had questioned Bishop's virtue, it was highly unlikely that any substantive disciplinary action would have materialized from such a disclosure. His reputation was practically unshakeable.

Melissa, Bishop's former client, came forward with a complaint that he had breached his ethical duties by sleeping with her during the course of her representation. Things got even more complicated when she later alleged he had faltered into a brutally violent state and beat her when she denied his unwelcomed proposals. Instinctively, Kaitlyn was hesitant to believe that an eminently revered person like Bishop could have committed such an atrocious act, but Melissa's cowardly demeanor during her jittery testimony was the only proof Kaitlyn needed to credit these allegations. Within minutes of glimpsing Melissa's terrified face, it became evident to Kaitlyn that Bishop was falsifying the nature of their relationship. She urged the rest of her unsuspecting colleagues to extend their investigation beyond the obviously partisan hearing, but the board was reluctant to push for any additional information. All she had was an admittedly modest hunch, which paled in comparison to Bishop's impeccable reputation and band of loyal admirers.

At the hearing, Bishop admitted that in a fleeting lapse of judgment he had engaged in "consensual relations" with Melissa. He testified that it was the first time he had ever given into such temptations with a client and that he had no intention of ever violating the rules of ethical conduct again. He explained that Melissa had repeatedly tried to initiate an improper relationship, and that he had again and again refused. Finally, when Bishop successfully argued and won her case, after a few celebratory drinks he weakened to her advances in what he described as a "regrettable moment of temporary moral fragility."

Three months before the hearing took place, Melissa had submitted a meticulously detailed written testimony which specified the extent of Bishop's tasteless etiquette. She alleged that Bishop had relentlessly pursued her for months with "uncompromising persistence." She purportedly refused his advances, explaining that she had a serious boyfriend and wasn't interested in dating her lawyer, but he dismissed her rejection with callous detachment and continued to incessantly push her boundaries. She claimed that he had asked for sex in exchange for his services in lieu of payment halfway through her representation, and threatened to drop her entire suit if she refused. At the end of their professional relationship, he insisted that they have a drink in his office to clear up any misunderstandings. She joined him willingly, anxious to put their past behind them, but after she arrived at his office Bishop blocked the door and repeatedly demanded that she sleep with him. This eventually led to him viciously attacking her until she at last yielded to his heinous request.

However, when she finally got a chance to speak to the ethics board about this encounter, her oral testimony drastically disjointed from her written statement. Suddenly their affair fully mirrored Bishop's mild account of events. When asked why she had filed such a frivolous complaint in the first place, she stated that she was bitter because he rejected her early in their relationship, and wanted him to suffer by attacking his reputation. Most on the ethics board blindly accepted this explanation without further inquiry, and agreed that a short suspension was a fair punishment for this level of inappropriate client relations. Despite Kaitlyn's objections, it took them less than an hour to reach a decision.

After the hearing had reconvened and the ethics board head announced to Bishop and Melissa that he would receive minor repercussions, Kaitlyn could scarcely watch the reconciled expressions of her colleagues. She turned to Melissa who was miserably staring at the floor, eyes wide with dissatisfaction and heartache. As Bishop victoriously smiled at his colleagues and went to shake their hands, Melissa slowly got up and sulked out of the room. Kaitlyn cautiously scanned the area to ensure no one was watching before she too got up and followed Melissa out.

Kaitlyn didn't know much about Melissa except that she was a beautiful, young immigrant from Eastern Europe who had been trafficked to the United States three years earlier. Although she was promised a job and an apartment upon her arrival, she was instead forced to clean houses without pay and live in a small, condemned home with nearly twenty other women. After years of forced labor, she was no closer to paying off her debt than when she had first arrived in the United States. Apparently she met a man during one of her jobs who would later become her serious boyfriend. In what would have been an all-too-perfect love story, he eventually uncovered the cruel reality of her situation and selflessly helped plan an escape. Their first step was hiring

Anthony Bishop, a world-renowned civil rights attorney who specialized in human trafficking lawsuits.

A full-fledged FBI investigation sprung from Melissa's case, resulting in the exposition of an advanced human trafficking ring. At the close of their investigation, four men were arrested and thirty women, all of whom been working for years as labor slaves, were set free and given immigration amnesty. In its entirety, Melissa's representation took close to two years, but in that time Bishop had secured her legal status in the U.S. and helped her testify against her traffickers in criminal court. The case became one of Bishop's most acclaimed legal victories, and brought Brooktown a flood of affirmative publicity. Nearly every day of the criminal trial, stories ran about Brooktown's star professor, and how he had humbly accepted a complex trafficking case that resulted in their team valiantly exposing and freeing a large group of victimized women. Once again, Bishop was portrayed as a hero in the legal field, and Brooktown fantastically benefited from the institution's association with his name.

Kaitlyn thoughtfully considered the peculiar way these events had unfolded as she followed Melissa out of the Brooktown and into the surrounding neighborhood in downtown Washington D.C. After several blocks on foot, Melissa finally sat at a bus stop and allowed her head to drop into her hands in a solemn display of devastating defeat. Gradually, Kait approached her and settled into the adjoining seat. Melissa was so afflicted with her overwhelming grief she didn't seem to notice Kaitlyn's presence.

"Hi," Kait finally said cautiously, suddenly very aware of how inappropriate and odd it was to have followed Melissa like she did.

"Oh," Melissa jumped at her voice and eyed Kaitlyn with a confused, suspicious stare. "What do you want?"

"I was on the ethics board for your case."

"Obviously. I just saw you," Melissa spat impatiently as she nervously scanned the area with a paranoid glance over her shoulder.

"I need to ask you something."

"Ok..."

"I just wanted to know why you... well I want to know if you lied in your testimony?"

"Does it matter?"

"It does to me."

"Why?" Melissa huffed and stared at the floor, hunching her shoulders like an angry toddler.

"I don't know. I just feel like something isn't right with you and Bishop. Why would you change your story like that?"

"I already told you that during the hearing."

"Did you really though?" Kaitlyn asked, mindlessly fiddling with the set of bracelet on her wrists so she wouldn't have to look at Melissa's solemn face.

"Yes."

For a while the two sat in a cold silence as Melissa frantically checked the time and impatiently watched for her bus to appear from around the corner. Kaitlyn let out a deep breath and tried to stress her supportive position, "Miss Antemie, I'm just trying to help. I've known this man for years, he's been my friend and colleague. I've trusted him with students I care for, and I've worked with him on several cases. If he did something to you, I need the truth. He could be dangerous." She stared at Melissa with maternal affection. The look of pain that crossed the girl's face struck Kaitlyn deeply, and she felt the urge to reach for Melissa's shaky hand.

"Have you ever been scared of someone?" Melissa whispered as she again glanced around with a nervous twitch.

"Not directly," Kait admitted, "but I've been scared of people generally. I understand what some humans are capable of, and I know a victim when I see one."

"Trust me, there's nothing you can do to help. There's nothing anyone can do. I just want to escape and live my life like this whole thing never happened."

"I can relate to that," Kait nodded thoughtfully, "but even if I can't help you, I still just need to know the truth."

"The truth is that he's not someone you want as an enemy. For your own sake and mine, I suggest you leave this alone and forget about it." Melissa looked up as her bus finally surfaced from around the corner. Kaitlyn saw her shoulders drop with relief at the sight. The two didn't exchange another word as Melissa climbed onto her bus, leaving Kaitlyn alone on the bench in a confused state of regret and isolation. Melissa gave Kait one sad glance from the window and slowly lifted her hand with a small wave of goodbye. Two days later, Melissa's boyfriend reported her as a missing person.

As Kailyn sat before Dean Herrera, she shivered at the memory of Melissa's last chilling look. She knew something was unmistakably wrong with their conversation, but her thorough confidence in this discrepancy was impossible to reasonably articulate. "There's something else," she mumbled, "I can't explain it, but I think he had something to do with Melissa's disappearance."

"You make it sound like she's dead," Herrera sighed, "Melissa didn't disappear. She just skipped town. She left a note explaining that she was ashamed of her testimony, and quite frankly that's something I can believe. That level of guilt would be pretty wounding if she did in fact lie just to slander Bishop's reputation."

"Are you not worried that no one's seen her in weeks?"

Herrera tried to convey her skepticism and dismiss Kaitlyn's concerns with a small shrug of dissolution, but underneath this unsympathetic exhibition Kaitlyn could see Herrera's uncertainty. Kaitlyn sensed the possibility that a small part of Herrera was equally mistrustful of Bishop's alleged incorruptibility.

"Please Adrian," Kaitlyn pled, "is there something *you're* not telling me? I need to know. I just... I want to protect my students."

She sighed, "I can't, Kait. All information that could possibly be relevant is confidential, you know that."

"Well I trusted you, so you should trust me. I just want the full story. Now it's your turn to treat me like a friend."

"Ok... yes, there was a student who came forward a few years back and said that Bishop made her feel uncomfortable in a meeting. But, she withdrew her complaint in a matter of days before a full investigation could even begin to take place. Honestly, her story didn't seem to have a lot of substance, and I thought the most likely conclusion was that she was being a tad overly sensitive."

"You really think she would make something like that up?"

"Unfortunately I do. She wouldn't have been the first student to misinterpret things. It's quite common in high-pressure academic situations. Professors hold so much power over their students, sometimes feelings get confused. It's very easy to idolize someone in that position."

"But... how could you not investigate further? You didn't even ask him about it?"

"I have to be fair, Kait. What if someone had accused you of something like that? Would you want me to automatically take the student's side or give an honest, objective analysis of the situation? I have to evaluate both sides, even when it's not easy-"

"-Even when it's not right!" Kaitlyn interjected with an exaggerated huff.

"Hey!" Herrera shot back firmly, "That's not fair and you know it. We have no definitive evidence that he did anything wrong. Now we don't even have a witness."

"He admitted to fucking a client! You don't think that's wrong?"

"You're getting worked up, calm down and I'll explain. I think strong feelings can develop over the course of representation, and it's not fair to deprive a man of his trade for one slipup. A lot of lawyers develop connections with their clients and sometimes certain lines get blurred."

"You have a daughter, Adrian. What if that had been her?"

"I have a husband too. Sometimes professors are wrongly accused. I have to be fair, and that's all there is to it."

"If he did it once, he'll do it again. There are some lines that you don't cross. It wasn't just a client, she was a child. Melissa was eighteen, for God's sake! If she was six months younger, it would have been rape."

"But she wasn't, and we have to abide by the law, even when it doesn't make sense."

"That's bullshit! What does that even mean to abide by the law even when it doesn't make sense? There are some situations when reason should prevail over some bullshit legal argument."

Adrian laughed at the irony, "That's not your usual attitude, Kait. I've never heard you even suggest a deviation from black-and-white justice."

"I never had to until I met Bishop."

"Well we can't fire him. We can't, and I won't. You understand that he's tenured, and we could be sued if we fired him without a pretty damn good reason. I'm sorry but a 'feeling' from a fellow staff member would not constitute a damn good reason, and a lawsuit is simply not something the school can afford."

"Can't afford? I'm sorry, but how many donors did Brooktown have last year?"

"I don't mean financially. If word gets out that our celebrity professor has been accused of inappropriate relations, our school might be portrayed as an unsafe place for women. It could hurt our ranking."

Kaitlyn inadvertently clenched her fist in frustration as anger overwhelmed her external poise. "Are you kidding me? What if he really is dangerous? What if something is really wrong? What good is a reputation of being a safe school if our students aren't actually safe?"

"You really think he's a predator? There's no way that you've jumped to a conclusion or are being unfair in your analysis?" Herrera let out a long breath and softened her tone, "Kait... we both know what this is really about. I'm so sorry for everything that happened to you, but don't you think your judgment is being a little overshadowed by the tragedies in your past?"

Kait gulped in shame and hesitated a little too long to answer.

"That's what I thought," Herrera snapped."I need you to respect me enough to accept this decision."

"Like I said, if he's crossed a line once, he'll do it again. I'm positive something's wrong, and I'm going to find a way to prove it."

"Well if you do, come to me and we'll take action."

October 7, 2015
Julia

Julia had breezed through law school, easily outperforming and surpassing most of her zealous peers. She found the struggle surprisingly gratifying, but her success in academia was only a small influence behind the fondness she felt for Brooktown. The honest reason behind her optimism throughout the program was her relationship with Daniel. His affection, steady and invariable amidst the inevitable weight of the rigid curriculum, kept her grounded and firmly levelheaded despite the crushing stress. As she reached her final year in the program, after years of wading through the chaos of her once disorderly life, things were finally falling into place. Then, as if on cue, Julia received the drastically upsetting call about her mother.

To say that Julia's mom, Diana, was emotionally unstable would be a gross understatement her plight. She had never been entirely balanced, but lately the daunting state of her disorder had grown especially dark and unmanageable. After mixing different doses of her medication, Diana had a psychological breakdown, inexplicably causing her to run through the streets of Julia's hometown, screaming at strangers for help in "finding her lost daughter." When police arrived and tried to diffuse her incomprehensible state of alarm, she lashed out and assaulted an officer with a knife. He only suffered minor wounds, but the act was enough to get her sentenced to four years in mandatory psychiatric care. Now, with her mother officially institutionalized, Julia was tasked with the job of sifting through her mother's things and packing up the remnants of their old apartment. To do this though, Julia would have to miss a full week of school.

The thought of asking for time off made her ache with anxiety. Rarely were law students granted more than a couple of days leave without a blatant emergency. As she calculated her options though, she found her choices unpleasantly narrow. She was a notoriously guarded person, and hated disclosing intimate details of her life with anyone, much less her professors. In a meek attempt at obtaining some guidance in approaching her uncomfortable dilemma, she made an appointment with Bishop, her favorite professor, to ask his advice. Throughout the semester, their professional relationship had matured to the point that she hesitantly determined he would be the most sensible person to approach with this issue. Although they had rarely visited any topics outside the law, he noticeably favored her in class, leading her assume he had some level of affection towards her outside her role as his student.

"I have to take a week off of school," Julia shyly explained as she sat across from Bishop in his office.

"Ok," he nodded patiently, "why is that?"

"Honestly, it's personal which is why I came to you first," she admitted with an uncomfortable quiver in her voice. "I'm not sure how much of this story I want to disclose."

Bishop eyed her thoughtfully, "Honestly, Julia, if I'm going to grant you a week of leave, I need a little more information than 'it's personal.'"

She sighed and contemplated the awkward task of untangling her torturously complicated past, "I don't even know where to begin."

"Would you feel more comfortable with a string of light chit-chat first?" Bishop asked with a gentle smile. Julia nodded for him to continue. "Good, because I have a question for you that's plagued my own curiosity."

"Of course."

"You're only 22, correct?"

"Yes."

"How did you make it to graduate school at this age?"

Julia let the question awkwardly hang in the air for a moment as she formulated a response. It's not that she hated the story, but it was difficult to craft an appropriate answer without the anecdote rolling into the complexities of her personal life. Generally she avoided the subject with vague and hollow remarks, quickly fending off the conversation with a trivial explanation, but she suspected this approach would be lost on Bishop. Even as she considered her options in distracting his curiosity, she could sense him reading her, already prepared to pierce the veneer of a shallow explanation. Besides, it felt wrong to dodge the question if he was sincerely seeking an honest glimpse into her personal background with the intention of ultimately helping her obtain a week of leave.

"To make a long story short," she explained with a bit of hesitation, "I dropped out of high school. I started college really young and finished early."

Bishop leaned back in his chair and nodded with growing interest. He discreetly glanced out his office window as he processed her answer before slowly turning back to her with a response, "I'm sure there's more to that story, but I won't push you if you don't want to tell me. If you do feel inclined to say more, I'm intrigued, but only out of shameless curiosity. Also, if you were able to disclose a little more about your background, I do think gaining some insight into your situation would help me justify granting you time off."

Oddly enough, something about his candor made her want to unfold pieces of her story, a remarkably uncommon phenomenon for Julia. While she considered overcoming the immensely damaged ruins of her childhood a significant personal accomplishment, the residue of her past was also her greatest insecurity. The bleak story left most listeners with an unbearable sense of pity for her struggle, a reaction she stomached with stiff distaste and intentionally avoided.

She knew Bishop had already glimpsed small pieces of her past through casual questions, but those stories were in small, isolated parts of a more complicated whole. A couple of months ago, he had asked about her father while they were going over one of her papers, and she explained that her father had passed away when she was five. Bishop asked if she remained close with her mother and she answered with a brisk, "it's complicated," before quickly changing the subject back to the assignment at hand. Even though her instincts told her not to delve deeper into her past, there was something oddly comforting in the thought of building their relationship past a hollow student-teacher dynamic.

"Ok," she said at last, "but it's kind of personal."

Bishop waited patiently for her to begin.

When her father was diagnosed with cancer, Julia was too young to initially grasp the unfortunate gravity of the situation. The word "cancer" inherently invoked a serious response, but the invincible facade of her father's strength was a difficult impression to break. As he grew weak and began to fade within months of starting his treatment, the idea of his death started sinking into her reality. The thought of his demise rolled around in her head and stayed with her. It wasn't until they lowered him into the ground, only eight months after receiving the news of his illness, that she fully understood the finality of his passing.

Very few people attended his funeral. Although Julia's father was a relatively successful IT consultant and a consistently well-liked figure by those who knew him, his wife's set of mental illnesses had isolated their entire family from any in-depth social interactions. Once her father had tried to throw Julia a birthday party, insisting that she compile a list of everyone from school she wished to attend. Her father had bought her a giant cake, hung decorations, and cooked all day in preparation for the event. However, when the guests arrived, they were met with the sight of Julia's mother, drunk off whiskey and delusional from taking too many anxiety pills.

Diana harassed each guest with personal questions and inappropriate comments, and further humiliated her daughter with embarrassing anecdotes about her childhood. Although her father tried to curb his wife's behavior by enthusiastically guiding the guests through various activities, ultimately the party was a wash and everyone in attendance felt a sigh of relief when the guests finally began trickling out the door. They never spoke of her birthday again, but after the incident there was a clear understanding that their family would from then on refrain from throwing parties and ultimately avoid social engagements at all costs. Julia learned to compartmentalize the embarrassment she felt for her mother's illness, and guard herself and her family from humiliation by putting up physical and emotional barriers.

Julia was twelve when she lost her father, and a piece of her died that day with his empty body. She cried not only for her loss, but also because she understood his death would surely serve as the beginning of her mother's ultimate demise as well. There are a lot of words for "crazy"- bipolar, schizo-phrenic, unstable, delusional- Julia had studied them all throughout her childhood. She suspected that if she could somehow educate herself and fully understand the illness, she could break through the barriers of her mother's brain and reason with the somewhat sensible woman underneath. There had been periods of her mother's lucidity throughout Julia's childhood, but they were inevitably replaced by a wave of hysteria and long stretches of delusion.

Her father had always been able to take care of Diana, even when she was at her worse. He was patient and brought a much-needed sense of stability to the household, a feeling that quickly dispersed after he was gone. When the burden of her mother's care fell on Julia's shoulders, she was never able to match her father's comforting abilities.

It's not that her mother was incompetent. She could function relative-ly well considering the state of her mental disorder. Her illness was subtle enough so that she could hide it from their neighbors, but prevalent enough to permeate every aspect of her life outside the public's eye. She had long periods of mania where she wouldn't sleep or eat for weeks at a time. During these episodes, she would lose all rational notions of consequences, resulting in delusional gestures like investing the entirety of Julia's college fund into a jewelry scam she found on the internet.

Within a year of her father's death, Julia started noticing calls from cred-itors, and understood enough about their situation to ask her mother about the status of their finances. Her mother grew agitated at the "accusation" and told Julia that their money was none of her concern. Within months though, it became clear that their house would soon face foreclosure, so Julia started shopping around for apartments nearby. Diana pretended not to notice as Julia began sorting through her childhood home, boxing up whatever was necessary to keep and discarding non-essentials. She cried when she finally went through her father's closet and was forced to throw out the majority of his precious belongings. It was around that time that Diana shut down and disengaged completely from her surroundings. She became too sick to work, and started living off of the disability checks Julia had secured for her through months of ongoing applications and interviews with local social workers. Diana began drinking nearly everyday, and was generally passed out by the time Julia got home from school.

Refusing to give up, Julia forced her mother to stay afloat. Even when Diana had lost her will to function, Julia had enough strength for both of them. She forced her mother to eat, helped her dress every morning, and started applying for jobs on her mother's behalf. Slowly Diana's brain began adjusting as her depression lifted, and for a while it seemed as though things were getting better. That changed when her mother met Blake Miller.

It wasn't exactly clear how her mother had come to know Blake, which Julia found suspicious in itself. In her darkest moments she worried he might have been a drug dealer, as he often carried large amounts of cash and generally had vague responses when asked about his line of work. Julia knew her mother often took pills, but she had never thought of her as an actual drug user until Blake came into their lives and Diana's problem grew too obvious to ignore.

He was nice enough at first, even to Julia who could only see his presence as an intrusion in their home and an affront to her father's memory. He was almost handsome, exceptionally tall with large, stocky shoulders which seemed to compensate for Diana's body which was shrinking with age and drug use. He sometimes brought groceries to their apartment and always tried to take an interest in Julia's life, even though she suspected his curiosity was just an act to appease her mother who enthusiastically encouraged them to forge a friendship. Even at his best, Julia didn't particularly care for Blake, but because her mother was finally showing small signs of happiness, she bit her tongue and ignored her own growing bitterness and the inexplicable sense of uneasiness she felt towards his company.

Blake and Diana dated for about a year before it became clear that Diana's mental health was fully disintegrating from bad to dysfunctional. To

Julia, this demise was particularly infuriating as so much of her illness was now self-inflicted. Julia knew this from the amount of pills she found around the house, and the uncomfortable blank stare her mother had adopted as a permanent expression. Whatever small semblance of a personality Diana had possessed during her husband's life and now been numbed into oblivion after years of detachment and drug use.

A week after Julia's fifteenth birthday, Diana announced that Blake would be moving into their apartment. Julia tried to dissuade her from this step, arguing that it was a drastic move considering she had only met him six months earlier, but her mother's stubborn disposition remained unyielding. With a dismissive smile, she assured Julia that this was the best thing for both of them and promised she would learn to think of Blake as her father as more time passed. Julia scoffed at the thought of comparing anyone to her father, much less a bumbling lowlife like Blake who likely made his living by selling drugs.

His arrival to their home was fine at first, and Julia did her best to tolerate his unwelcomed presence. But then, after several short months of his arrival, Blake put his hand on Julia's knee as they watched TV. He shrugged when she shot him a look of disdain and immediately got up to leave. She almost spat on the ground out of anger and spent the next several days sulking over the disgusting nature of the incident.

After that, Julia began avoiding home by spending long hours in the public library around the corner and taking on additional shifts at the restaurant where she worked as a waitress. Eventually, both out of loneliness and in an attempt to further escape her home, she broke her routine of habitual social isolation and started consciously making an effort to reach out to new friends. To her surprise, socializing actually came naturally for Julia, and she found that her guarded nature somehow benefited her in the realm of human connection. She quickly learned to avoid talking about herself by asking pointed and direct questions about others, finding that most people enjoy the heightened attention of having a friend so genuinely inquire about their thoughts and backgrounds. Ironically then, her attempts to avoid Blake had actually forced her to make true, genuine friends for the first time in her life and develop a set of social skills that would become a notorious fixture in her personality.

One rare and unfortunate evening when Julia was home before midnight, she watched her mother and Blake enter their apartment in a troublesome state of disarray. As soon as the door opened, her mother immediately fell to the floor and half-laughed at herself as she struggled to stand. With a sigh, Julia went to her aid and gently tried to put her to bed. At first Diana refused and kept repeating, "I want to spend quality time with my beautiful daughter," in such a slurred tone that her words were almost incomprehensible. "We can hang out tomorrow, Mom," Julia suggested as she struggled to carry her mother's limp body to bed.

As she laid Diana down and covered her with a blanket, Blake appeared in the doorway and watched with interest at the sight of Julia tucking in her mother into bed like a child. "You know," Blake slurred from behind her, "the two of you look alike."

"Is that so?" Julia replied coldly, refusing to look up as she gently turned her mother onto her side.

"Sure," he slurred, "when I look at you, I think of how your mother must have looked when she was young, even more beautiful than she is now. Am I right? You both have freckles and that red hair, but I must say that they look cuter on you."

Julia ignored this comment with a dismissive shake of her head as she attempted to maneuver around Blake to escape the confines of her mother's bedroom. He held his arm across the door to stop her and suddenly scanned her body up and down with a hungry, half-smile. "Does that make you uncomfortable?" he laughed as he stumbled a bit in the doorway, swaying a little as he tried to meet her eyes with his own.

"Just let me go. I have homework to finish," she huffed. She threw her shoulders back with confidence and tried to make herself seem stronger under his gaze, but she could feel her heart beating faster out of fear.

"You always say you have so much to do, but do you even do your homework?"

"Yes," Julia stated simply and crossed her arms across her chest in indignation. "What's it to you?"

"Beautiful, little Julia." He slurred as he unsuccessfully reached out a hand to grab her. She stepped back and shot him a look of disgust, intuitively scanning the room for an escape route. "You're just always gone. What do you really do when you're not home? Because I highly doubt you actually spend that much time at the library. So... just between us, where do you go?"

"Leave me alone," she shot back through gritted teeth.

"Only if you give me a kiss."

She slapped him with a harsh swoop of her wrist, but this only served to stun him for half a second at most. He immediately grabbed her hands and thrust her against the wall with a heavy thud of her body. She managed to escape his grasp, clumsy in his drunken state, and pushed him away as she ran to the next room. He swayed and nearly collapsed at her charge, but it only took him a moment to catch his bearings as he quickly scrambled to follow just steps behind her. When she reached the kitchen, she grabbed a knife and pointed it in his direction. He stopped just inches from the blade and looked up at her in an angry state of disorientation.

"What the fuck?" he yelled, his gaze still fixated on the sharp blade in front of him. "Are you actually threatening me?"

"Stay away from me!" she screamed as she continued to point the knife in his direction. "I promise I'll hurt you if you take one step closer."

"What's happening?" a weary voice suddenly shot from the corner, making them both jump in surprise. Diana had emerged from her bedroom and stared at the two of them with a look of raw horror.

"He tried to kiss me and attacked me!" Julia yelled, her voice shaking with adrenaline and rage. Blake started backing up, but she still held out the knife with unwavering conviction.

"I did not!" Blake protested, "This bitch is just crazy."

Diana approached them both and placed a hand on Blake's shoulder, suddenly fixated on the blade with an alarmed expression plastered on her sunken face. Julia watched in horror as her mother gently started to rub Blake's back in a manner that seemed almost maternal and calming.

"Mom, did you just hear me? He tried to attack me. He probably would have raped me if I hadn't stopped him."

"It sounds like a misunderstanding, my love. Let's just all calm down."

"Calm down?" Blake spat. "She just tried to stabbed me. She should be institutionalized."

"She'll be punished," Diana assured him. "Julia you did a terrible thing. You crossed a line and you need to apologize."

"Fuck you both!" She yelled as a fresh wave of rage washed over her body. "What the hell is wrong with you two?"

"Calm down," Diana responded calmly. "Go to your room, get a good night sleep, and we can all work this out in the morning." Julia did go to her room, knife still in hand, slamming the door with indignant force and locking it behind her. She stayed up all night, watching the doorknob with dogmatic adherence in case Blake dared to challenge her again.

That was the last night she ever spent in her mother's house. The next morning she quickly packed a few of her most valuable belongings, of which she had very few, and left a note explaining that she was running away and that they shouldn't bother trying to find her. She wasn't sure if her mother actually did try to look for her in the first several days of her absence, but something told her that was an unlikely case.

After this departure, Julia dropped out of high school and started working full-time. She moved into an apartment on the other side of town and avoided places she knew her mother was likely to be. She hoarded money in a way that it became a somewhat unhealthy obsession, and started looking at options to continue her education, which at the moment looked quite bleak. In a move that seemed almost helpless at the time, she started start attending a local community college and dedicated herself to making decent grades. She signed up for the SAT on a whim and to everyone's surprise, including her own, made a nearly perfect score. Not long after, she applied to transfer to a top university just outside the state and miraculously received a scholarship based on her personal statement. She wrote about her father's death.

When she pictured the life she wanted after college, she longed for some form of financial and social empowerment which would allow her an unshakeable level of independence. She couldn't remember the exact moment when she decided to become a lawyer, but by the time the first semester at her new university had come to an end, getting into law school had become her new obsession. The profession felt safe, respected, and valued, the exact elements of a career she longed for after spending so much of her past in chaos.

When she got her acceptance letter to Brooktown, for the first time since her father's passing, she finally felt as though she could breathe. As the number one ranked school in the country, she pictured herself with a top degree from a top university and suddenly felt that her desire for independence and consistency was finally secure.

She recited this story to Professor Bishop, leaving very little out as her life history surprisingly cascaded from her mouth in uncontrollable impulse that oddly left her feeling relieved. She shocked herself with the details she disclosed to him, almost expecting him to grow bored with her ramblings and ask her to stop. Instead, Bishop stared at her with an unshakable interest, and not a hint of disbelief. "Your dad sounds like a man of good character. I'm glad he was in your life, even if it was for a short while," he said at last after her story had reached a natural stopping point.

"I am too. This might sound strange, but you actually kind of remind me of him." This integral connection was probably the root of her endearment towards Professor Bishop. Although he was undeniably and objectively fascinating in a number of ways, his demeanor mirrored that of her father's, making the relationship with her professor feel unusually steady and familiar.

"That's very kind considering how highly you speak of him. Honestly," he replied after a short pause, "it's an unusual story but not terribly surprising. It actually makes sense how you ended up so... intense."

Julia laughed, "Um... thanks?."

"It's a compliment," Bishop assured her with a boyish smile. "I'm still curious about why you chose Brooktown though. I've seen your grades, and I'm sure you had your pick of schools."

Julia smiled, "I mean, it was never a choice for me. It's the best school in the country. I've been obsessed with the idea of coming here since I first decided to be a lawyer. I didn't even apply anywhere else."

"Interesting. So what happens after your legal education? The narcissist in me hopes you go into civil rights law, but only because my work is the true love of my life."

"I wish," she sighed. "I'll have to go into a firm though. I need a high salary."

"Why is that?"

"The debt," she said flatly with a small shrug. "It's terrible. I mean, even with my scholarship I'm already $150,000 under. Once I have to start paying it back, I won't exactly have the luxury of following my dreams. I need just need a decent paycheck so I can pay it off."

"I was afraid you'd say that. I suppose that's the downside of Brooktown. It's an unreasonably expensive program. Do you ever regret coming here? You could have gone somewhere with better financial aid."

"Not at all."

"Why's that?

"For a lot of reasons."

"Name one-"

"-My boyfriend," she blurted out impulsively, almost blushing at her mistake.

He chuckled. "I can see why. Daniel seems like a really great kid. Anyway, your story is interesting, Julia. It helps me make sense of you as a person."

"What do you mean?" she asked out of curiosity.

"I understand now why law school means so much to you. You work harder than any of my other students. It's clear you've had this goal for a while."

"I've thought of nothing else since starting college. This place means everything to me. I just hope... I hope that story didn't make you feel uncomfortable."

He threw up his hands in protest, "Not at all, I'm the one who pushed you to tell me. If anything Julia, I'm just more impressed with you. I think it's amazing what you've accomplished at such a very young age, and I'm proud to have you as a student."

His response was simple, but exactly what she needed to hear. Suddenly, every decision she had made throughout her education felt validated by his approval. It felt surreal speaking to a professor like a friend, but she also felt honored and admittedly special by his interest.

"Ok," he said abruptly, returning to his professional tone, "you'll take a week off. I'll talk to your other professors. I'll let them know that you're having a personal issue and that you don't wish to disclose anything further. If it comes from me, I'm sure they'll all agree."

"Thank you," she sighed with relief as she sank back into her chair. "You have no idea how much that means to me."

"I have something else to ask you though," Bishop continued, "but don't feel obliged to say yes, especially if you think your personal issues will get in the way."

"What do you mean?"

"I'm currently working on a pro-bono human trafficking case involving an immigrant from Guatemala. She was charged with prostitution, which I'm hoping to get dropped by December. She applied for asylum a while back, and I'm going to help her put together a claim. If we win her charges will be dropped and she'll get to stay in this country as a citizen. If we lose, she'll be deported."

"That sounds like an interesting case, but what does that have to do with me?"

"I need a research assistant. I'd like you to help me with it."

"I don't have a lot of experience with the subject," Julia sat in disbelief, immediately cursing herself for not masking her hesitation. Something told her this was the wrong response. Any other student would have jumped enthusiastically at the opportunity to work under Bishop.

"Why should that matter?" Bishop laughed.

"Well, why wouldn't you want a research assistant with more experience? I don't understand."

"To be honest," he chuckled, "No law school student has genuine 'experience' with any subject. I need someone competent, with good research skills, and a fresh take on the case. I've done this a couple of times in the past, and I've been very pleased with my students. If it's too big of a commitment though, I don't want to put more on your plate than you can handle."

"Who's the client?"

"She's a very young girl who ran away from Guatemala and was trafficked through Mexico. When she crossed the border, she was sold to a man named Roberto Hernandez who forced her into prostitution. She's barely eighteen now. Her brothel got raided last year, and for some ungodly reason she was charged with a crime. She's a victim, but the system decided to label her a criminal. It's disgusting, really."

"What exactly do you need from me?"

"I've done most of the research already. I just need a fresh pair of eyes to bring a human element to my argument. I'll also probably ask you to draft part of her written testimony. Are you interested?"

"Absolutely, I'm honored that you even asked."

"It's not too much work?"

"No. I can handle it. I would tell you if I couldn't."

Bishop smiled at that and nodded with a satisfied grin, "I assumed you would. I really look forward to working with you on this."

"What's she like? Our client, I mean."

"Hmmm," he pondered with a light stroke of his chin, "it's difficult to explain. She's a very sweet girl. It's obvious she's been through a lot of trauma, and I suspect she suffers from PTSD and possibly a few other mental issues. She's a little unstable, but that's partly why I took her case. She has no one else to help her."

"What's her name?"

"Gabriella."

MAY 21, 2016
Julia

"So you couldn't think of a friend to bring with you?" Detective Weir asked as he pulled out a chair for Julia across from his own. They were in his office, which was a relief considering Julia had spent all night dramatically envisioning their conversation taking place in a small interrogation room. His office was transparent and uncomplicated, but in a way that was comfortable in its own simplicity. She studied Weir, who almost seemed bored at the familiar strides of the investigatory process.

"I told you I wanted to come alone. I haven't done anything wrong so I have nothing to hide." Her body grew tense as the words slipped from her mouth in a rehearsed dribble.

"Ok, well I invited you down here to talk about a project you were working on last semester with Professor Bishop. I understand you were helping him with Miss Gabriella Rodriguez's case?"

"Yes, but what does that have to do with Bishop's murder?"

"Well, Gabriella is currently a person of interest."

"Why?"

"I can't disclose any additional information about that at this time. I was wondering if Professor Bishop every spoke of his relationship with Gabriella. Did he ever mention if she was mentally unstable or maybe even just a little off?"

"Not that I can recall..."

"Did he talk about her at all in a personal capacity?"

"He felt sorry about what she went through," Julia answered. "I think he had a lot of sympathy for her as a victim."

"So he never mentioned that Gabriella might have been stalking him or-"

"-Gabriella was stalking him?" Julia quickly interjected with a befuddled sense of urgency.

"Did you know her?" Weir asked, his eyes flickering with subtle interest.

Suddenly Julia felt her cheeks grow red, and for a moment she worried she had said something wrong. Then she remembered that she had in fact met Gabriella in a professional capacity, and she breathed in a sigh of relief. "Yes, she came to Bishop's office a couple of times while we were working on her case. I didn't know her well, but my personal assessment is that she was very stable and professional. I know my opinion probably doesn't mean anything to you though."

"Everything *could* mean something at this point, Miss Harrison. Your opinion matters very much. You see, not a lot of people knew Miss Rodriguez. After her brothel was raided and she stopped working as a prostitute-"

"-You mean after she escaped from being forced to work as a sex slave."

"Yes, my apologies, I meant after she escaped from her trafficker. I see how my wording misconstrued the situation. I agree that she is very much a victim. Anyway, she didn't have any friends or other contacts outside of the brothel. She lived in a halfway home as her case progressed, but she didn't talk to anyone during her stay. Now she lives alone in an apartment in Southeast, and doesn't seem to have a lot of contact with anyone outside of work. We can't find a single person who can accurately assess her personality."

That's because she didn't trust anyone after what happened to her, Julia thought with pressing revulsion, *she was terrified.*

"Oh, that's unfortunate," Julia finally mumbled, fidgeting with the ends of her curls like she always did when she was nervous.

"How long did you speak with her during your meetings?"

"Each one lasted about an hour."

"And she never did anything to indicate that she was at all interested in Professor Bishop in a personal capacity?"

"Never... not that I can remember. It was a while ago, but I think I would have noticed something like that."

"Did she mention anything about her personal life?"

"Of course, our case was about her personal life."

"Did she mention any men or anyone she was dating?"

Julia felt her bubbling resentment rise with each provoking question. "I feel like you're trying to coax something out of me, and I don't understand what you're fishing for. Maybe if I knew the context behind your questions I could better assist you."

Weir sighed, "We have reason to believe that Miss Rodriguez and Professor Bishop were engaged in some kind of personal relationship. It also appears as though she might have been in an unhealthy mental state at the time of his murder. Miss Rodriguez was showing textbook symptoms of PTSD, and it appears as though she latched onto the first person who showed her any sort of positive attention, that person being Bishop."

"Attention? What kind of attention? Anthony was her lawyer."

"That's what we're still trying to figure out. He might have been more than just her lawyer." Weir stated with a shrug and small shake of his head.

"Honestly, I don't think I'll be much help with that," Julia responded after a momentary pause. "We were collecting information for her legal argument. Her mood around me was very professional, and I truly didn't notice anything out of the ordinary. I think I would have remembered something like that, I have a decent sense of perception."

"What about a good judge of character?" Weir asked coldly.

For some reason the question made her feel sick. Before this year, she would have answered with a confident and unequivocal 'yes,' but now she knew her intuition had a few inherent flaws. "I guess so," she admitted, "but not in a way that would allow me to predict if two people, who had been nothing but professional around me, were secretly having an affair behind closed doors. Besides, Anthony was incredibly secretive about that stuff. I highly doubt he would have let it surface. I took notes during our meetings. You're welcome to look over them."

"That would be helpful. Well, I think I understand. I appreciate you coming to chat."

"Is that all you need?"

"Yes, I believe so."

"Thank you for your time, Detective Weir," Julia said as she got up to leave.

Before she reached the door, Weir spun around in his chair with a jolt and suddenly stared at her with blatant suspicion. "By the way, it's interesting to me that you called your professor by his first name. Most of his colleagues didn't even do that."

She almost lost her breath at this sharply unexpected observation. "Oh... I don't know," she stammered, "I guess it just slipped out."

"Indeed it did," he nodded. "You know what's funny? I had almost forgotten his first name completely. I never noticed this until now, but it's a little cold the way everyone in his life calls him Bishop. Well, *called* him Bishop, I suppose."

"That's not that uncommon with professors. Everyone referred to Bishop by his last name."

"Except you. You were on a first name basis."

October 15, 2015
Kaitlyn

After their public argument, Kaitlyn could sense that it took all of Julia's willpower each day to attend her class. Their relationship was progressively deteriorating with each transient day of the semester as their interactions melded into a series of impassioned disputes. While most students would have humbly withdrawn after their initial outburst, Julia stubbornly continued to push Kaitlyn through her lectures. Consequently, their debates spilled over into every area of law and life generally, making their arguments innately personal. Today what started as simple case analysis, somehow spiraled into a heated debate over affirmative action and the question of racism in modern America. The ardent discussion, now wildly off-topic, ended in Kaitlyn respectfully requesting that Julia stay after dismissal for a brief chat.

As class ended and the final lingering students filed out of the room, Julia remained as instructed, obviously anticipating yet another lecture on how her behavior demonstrated inappropriate classroom etiquette. Generally, Kaitlyn would have freely picked apart Julia's opinions and undermined her theories by insinuating the unrealistic nature of her arguments. In turn, Julia likely would have hinted at Kaitlyn's bitter disposition, hardened by her years of dismay in academia. Both would walk away seething in anger, further enforcing their web of conflict which was steadily escalating throughout the year. Today, however, Kaitlyn held her tongue, plagued with an alternative motivation to their meeting.

"Listen," Kaitlyn began, "I need to talk to you about-"

"-I didn't mean anything by it," Julia cut her off before uncontrollably spiraling into a passionate rant. "I was just trying to prove a point... although it is a point I will stand by until my last dying breath because anyone who can argue against the necessity of affirmative action, in my opinion, is consciously blinding themselves to the heart of injustice in our society. I know what you're going to say, but it's not that I don't understand the law or the need for uniformity, but considering-"

"-Julia!" Kaitlyn held up a hand as a signal to stop, "That's not what I want to talk to you about. Your points were fine. Actually they were better than fine, but it's not my job to tell you that your points are fine. It's my job to strengthen your arguments through criticism. That's the way this works, damn it. Have you not figured this out by your third year? I wouldn't call you down here for making a decent point in class."

"To be fair, you have before... several times, in fact," Julia said skeptically as she crossed her arms across her chest with the indignant look of a rebellious child.

Kaitlyn's face grew stern with warning, "Don't test me Julia, not today. I need to talk to you about something important."

"Oh, I didn't realize. I'm sorry, I just assumed you were angry about class... like always. What's going on?"

After the unwarranted victory in Rowland's case, Kaitlyn developed a painfully bitter taste for criminal court. She was traumatized by the injustice, but stubbornly clung to the bits of morality that loosely held together the foundation of the legal profession. She still passionately preached the importance of consistency within the law and the idea of an inherent truth buried beneath the biases. She was infamous amongst her colleagues as a passionate advocate for "black and white justice," and for a fairly lengthy period of time refused to forsake the notion that, despite its imperfections, the core of the legal system remained ultimately pure.

With Kaitlyn's background in criminal law, it was natural for Dean Herrera to ask for Kaitlyn's assistance in running the school's criminal justice clinic. Apparently Brooktown was trying to heighten its reputation by instigating a program to assist sexual assault victims in obtaining free legal advice and representation from the school's array of competent lawyers. Although Kaitlyn initially refused to take on this role, after a little coaxing from her favorite colleagues, including Anthony Bishop who assured her that she was a perfect candidate to lead the clinic, she eventually accepted and started regularly taking on pro-bono cases involving the most heinous claims of sexual assault.

She grew attached to nearly all of her cases, carrying a deep emotional burden with every new victim, but she energetically pursued each allegation with a renewed sense of optimism in the legal system. These women had experienced the depths of oppression and inequity, and she blindly believed that with the right amount of work she would be able to obtain some form of justice to offset their pain. She was wrong.

She served six years as head of the criminal justice clinic, and in that time took on eight different pro-bono cases, all with dreadfully anguished victims and seemingly clear attackers. She aimfully fought to get these cases into court, and put together perfect arguments on behalf of her clients. Although she began each new claim with a sense of misplaced hope, one-by-one each of her clients lost their cases and watched as their attackers went free.

The inherent injustice of the system drove her into a state of hysteria and inspired her into the role of an activist. She wrote various papers on the deep-seated inequity of the justice system when it comes to cases of sexual assault victims, she spoke at various events and helped organize protests against the most discriminatory laws on the subject, and she even testified in front of Congress about her experiences in the field. Nothing she did served to move the needle even a little towards a just result, and slowly she sunk even deeper into her own bitterness. She eventually resigned as head of the clinic and swore off pro-bono cases altogether.

Now she eyed Julia, carefully searching for an appropriate way to impose a subtle warning. "I heard you're Professor Bishop's new research assistant," she said slowly.

"Yes ma'am, he asked me last week."

"And how many hours a week will you be working with him?"

"Not many, he's done most of the groundwork already. I'm just doing minor research, so it's not really a burden. Why do you ask?"

"Listen," Kaitlyn continued, "I want you to really think about whether or not you can handle that level of a workload right now. We usually discourage third year students from taking on additional responsibilities. You're still hunting for a job, and your grades this semester should be your top priority. You have a chance of getting an offer from a top firm, Julia, that should be your focus."

She could see Julia growing offended. "Honestly Professor Tryst, I appreciate what you're saying, but it's not like I'm a first year student. I have a pretty good gauge on how much work I can handle. Plus, to be frank, I've been coasting through third year anyway. Law school is practically done."

"Ok... I know Professor Bishop can be a hard person to say no to. He expects a lot from his students, and it's an honor to be chosen to assist in his research. However, I want you to know that if you ever have problems with the workload... or him... you can come to me. I won't tell anyone else. Do you understand?"

Julia couldn't mask her confusion. It was no secret that Kaitlyn didn't care for Julia and it must have felt curious for her seemingly cold professor to reach out like a friend. She watched as Julia squirmed with obvious discomfort at Kaitlyn's offer. "I appreciate you saying that," Julia responded with hesitation, "but I'm positive I can handle the work. If I can't, I would probably go to Bishop directly. He's been very reasonable in working with my schedule."

"I understand that," Kaitlyn sighed, "but I want you to know that if you ever need help with anything, not just the workload, you can come to me. Alright?" Kaitlyn studied Julia's features, and for a moment a hint of desperation inadvertently crossed her face.

"Is something wrong, Professor?" Julia prodded with a confused stare.

Kaitlyn shook her head, "No... sometimes I just forget how young you are. You look like you could be in high school... like a child." Julia was taken aback, clearly unaware of how to appropriately respond to this unexpected inquiry. "Sorry," Kaitlyn broke the awkward moment with a weary smile, "I just want you to be careful. I would dissuade you from putting too much on your plate."

"I understand," Julia answered firmly, "and again I appreciate your concern."

August 15, 2016
Gabriella

"Do you think I'm crazy?" Gabriella asked Dr. Estes in a feeble voice.

"Why do you ask that?" he replied calmly, as he subtly made a note on his clipboard.

"Well, I've never been totally honest about this story with anyone and I'm realizing now how crazy it sounds... but it didn't feel that way at the time."

"Why didn't you tell anyone before me?"

"Well I guess I did tell one person bits and pieces, but never the full truth."

"Was this person a friend?" Estes prodded.

"No... I wouldn't say that. The person was more like my lawyer, but obviously not the one I was in love with." Gabriella pondered this for a while, "Now that you mention it, I guess she was more like a friend than my lawyer, but I've never had any friends so I wouldn't know. Anyway, do you think I'm crazy?"

"Well to be totally honest, you are describing some irrational behavior, but that doesn't mean you're crazy. I do think it might be possible that your mind periodically disassociates from reality. That's an issue we need to address."

"With medication?"

"Maybe but this is only your third week of institutionalization. I want to know more about your background and current state of mind before I make a diagnosis that would require any additional medication."

"That sounds fair... where was I?"

"You were just telling me about when you started to develop feelings for your lawyer."

Gabriella genuinely liked Doctor Estes, but the way he used the word "feelings" sounded strangely robotic and made the entire ordeal seem unjust-

ly trivial. Anyone could develop feelings. She had irrefutably developed serious feelings during her time in Virginia, but the way she felt about Anthony
Bishop was much deeper than what she could accurately describe. She didn't
just want to be with him, she wanted to be like him. She had never developed
such profoundly intense emotions about anything or anyone. The further her
case progressed, the deeper she had fallen for him. She became obsessed, she
understood that now. It became clear later that she crossed some arbitrary
line of professionalism, but at the time it didn't just feel natural, but also
inevitable.

After the raid and Roberto's imprisonment, she was jailed for three days
before being sent to a group home in the outskirts of D.C. She was charged
with prostitution, and started surveying her options, which seemed hopelessly bleak at the time. One of the girls in the home told her that she needed
a lawyer, and suggested eliciting pro-bono counsel, even though they were
rare and usually provided low-quality work. She wrote a number of letters
to different attorneys in the area, in a desperate attempt to gain competent
representation. However, each request she sent was met with a harsh silence.
She had almost given up hope completely when one man, Anthony Bishop,
finally responded.

He met with her at a small restaurant in downtown D.C. After their
initial awkward greeting, he bought her lunch and asked to hear her story.
He listened intently, nodding as she blindly tried to recount everything that
could possibly be relevant to a legal claim. She wasn't sure what she needed to
disclose, so he guided her through their conversation and graciously listened
like an old friend. She saw the sympathy in his eyes as he gently patted her
hand. He explained that she would need to apply for asylum, and told her
that he would undoubtedly take on her case for free.

"I don't have a lot of money," she explained. "Roberto kept all of my earnings, so I have no savings."

"I have enough money," Bishop stated blankly, "I want to help you because it's the right thing to do. You can pay me back by making a good life for yourself after we win."

"That's when you fell in love with him?" Estes asked after Gabriella dreamily recited the details of this first encounter. Her eyes were watering by the time she reached the end.

"Yes," she choked through tears, "and it only got worse from there."

"Worse on an emotional level?" he asked curiously.

"Obviously, that's why I'm here, isn't it? Because I got too attached?"

Estes sighed, "No Gabriella, that's not why you're here. You're here because you committed a crime."

November 2, 2015
Adrian

"Good afternoon, Dean Herrera," Bishop smiled as he strolled into the dean's suite at Brooktown with an air of easy confidence.

"Hi Anthony," Adrian echoed, noting with a small pulse of satisfaction the cringe Bishop tried to hide in response to hearing someone call him by his first name. Adrian didn't know of a single other person who dared refer to him with such an informal tone. "How are you today?"

"Oh, just great. You know I always look forward to my evaluation."

"Yes, I understand you look forward to this as a subtle boost of your already inflated ego," Adrian mumbled, only half-joking. She had known Bishop for over ten years now, and while he was one of the school's most coveted professional assets, their cordial relationship had always been riddled with pieces of uncomfortable connotations. Before she came to Brooktown, Bishop had been offered the position of dean, but turned it down because of his "unyielding dedication to his job as an educator," as he so humbly phrased it in his rejection to the job which had conveniently been leaked to the press the following day. He liked to remind her of the fact that he was Brooktown's first choice whenever he got the chance, but in a way that was so subtle it was hard to pinpoint and reprimand.

"Well craving positive re-enforcement is only human, don't you think?"

"Sure, Anthony. Please, take a seat," she said with a dismissive gesture of her hand.

Bishop sat across from Adrian with a deep, smug smile. "So, how were my student reviews?"

Adrian sighed, "You know they were excellent, like every year. Of course your students love you." She slid the evaluation notes across the table so that he could see the results directly, "You nearly received a perfect score in every category."

Bishop made no attempt to hide his amusement, "So who didn't give me a perfect score? I need to put them on my list."

"You're aware that the evaluations are confidential, and I also hope you're aware that that comment really isn't funny," she groaned with a genuine sense of annoyance.

"Oh come now, you know I'm only joking. It takes a lot more than that for someone to get on my bad-side."

Adrian rolled her eyes.

Bishop's "bad-side" might have seemed humorous if there wasn't so much truth behind the awkward sentiment. Rarely did she see glimpses of his wrath, but when it did surface, it was generally an unforgettably troublesome ordeal. Before taking the job as dean, she had heard rumors that Bishop could be professionally vindictive, but after ten years as his superior, she had seen his work firsthand and found it to be far more distressing than she had initially anticipated.

The most rattling example Adrian had experienced occurred eight years ago when a Bishop published an article about an upcoming Supreme Court case involving affirmative action at the university level. Although most praised his writing as brilliant, one fellow Brooktown professor, Kyle Thompson, wrote a rebuttal piece in the same journal harshly criticizing Bishop's legal argument. He went as far as calling the article "naive" and "unsophisticated," and suggested a rewrite of his entire proposal.

Bishop was enraged when Thompson's rebuttal was published, and immediately called a meeting with Adrian to demand repercussions, claiming that Brooktown professors shouldn't be publically criticizing each other in what he referred to as "A childlike circus of unacceptable levels of ineptitude." Although Adrian agreed that the article was published in poor taste, in the name of freedom of expression, she refused to punish a member of her staff for openly expressing a controversial opinion. Outraged, Bishop swore he would not work with someone capable of such infantile remarks. "Are you quitting then?" Adrian had asked calmly in response to his rant.

"Absolutely not," Bishop stated in an oddly foreboding tone. "I'll just have to find a way to convince him that this school is too fine of an establishment for someone of his distasteful standards."

Adrian shook her head at that, refusing to indulge such a frivolous threat. He had left her office in a rage, but then never spoke of the incident with her again. One month later, she received an anonymous letter informing her that Professor Thompson had a pervasive problem with the use of cocaine. The letter also included photos of Thompson purchasing the drug and several shots of him obviously partaking of the substance in a public setting. Shocked and outraged, she immediately suspended Thompson with the intention of firing him after a formal hearing, which ultimately proved to be an unnecessary measure. As it turns out, whoever sent Adrian the anonymous letter and photos, had also sent identical copies to the bar association and a local paper. Thompson was banned indefinitely from practicing law, and the story about his drug addiction ran rampant through the legal community like a cheap gossip tabloid. Thompson left town that next day and eventually fell off the grid completely.

After the incident, Adrian called Bishop into her office and asked if he was responsible for publically uncovering Thompson's addiction. "What are you talking about?" Bishop had responded indignantly with an undeniable air of satisfaction. "Thompson is the only one responsible for his actions. He was a drug addict. I thought you would be thrilled to be rid of him."

"Of course I don't want a member of my staff to be engaged in such unruly behavior, but it's a nightmare having a public disgrace pasted all over town with Brooktown's name attached to it. This unfortunate mishap could have been disclosed in a dignified and confidential way. Now, I'm going to ask you again, did you do this? Please tell me you did not hire some private detective or someone else of that nature to tail Thompson out of spite."

"Of course not, Dean Herrera," Bishop responded blankly, but Adrian could sense a hint of smugness underneath his unwavering stare. "Although,

I will say this is a satisfying turn of events as far as I'm concerned. I can't say that I'm sad to see him go."

Adrian sighed, "What an untasteful thing to say. He criticized your writing. Is that such an unforgivable sin?"

He shrugged, "It is to me. And again, why do you care? You had an unstable drug addict working in your school, and now he's gone. The integrity of Brooktown employees has now been reinforced."

"Yes, I suppose I should thank whoever caused this, even if it's been nothing but a public nightmare for everyone in this school," she quipped sarcastically.

Again Bishop gave her a seemingly unempathetic stare. "I still don't really see what this has to do with me. I already said I wasn't responsible. What else are you asking?"

"I'm asking that next time you have a vendetta, you react proportionately instead of annihilating your enemy like a vindictive child."

Bishop let out a half laugh, "Now you just sound paranoid."

"Anyway," Adrian said as she looked over her notes for Bishop's evaluation, "like always, your marks are impressive and the progress you've made on your research is certainly up to Brooktown standards. I guess there's not much else to go over."

"I'm always glad to hear it, Dean Herrera. Your opinions really do mean the world to me."

She gave a weak smile and rubbed her forehead, a stressful gesture she often employed in his presence. She had never openly admitted concern, but Bishop had always made her feel a restless sense of unease, especially since one of his female students had come forward with a minor allegation against him in the years before. The complaint was almost immediately dropped, but it was always a tense reality in the background of her personal opinion of Bishop. Then, after Melissa Antemie's hearing, she had made it a point to keep a close eye on him and his interactions with younger students and clients. "One more thing before you leave. I heard Julia Harrison is your new research assistant."

"That's correct. She's been quite impressive. She's truly a remarkable young talent."

"Yes, she is very young."

Bishop raised his eyebrows and shot her a suspicious glare, "Do you have an inquiry about this subject, or is this just an aimless observation on your end."

"No inquiry, I just like to keep tabs on who is working with whom in my school, especially with a student like Julia. She's been a rising star throughout her time here."

"I understand."

"I'm sure you do. Is that why you specially requested a spot for her in your class?"

"I requested a spot for her because I appreciate talent when I see it. I like working with talented students. Do you have something to ask me, Dean Herrera?"

"No, I don't suppose I do."

"Great, then I'll be on my way. I have a lot of work to do. Have an excellent evening, and, as always, it was lovely chatting with you."

"And you as well," she sighed with exhaustion as he left her office with a chipper last wave of his hand.

November 7, 2015
Julia

"What else should we go over?" Bishop asked Gabriella and Julia as he shuffled through the stack of research in front of him.

"If Gabriella doesn't have any more questions, I think we covered everything," Julia announced with a relieved smile. For an hour they had gone over Gabriella's asylum case in preparation for her processing interview next week. If all went according to plan, she would be granted asylum by next month, obtain permanent status in the U.S., and her deportation proceedings would be dropped indefinitely. Gabriella was shaking with nerves, and Julia felt an almost motherly instinct to reach for her hand in comfort. Instead she gave a reassuring smile and turned back to Bishop for guidance.

"I know you're worried, but there's sincerely no reason to be nervous. I've done this a long time, and I'm really confident that you have an easy case," he reassured her with a positive nod of his head.

This seemed to put her at ease, "I believe you. There's just a lot on the line. I can't help but feel a little nervous. Thank you both so much though," she related while teetering her stare back and forth from Julia to Bishop, "for everything you've done for me. I know you didn't have to."

"There's no need to thank us," Bishop smiled and Julia nodded in confirmation. Julia admired Bishop's ability to calm Gabriella, whose natural temperament was punctured with nerves so that she always seemed a little unhinged. Sometimes she would ramble for minutes at a time, and other times she would just stare in awkward silence with her head hung to the floor. She wasn't the easiest client to elicit information from, but regardless Julia found her sweet, unsteady nature altogether endearing. The more Gabriella's life story unfolded, the more Julia was captivated and invested by the intricacies of the case.

"Oh hey, Julia! Before I go, I read that book you recommended," Gabriella stated suddenly with a large smile. "The one about the older guy and the little girl." Upon their initial meeting, Gabriella had been expressly reluctant to accept Julia's assistance in her case. She had grown to trust Bishop throughout her representation, but Julia's presence brought a renewed sense of harrowing turmoil. Julia had struggled to break her new client's seemingly impenetrable shell and instill a steady level of confidence in their relationship, but Gabriella innately refused to open up. Finally, after Julia spotted "Jane Eyre" in Gabriella's backpack, the two discovered that they shared a long-standing and adamant love of reading. Unearthing this simple, common ground at last spurred their relationship from a series of tense exchanges to an easy bond.

"Lolita? You read it already? I just told you about it last week."

"Yeah! I loved it. The characters were great together. You should give me a list of other books. Now that I can go to the library when I want, I have too many choices to sort through. I keep getting overwhelmed and walking out with ones I've already read."

"Sure, I'll have you a list by our next meeting."

Bishop leaned back and smiled at their interaction with a small, gratifying nod of his head. Gabriella had taken to Julia with both a sense of gratitude and fascination. Julia could see he was proud of her for finding a way of connecting with their timid client despite her skittish nature, and had made a couple of comments in passing about how Julia had exceeded his expectations in both legal research and client interaction.

"Maybe by our next meeting, you'll have both your green card and a new reading list then, Gabriella," Bishop affirmed with a look of pure contentment. "Is that it then?"

"I think so," Gabriella smiled and collected her things to leave. "I'll see you in a couple of weeks."

Julia started doing the same, but Bishop motioned for her to stay. After the door closed behind Gabriella, he gave Julia another satisfying smile. "So you like her?"

"I really do. She's so interesting."

"Yeah, she's my favorite kind of client. I've enjoyed working on this case."

"I have too, thank you so much again for asking me to help."

"Absolutely. That's why I wanted you to stay. Her case will probably wrap up in about a month, and I wanted to acknowledge that you've done an incredible job."

"Thanks," she said sheepishly and incidentally felt a bit of color rush to her face.

"How's everything at home?"

"Um... much better. Thanks for asking," she nodded with brisk dismissal. She appreciated the sentiment, but she still hadn't grown accustomed to the idea of Bishop knowing so much about her past.

"And the boyfriend?"

"Great, like always."

"I figured, he's really lucky to have you."

"I'm actually the lucky one."

"I doubt that, Julia. I'm sure every man wants a girl like you."

"Um... thanks. I appreciate that. Daniel is really great though."

Bishop stroked his beard in polished contemplation, "So you're satisfied in your relationship then?"

"Yeah... Why do you ask?" Julia inquired with a small hint of apprehension.

"Oh! No reason. I'm just always curious about your life. I like to hear updates."

"Thanks. I'm really good though."

"Great to hear," Bishop declared with a warm smile. "I'll see you tomorrow in class." For half a second Julia turned her head and stared with slight traces of modest skepticism. Quickly though, she smiled back and gave a brisk nod of agreement.

November 12, 2015
Daniel

"Is something wrong?" Daniel asked as he followed Julia out of the library. The icy air hit him with a small jolt of surprise. Even after three years on the East Coast, the bitter transition to the cold always stunned him into a small state of seasonal depression at the outset of every winter.

"No, I'm fine," Julia responded with a dismissive wave of her hand as the two made their way through campus and started the brief walk to their apartment down the street.

"You've been acting weird all day."

"I promise it's nothing, I'm just stressed with finals coming up, and Gabriella's case is getting intense."

"But you said you're really confident she's going to win."

"I am, but it's still a lot of pressure. I feel connected with this case now that I've met her. She's really sweet."

"What did you guys talk about?"

"Everything... her life story is absolutely devastating. She was forced to have sex with like fifteen men a day. It's disgusting. Now she might be deported. Can you imagine going through something like that? She has no education, no real family, and no money. It's terrible. That's what's weighing on me."

"Honey," Daniel said in a concerned tone, "I know you just want to help, but are you taking on too much? I mean this on top of law school and trying to find a job-"

"-I can handle it!"

"I wasn't saying that, Julia! Of course you can handle it, but this is a really critical time in of your life. Plus... sometimes you get a little too attached to your work."

"You're saying that like it's a bad thing."

"Of course it's not! I love how passionate you are. It's just, if this case is affecting you emotionally-"

"-Then that's something I'm going to have to learn to fucking deal with if I'm going to be a lawyer, now isn't it?"

Daniel sighed, "What's wrong, Julia? Where's your head? You've never talked to me like this. I'm not mad, I just want you to talk to me."

She sighed and gave a small shake of her head. "I promise it's nothing. I'm just stressed and reading too much into everything."

"What do you mean? What are you reading into?"

"Nothing."

They spent the remainder of their short journey in a disagreeable silence, both stubbornly staring ahead with unshakeable indignation. When they finally made it back to their shared apartment, Julia casually threw her backpack on the table and immediately dug out her laptop. Without a word, she briskly began clicking through her emails.

Daniel quietly watched her from the corner as she settled on a page with a small, distressing gulp. Suddenly her eyes began warily darting back and forth, compulsively reading and rereading the same line in an ominous manner. The longer this went on, the more visibly agitated she became. He could almost see her mood collapse as her face turned red with embarrassment. He noticed a subtle shudder, and for half a second, he thought she might cry. Daniel tried to formulate a way to investigate her flagrant state of disarray, but decided not to push the subject any further.

"I'm going to take a shower," she said at last, throwing her laptop on the table and turning towards the bedroom in a single, stiff motion.

"Hey," Daniel said as he decidedly moved himself between her and the door, "come here." He held out his arms and pulled her into a long, encompassing hug, stroking her tangled hair with gentle compassion.

"I'm sorry," she finally sighed. "I'm so, so sorry. I don't mean to take anything out on you. I have a lot in my head, and I just don't want to talk about it right now."

"I know, baby. It's a hard year for everyone, but we're almost done. I love you so much, I wouldn't have survived this place without you. You have to let me in your head though. I've never seen you like this, just tell me what's wrong so I can help you."

"It's just... nothing. I would tell you if there was something wrong, but there isn't," she promised as she leaned in to kiss his cheek. "I'm going to go shower now and then we can find something stupid to watch on Netflix, ok?"

"Of course."

She smiled and left the room as Daniel laid down on the couch in a restless discomfort, his relief fading within seconds of her departure. He couldn't shake the feeling that something offbeat was lurking at the root of her sour mood. Julia was notoriously passionate, but had never snapped at him in such an unprovoked state of irritation. It was a strange side of her to uncover. The poignant image of her face as she clicked through her emails replayed in his head like a broken record. After he heard the shower snap on from the adjacent room, he cautiously picked up her laptop and flipped it open with minor hesitation. He typed the word "Daniel" into her lockscreen, the universal password she used for all of her accounts.

A pang of guilt hit his stomach as her screen lit up. He had never been a notably jealous boyfriend, so he had never had a reason to infiltrate her privacy. This was different though, he rationalized, in that his curiosity didn't really stem from a jealous nature. He instinctively trusted Julia, but he also knew her well enough to understand her hesitation in burdening others with her problems. With refined vindication, he opened her emails and slowly began clicking through her inbox.

Initially, to his relief, most of the messages seemed shallow and surprisingly ordinary. He was about to give up completely when an exchange with Bishop flashed across the screen.

To: jharrison@brooktown.edu
From: abishop@brooktown.academics.edu

Julia,

Hope all is well. I received the email you sent earlier. I only had time to scan it, but, as always, I think your research is correct. Excellent work.

For your own pleasure, I'm attaching my latest article I wrote on human trafficking. I'm planning on getting it published and I want your opinion. You always have a fresh take. I like the thought of you reading and enjoying my work... read it when you're in bed.

Sincerely,
Bishop

The undertones were so subtle that Daniel had to read it twice to fully grasp the tasteless traces of an inappropriate exchange. His eyes were swiftly drawn to the last sentence and remained glued to its wording. He found himself reading it repeatedly until the connotations fully took shape amidst his understanding. His heart sank with the sickening realization that Bishop was ruthlessly and undoubtedly hitting on Julia. He tried to imagine some sort of alternative context that could possibly make the phrasing of the email fit into some appropriate box of professionalism, but eventually he accepted that there was no other possible substitute for this blatantly unwelcomed advancement.

To Daniel's humble knowledge, Bishop had always been entirely appropriate with Julia during their exchanges. If Bishop had ever crossed a line with her, she hadn't shown even a small hint of discomfort. The two of them had spent hours alone together as mentor-mentee, but the thought of Bishop laying a finger on her seemed thoroughly impractical.

He scanned the email again with a somber shake of his head. The wording was deviously subtle. Yes, he was undoubtedly hitting on her, but in a way that was almost ingeniously unnoticeable. He could probably talk his way out of any repercussions should Julia try and retaliate against him for inappropriate behavior. It was suggestive enough for Julia to understand his intentions, but not enough so that Bishop could be held liable. No wonder Julia was hesitant to voice her concern.

Daniel heard the shower turn off, and quickly closed out of the incriminating window on Julia's browser before carefully placing her laptop back on the table in the exact position where she had left it before. Julia had an incredible knack for picking up on small details, and the last thing he wanted to do was give her a reason not to trust him. Another pang of guilt hit him at the thought.

He went back to the bedroom to find Julia already in pajamas, loosely drying her hair with a towel.

"Do you feel better?" he asked as he shut the door and gently moved towards her.

"Much... I'm sorry I was in a bad mood."

Daniel smiled kindly, "You're forgiven. I want you to know something though."

"What's that?"

"I get that it's hard for you to trust people, but if you ever need to tell me something, I would never hurt you with it. Just... if you ever need to talk, I'm here."

She chuckled warmly behind a hint of masked confusion, "Where is this coming from?"

"It's not coming from anywhere," he answered calmly. "I just want you to know that you can talk to me about anything. I would do anything for you, Julia. I hope you understand that."

November 20, 2015
Julia

"Is that it then?" Julia asked coldly. For the first time she was overtly uncomfortable as she sat across from Bishop in his office. Instead of looking him in the eye, she pointed her gaze towards the window with a heated glare. His oversized windows on the top floor of the law school overlooked the spacious campus, and she could see snow beginning to gently fall across the courtyard. It had been a mild and mostly pleasant fall, but winter swiftly came with a biting frost.

"Pretty much, but I also want you to proof this argument and make sure all the dates are correct," he answered cheerfully. "With any luck, we can still wrap this up by next month. We make a good team, Julia."

"Yes, the three of us do-you, me, and Gabriella," Julia replied without looking up from her notepad. She had barely glanced at him since the start of their awkward meeting.

"Is something wrong?" Bishop challenged with what appeared to be a genuine sense of worry. "You seem a little off this week."

"I'm doing fine, thanks."

"I imagine holidays would be tough for you, what with your family's past and all. It must be a difficult time," he noted casually. Julia felt her cheeks flare and burn red with his unwelcomed inference. Perhaps the suggestive nature of his email had been an innocent mistake, but he had said enough for her to justifiably keep him at arm's length. She suddenly regretted everything she had told him about her troubled past.

"No, the holidays are fine. I'm going home with Daniel. I spend the holidays with his family now in Seattle."

Within the first few months of their budding relationship, Daniel had promptly insisted that Julia meet his parents with an uncharacteristically forceful sense of impatience. Initially, his blatant display of eagerness had turned her off to the idea, as she almost felt like a standard prize he wanted to show off. However, after spending time with his profoundly intense parents and reflecting on the intricacies of their family dynamic, she admittedly understood why he had been so adamantly pushing for the two parties to meet.

Daniel's shallow conversations with his parents were distinctly uncomfortable and seemingly forced. They incessantly bombarded him with questions about Brooktown, pushing him on what areas caught his attention and how he grappled with the sophisticated theory behind each course. He awkwardly sought to appease them with charming anecdotes from class, but he would inevitably fail in matching their flagrant enthusiasm. Consequently, their conversations were sadly incomplete and torturously uneasy. Julia could almost sense their lingering disappointment as Daniel steered the conversation into realms he found bearable.

Julia, on the other hand, adored every convoluted aspect of the law, and indulged in deeply complex conversations about entangled legal theories. His parents were almost immediately taken with her ability to argue, articulate, and pander to every dimension of the areas they found most interesting. Daniel watched with long-awaited relief as they debated upcoming Supreme Court cases, naturally spiraling into civilized disputes, in a way that Daniel had always envied. For once, instead of dreading his parents' visits, Julia could see him physically relax in their company. As she took the lead in their conversations, she would intentionally ask his input on subjects she knew he was most comfortable in arguing, finally allowing him to enter his parents' worldly discussions without bringing their debates to an unbearably graceless halt.

Daniel's family had practically adopted Julia as their own. Sometimes he joked she was their new favorite child, which made her feel uneasy against the tragic backdrop of his past. She had never had a family like his, and almost marveled at the way they functioned with such manageable normalcy. She envied the intimacy of their shared experiences, and the way they cared for one another with such genuine interest. The more they welcomed her into their family, the more complete her life became. This was just one more exceptional component of her relationship with Daniel.

"Oh yes, the boyfriend," Bishop said flatly, making Julia feel awkward against the bitterness of his tone. "How's he doing? I miss his insights in class. He always did give such well-articulated answers."

Julia fell silent with the sting of his derogatory insult. His ridicule was so subtle that it almost slipped into the conversation as an unnoticeable side note. The very thought of him undermining Daniel intuitively flared her rage.

"It's amusing how your cheeks turn red when you get angry," he said with a devilish smile.

Julia snapped in disbelief, "What is that supposed to mean?"

"Nothing," Bishop shrugged innocently. "Is something wrong?"

She let out a long breath to calm herself. "I have to go," she announced as she briskly picked up her bag and brutally swung it around her shoulders. "I'll get that research to you by Thursday. I'm looking forward to the end of this case... and semester."

"Me too," Bishop said thoughtfully. "Although I will miss having you as my research assistant."

"Goodbye, Bishop," she spat.

"Have a great evening. I'm sure we'll talk soon."

August 15, 2016
Gabriella

"What was I saying?" Gabriella asked Doctor Estes after a long pause.

"You were telling me about when your feelings for Bishop crossed the line from a passive interest to an active obsession," he replied calmly.

"I didn't use those words."

"What words would you prefer to use?"

"I don't know, but why did you just say it was an obsession?"

"Does that word bother you?"

Gabriella chuckled, "You remind me of my lawyer."

"Why's that?"

"Because you never really give a straight answer to anything, just like her."

"You're not talking about Bishop?"

"No, I had a different lawyer. She was the one who was kind of like my friend."

"What happened to her?"

"I don't know, and I don't care."

"I thought you liked her," Estes prodded.

She fidgeted in her chair as she tried to formulate an answer, "It's complicated. Let's get back to Bishop."

It started with a girlish infatuation that very gradually spun into a more sinister entanglement of emotional obligation. It wasn't a rush, but rather a slow build of misplaced passion, asserting itself piece by piece so that she didn't even notice how enslaved she had become to her own fantasies. At first, Gabriella merely felt awestruck that someone of Bishop's status would so selflessly navigate her through the intricacies of the American legal system which felt impossibly cryptic and unattainable. This disbelief turned to gratitude, which then faded into admiration before spinning into something that felt somewhat discomforting and uncontrollable. She was lost within a spectrum of confounding emotions and had a difficult time piecing together rational thoughts.

Bishop was her lawyer, but their relationship developed in a way that landed him somewhere between a mentor and friend. Her life, which had practically been fragmented into unmanageable shambles, started piecing together under his guidance. First, he contacted immigration services and helped her gain work authorization. He told her how to fill out job applications and even offered to serve as a reference. Eventually she did get a job at a coffee shop in a small suburb just outside the city. She was a fast learner and had never minded hard work. If anything she welcomed the distraction from the violent memories that still crept into her head at various moments throughout the day. She cried when she got her first paycheck, and cherished the sight of her name next to an actual dollar amount before realizing she had no way to cash a check. When she explained this to Bishop, he helped her set up a checking account at a bank across from her work.

Within months, she had saved up enough to start renting an apartment. Bishop helped her find places online, directed her to neighborhoods he felt were safe, and looked over her lease when she finally found a suitable place to make sure it was a fair arrangement. It was a small, musty studio on the outskirts of the city, but Gabriella immediately fell in love with the apartment. For the first time in her life she experienced true independence and the freedoms that accompany a certain level of autonomy. Her life was looking up with so much advantage that it almost felt fictitious, like she was playing out a rather unbelievable plot twist in one of her books. The better her life became, the deeper indebted she felt to Bishop for taking such an active role in her well-being.

Staying level-headed in his presence proved nearly impossible, but as her case progressed through the immigration system she never broke character. He treated their meetings like an emotionless transaction, so she tried her best to mirror his professional demeanor. After each interaction though, she would swoon over him like a little girl, cataloging every word he had said to her that day and replaying it over and over as she indulged in the memory of their meeting. She had a suspicion that he felt something for her too, but he never gave her enough of a definitive hint to confirm or deny that there were in fact lingering feelings beyond their formal relationship. Sometimes, she felt him staring a little too long or noticed small traces of nerves in his mannerisms when she was around, but she also worried that these signs were a product of her own longing. Maybe she wanted him so badly that she was reading into feelings that weren't there.

Everything changed the day she was granted asylum. The decision was delivered to Bishop's office in a simple letter, stating that she had been found eligible for permanent status in the United States and was no longer at risk of deportation. He called her immediately, referencing a piece of good news, but when she heard the excitement permeating through his voice she abruptly cut him off and stated that she would rather hear about the outcome of her case in person. The moment her case ended so did her excuses to see him, and she wanted to savor the gratification of having him in her life for just a little longer. It was the dead of winter and Brooktown's campus was on the other side of the city, but she didn't care. She had to work late and asked him to wait until she got off. He hesitated for a moment at what must have seemed like a rather inconvenient request, but he finally complied and agreed to wait for her in his office.

When she arrived at Brooktown that evening, she found the campus nearly unrecognizable. She had frequently visited the grounds during the day to receive updates about her case, but she had never seen Brooktown so docile and eerily vacant. She had always felt out-of-place amongst the army of elite students that roamed the campus during the day with an easy confidence, but tonight the empty univeristy allowed her to fade into a subdued state so that she could relax and at last admire the gothic architecture and innate beauty of the ancient school. Bishop's representation gave her a right to be here, and again a swelling of gratitude overwhelmed her senses at the thought of his generosity.

She proudly marched through the desolate law school and slipped into his office without knocking, feeling bold amidst the end of their attorney-client relationship. He looked up and smiled, nodding as she nestled into a chair across from his own. "We won," he said without introduction as a boyish smile crept across his face. She studied his jawline and shape of his glasses, and couldn't help but swoon at his subtly handsome features.

"I know," she replied. "I could hear it in your voice when you called earlier. I could have let you tell me over the phone, but I still wanted to see you in person. I thought this called for a celebration."

"I agree," he nodded as he turned to pick up a picture frame from a shelf behind him, exposing two small keys underneath. He unlocked the bottom drawer of his desk and pulled out a slender bottle and two glasses. "Do you drink scotch?"

"Sometimes," she lied. She actually hated the taste of alcohol, but she was too intimidated to refuse his offer and wanted to seem older and sophisticated.

"How do you feel?" he asked as he poured them both a glass and slid one across the desk for her to take.

"I can't describe it," she squealed with an uncontrollable smile. "Honestly, I'm still afraid to be happy. I keep thinking they made a mistake."

He laughed at that, "They didn't make a mistake, Gabriella. You won! Be happy! Celebrate! Go live the American dream, whatever that's worth nowadays."

"It's worth a lot to me."

He took a large sip of his scotch, tilting back the glass until it was almost empty. She did the same, trying to hide her discomfort as the harsh liquid hit her throat. He didn't seem to notice her obvious disgust, and instead poured them both another round.

"You know," he said with triumphant wave of his hand, "I never doubted we would win, not for a second. You were truly a great client to work with."

The past-tense made her stomach sink and for a moment she had to choke back tears. This time she was the one who tilted her glass back and in one motion swallowed its contents entirely. He looked surprised for only a second before he shrugged and did the same, pouring them another round with very little hesitation.

"So what are your plans now?" he asked enthusiastically.

"What do you mean?"

"I mean, will you stay in the area? Have you considered relocating? I'm curious where you see yourself in the future."

"You think I should leave?" her heart sank again at his dismissal.

He looked confused, "I just mean that you can do anything now. If you want to leave, I certainly think you should. Nothing is keeping you here, is it?"

"Well... no, I guess not."

He smiled with unhinged energy. "Exactly! You can do anything. So what is it that you want to do?"

"I want to thank you for everything you did for me." She stood quickly and motioned for him to do the same. As he stood with a confused tilt of his head, she walked around his desk and bravely threw her arms around him in an intimate hug. He looked down at her with a genuinely shocked expression. She held him there for a couple of seconds and allowed her body to melt into his. It was the first time she had touched him apart from brief handshakes and she wanted to savor every half-second of his embrace. She turned to kiss his cheek, allowing her smooth lips to gently brush against his beard as her hands reached up to cup his face.

"Gabriella..." he began and she could almost feel the enthusiasm drain from his body. A different emotion now lingered between them, one that Gabriella couldn't initially place. He took a deep breath and pulled away slowly, staring at her deeply with a heavy sense of tension. He was shaking, and at first she thought it was out of anger, but as he looked down at her body, allowing his glance to linger as his eyes traced the outline her figure, she suddenly understood his longing. Slowly she bent forward and let her lips touch his.

"Don't do that!" he snapped, suddenly releasing her with a shock and spinning himself around in exasperation.

"Why?" she asked shyly, letting her head fall to the floor out of shame.

"A lot of reasons, starting with the fact that I'm your lawyer. There are rules against these kinds of things. I could lose my job... I'm... I'm already on thin ice."

"Well it's not like I'll be your client for much longer," she pleaded as she looked up from the floor with a small flicker of hope. "I'm sorry, I thought maybe you felt it too, I guess I was wrong."

Bishop let out a long breath, "You're so young, Gabriella. You don't understand what you're doing. Trust me on this. You're a beautiful lady with a whole life ahead of you. I'm an aging law professor. I assure you that I'm quite boring, and in a different setting, I doubt you'd find much appeal in the thought of our courtship. You'll find someone a little more... age appropriate."

"I'm not smart enough for you..." she said as tears sprang to her eyes.

"That's what you're getting from this?" he sighed. "You know I didn't say that."

"You didn't have to, I just know. I might not be smart enough for you, but I'm not stupid either. If I was as smart as that girl Julia, you'd probably want me. I see the way you look at her."

"What does that have to do with anything? Look at me," he said a little more firmly than she had anticipated. "That is not it. I can see that you're a very intelligent girl. I knew that from the first time I met you. Like I said, I am on very thin ice with the Brooktown administration after an... incident. If someone caught us... I don't know. I am telling you the truth, but if you don't want to hear it, there is no point in me explaining things any further. Any sort of relationship between us beyond a professional setting would be inappropriate. Please, you need to leave."

He sank into his chair and immediately began sifting through papers in a cold gesture of dismissal. She was astonished by the sudden transformation in his demeanor. He had been so kind to her not even twenty minutes before.

She started to leave but stopped at the door, and let her eyes meet his for a final plea. "You know, my whole life I was treated like a whore... you treated me like a person. I just wanted to know what it would be like... to be with someone who wasn't terrible like everyone else."

He turned back to her, standing again and staring into her eyes with a confident glare that almost felt like a warning. "Gabriella, I am far more terrible than you can imagine. You have no idea who I am."

"Yes, I do. Please, I just want to know..." she slowly moved back towards him until their bodies were close enough to touch. He held her hand to his cheek and allowed her fingers to softly touch his chin. He closed his eyes and let his head rest against her palm.

"We have to stop," he whispered without backing away, "we have to stop now or I won't be able to-"

She leaned over to kiss him and this time he met her lips with his own. Slowly they touched as their bodies moved closer together. He wrapped his arm around her and pulled her towards him so tightly that for the first time she really felt his strength. For half a second it was satisfying, but almost instantly she recoiled at his touch. With a startling jolt, suddenly Gabriella's head began to swim with anxiety and a feeling of unmanageable vulnerability shot through her body as panic set in. Helpless to the wanderings of her own mind, miserable memories began flooding her head with the most unbearable scenes she had experienced in the brothel.

Her head felt heavy with these nightmares until she could no longer grasp the realities of her surroundings. She scrambled to get away in a manic frenzy, and suddenly looked around Bishop's office which now felt entirely unfamiliar and thoroughly stifling. "Stop!" She screamed with a jerk of her head, as she tore apart their embrace and stepped back a little to catch her bearings. At first, he only looked shocked, but he reluctantly obeyed and momentarily stepped away. Stunned by her own reaction, she started to cry in a state of dismay. He watched as she held her hand up, embarrassed by her inability to gain control. He reached out to comfort her, but she quickly slapped his hand away with an intuitive jolt.

Bishop studied the hand she had just slapped as if it was suddenly an unrecognizable part of his own body. She watched as a hint of a smile stretched across his face before his expression went blank. He moved again to kiss her.

"No!" she yelled, "stop!" .

"Say it again," he commanded in a voice that felt suddenly uncharacteristic and abrupt.

"Stop... I-I don't want to do this. I'm sorry I thought I did, but-"

Before letting her finish, he grabbed her and pushed her onto the desk, letting the contents of the desk's surface spill clumsily onto the floor. She tried to kiss him softly, hoping to slow him down, but he bit her lip and pushed her back. She closed her eyes and felt herself cringe as he started clawing at her dress. The sensation was all too familiar, and instinctively she began to shut down. Just like in the brothel, she let her brain detach from her body and wander to the past. Like so many times before, she began counting the seconds until it would end and thought of the latest book she had read from Julia's reading list.

December 10, 2015
Julia

They won the case. Gabriella was granted asylum and her deportation proceedings were dismissed. Julia cried softly with overwhelming relief when Bishop emailed her the outcome, and she could almost feel her whole body unwind and return to a state of tranquility she had not experienced in weeks. The earnest sense of elation she felt for Gabriella was nothing compared to the burden that was instantaneously lifted from her shoulders when she realized her commitment was fulfilled. It was official, she no longer had to be Anthony Bishop's research assistant. For several moments, she sat back with a fresh taste of closure and relished the presence of this new freedom.

Since their last strained encounter, she had tried to distance herself from Bishop which had turned out to be an oddly uncomplicated task. She claimed her classes were becoming unusually demanding, often excusing herself from their weekly meetings or her research deadlines. She even began to avoid raising her hand during class and let herself become invisible amidst her fellow pupils. If Bishop noticed these changes at all, he failed to acknowledge it. She was hesitant to accept his evident retreat, but decided not to question whatever motive was behind his new passive behavior. Their communications grew cold and transactional, and she welcomed the return of their formal etiquette.

When she heard Gabriella's case was wrapping up, Julia sent an email politely informing Bishop that she would not be able to extend their research agreement into the following semester, explaining that she needed to focus on her grades and finding a post-graduate job. She noted that it had been an honor to work with him and cordially wished him good luck with his future cases. Oddly enough, within moments for her pressing send, he replied by graciously accepting her resignation and thanking her for her work. He acted with such unwavering professionalism that for a half a moment she almost questioned whether she had imagined the depths of his inappropriate advances. Maybe she had just been sensitive and her hesitations were all a simple product of an innocent misunderstanding.

Julia pondered this from her seat in the Brooktown library as she looked out the towing glass windows and scanned the exquisite school grounds she had grown to adore. It was almost midnight on a Saturday evening. There were very few people in the large reading room at this time of night, or on campus generally, making it feel ironically serene despite the general chaos of the closing semester. As she glanced into the courtyard below, she saw a figure moving through the snow and narrowed her eyes to place the familiar stride. Almost instinctively, she knew it was Gabriella. Julia watched curiously, speculating why Bishop would invite Gabriella all the way to Brooktown for a five minute conversation. Even with such big news, she lived nearly an hour away and surely would have preferred a simple phone call.

She closed her eyes and took a couple of deeps breaths, immediately feeling uneasy at the thought of Gabriella alone in Bishop's office. She wasn't sure why it bothered her to the extent that it did, but her staunch apprehension drove her suddenly into a state of subtle agitation. For a while after she saw the figure pass and enter the building, she tried to go back to studying. She needed to wrap up anyway. Daniel had gone home early to make dinner, and she didn't want to waste any more of her Saturday night locked away in the confinement of Brooktown's library.

No matter how she tried to fight it, though, her mind inevitably spiraled into an inescapable, crushing anxiety as she weighed every possible dark scenario this situation could entail. She finally accepted the imminent distraction, abandoned her homework for the night, and decided to go after Gabriella. She would go up to Bishop's office, explain that she had seen Gabriella walking through campus from the library window and wanted to congratulate her in person. It was a believable enough story, and one she knew Bishop couldn't blatantly fault her for.

She climbed the stairs to the floor which hosted the staff lounge and offices. It was strange to see the hall, usually bustling with students and professors alike, completely abandoned like a dreary ghost town. Her pace quickened as she made her way to Bishop's corner office, and was practically at a run by the time she approached the door. That's when she heard the unmistakable sound of Gabriella's voice let out a small and harrowing scream. Julia cautiously then allowed her stride to ease and crept towards the entry of his office in a steadfast state of dismay. She touched her ear to the outside of his heavy door and felt her stomach turn to knots at the sound of their voices. Tears sprang to her eyes as her body stood paralyzed in fear.

"Stop!" Gabriella's voice said from the other side.

"Say it again."

"Stop... I-I don't want to do this."

Julia should have thrown the door open and screamed. She should have tried to fight Bishop to save Gabriella. She should have lunged herself at him, clawed at his eyes, punched his stomach, anything that could have possibly overpowered him for just a while so that Gabriella could have escaped. She was the only person on this part of campus, the only one who could possibly save Gabriella, but fear stopped her from doing anything but crying softly on the other side of the door and shake uncontrollably like a frightened child.

For the rest of her life she would replay this moment. She would hate herself for the way she stood in fear like a coward as she listened to Gabriella scream for help from the confines of Bishop's office. Instead of rushing in, finally all she could manage was a feeble knock. She lifted her hand, almost uncontrollably, and beat the door three times. She heard them startle, and slowly began backing away from the door before she took off running through the hallway. She ran through the corridor and into an empty office down the hall. She hid under a desk as adrenaline pumped through her body, making it difficult to think clearly or formulate her next step.

Every instinct told her to get out of the building, and she felt her brain enter an almost animalistic state of survival. Nothing mattered in that moment apart from safety and distance from Bishop, but she was still too shocked to actually move. She had a feeling like he was somehow in the room watching her, even though every time she turned around she was faced with the same abandoned office. She sank to her knees to catch her breath, and allowed herself a moment to calm. She concluded within seconds that she would have to call the police. She would never forgive herself if she stood idly by while Gabriella was raped just doors away from her. *Raped.* The word rolled around her head and settled as an immediate fixture in her conscience. She shuddered but quickly commanded herself back to reality.

She pulled out her cellphone and started dialing 9-11. Her phone beeped, signaling a weak reception. She moaned in frustration as she furiously waved it around the room, trying to find a signal, before accepting she would have to find another way.

She remembered triumphantly a public phone in the staff lounge, and she instinctively ran to it without any additional hesitation. It felt like a dream as she quickly made her way back through the hallway, so hyped with adrenaline and fear that she barely noticed the noise she made as she hurried to the other side of the floor. Her only thought now was saving Gabriella, which dulled her remaining instincts. So much so that when she picked up the receiver and quickly dialed 9-11, she didn't notice a figure emerge from the door behind her.

"Hello... I need to report a crime," she yelled into the receiver. Her voice quivered in a way that made it nearly unrecognizable.

"Where is your location?" the dispatcher responded quickly.

"Brooktown-"

She was cut off by an angry hand, grabbing the phone from behind her and slamming it onto the receiver. She turned to see Bishop's face just inches away from her own.

"Good evening, Julia."

"Hi," she stammered like an idiot, unable to see straight through her state of panic.

"What are you doing here this late?"

"I... I heard Gabriella-"

"-She went home. I suggest you do the same now."

She nodded with a quick breath and turned to leave, shaking her head in confusion and shock as she made her way to the door. Although she wouldn't grasp the full extent of her situation until much later, almost instantly she was hit with the realization that Anthony Bishop was going to ruin her for this. She thought of reporting him right away, but how could her word possibly hold any weight against his?

Before she left the room, she glanced out the window and watched Gabriella shuffling through campus, walking quickly with her coat tightly wrapped around her body. Julia gulped at the sight. Even from three floors above, she felt an odd bond with Gabriella already, and took a small piece of comfort in knowing that she wasn't the only one who now had a shattered impression of the professor she once adored.

"Oh Julia," Bishop called from across the room. She turned to him, still shaking in fear. "I suspect you won't be making any more phone calls tonight, agreed?"

She took in another sharp breath and tried to speak, but all she could manage was another a small nod in his direction.

"Great," he said again as his face changed to an ironically cheerful smile, "I'll send you an email soon. We have some things to discuss."

JANUARY 1, 2016
Julia

To: jharrison@brooktown.edu
From: abishop@brooktown.academics.edu

Julia,

I'm not sure if you're getting my emails, but I would really like to schedule a meeting. As your mentor, I'd like to discuss a few things about your future and possibly set up additional research for next semester. I noticed you switched out of my class, which I entirely understand was due to scheduling conflicts, but I really think you should reconsider. Please let me know when you are available for that chat.

Thank you,
Professor Bishop

- - - - - - - - - - - - - - - - -

To: abishop@brooktown.academics.edu
From: jharrison@brooktown.edu

Professor Bishop,

I'm sorry I have not responded to your emails. I have been dealing with some personal issues. I am very busy this week and I'm not sure I can set up a meeting. I have taken on a lot of responsibilities this semester. I will contact you later in

the year to set up a meeting when my schedule relaxes. Perhaps Daniel can come
as well.

Thanks,
Julia

- - - - - - - - - - - - - - - - - -

To: jharrison@brooktown.edu
From: abishop@brooktown.academics.edu

Julia,

I insist that you stop by my office this week. Friday at 6:30. I need to speak
to you concerning some loose ends from our case last semester. For confidentiality
purposes, please come alone. If you take your academic career seriously, I highly
suggest you find the time.

-Anthony

"Hello Julia, it's been a while. Please shut the door," Bishop stated casually
as Julia moped to his office on Friday evening. She complied after an awkward
moment of hesitation. "How's your semester going?" he continued in an eerily calm voice as he took a long drink from a cup of stale coffee in front of him.

"Fine, it feels good to be back at Brooktown after the break," she lied. It
was dreadful to be back on campus. She had spent the holidays with Daniel's
family in Seattle, but had been so sick with anxiety throughout the trip that
she hardly got out of bed. Daniel knew something was wrong, but had been
strangely understanding of her hesitancy to disclose the reasons behind her
dispirited nature.

"Great," Bishop smiled, snapping her mind back into their conversation. "So I understand that you're having hesitations about continuing your work as my research assistant this semester."

"Yes," she answered coldly. "I feel that I have too much on my plate right now. You told me when I started working for you that if my schedule got too hectic there was no pressure to continue. Unfortunately that's now the case."

"I did say that, and I completely understand your decision. You did an excellent job last semester, and I know it took up a great deal of your time. Plus, I realize certain cases can be very trying for someone with your history of emotional instability."

"What?" Julia gasped with an immediate sense of fury. "Emotional instability? Are you serious?"

"Oh, please don't take offense, it's nothing to be ashamed of. I just know with your background you have some issues in maintaining a rational pattern of behavior."

"I'm not at all emotionally unstable. I've always been professional. I really don't appreciate you insinuating otherwise."

Bishop shrugged, "Well I've heard some of the other professors talk about it. I know sometimes you're prone to having outbursts during class."

"What? Who? Which professors?" Julia responded as her fists clenched instinctively out of anger. "I don't have emotional outbursts! I speak up in class because I'm a good student."

"There's no need to get emotional, Julia, lots of people have problems with maintaining stability. It's certainly not a big deal."

"Are you kidding me?" she spat, crossing her arms in front of her chest like a rebellious child.

"You're taking this too personal. You've had an unusual background. Anyone who examined your past would likely conclude you had issues, but I'm not saying you don't conduct yourself in a decent manner most of the time considering your circumstances. It's just a simple fact that your family has a history of psychological problems."

Julia changed her tone and eyed him with seething distaste. "I know what you're doing Bishop-"

"-Call me Anthony. I think we've reached that point in our relationship, don't you?"

"Actually, I'd prefer to call you Bishop, if you don't mind. I refuse to play this game with you."

He threw up his hands, "What game? I'm not trying to play a game, Julia. I like you. I want to help you."

She closed her eyes and let out a long sigh, "Professor Bishop-"

"-Anthony-"

"-I don't want to cause you any trouble. I thought about this a lot over winter break. All I want is to go on living my life, and let you live yours. Is that fair?"

"Of course, but I think part of living my life is taking an interest in my students. Wouldn't you agree?"

"Like the interest you took in Gabriella?"

He stared at her for a few cold seconds. His nostrils flared like he was angry, but he continued in an alarmly calm voice. "Maybe," he said at last, "it depends."

Julia's heart dropped with an anxious sweltering of fear, but she focused on consciously hiding her intimidation. "That's comforting. What exactly does it depend on?"

"Your behavior, I suppose."

"You realize I'm the one who could be blackmailing you, don't you? I didn't do anything wrong."

"Of course not. It's normal for someone in your position to develop feelings for your professor. I'm sure you didn't see it as stalking when you came to my office that Friday night. You probably didn't even consider the fact that it was after everyone else on campus had left. I know you have a difficult time with boundaries."

Julia choked, "You wouldn't... Gabriella would testify-"

"-I highly doubt Gabriella would testify to much of anything, Julia," he smirked with a frustrating air of satisfaction.

"Listen Bishop-"

"-Anthony!" He yelled sharply as he pounded the desk with his fist. Julia jumped at the unanticipated thud and tried to stop herself from trembling.

"Ok. Anthony, you don't have to do that. I'm not going to tell anyone what I heard."

"I don't really think it's a matter of what I *have* to do. I think it's more a question of what I *want* to do."

"You're sick."

"That's not very professional."

"My apologies, *Anthony*, I didn't realize we were still in a professional relationship."

"We are until I say differently."

"Fine, what exactly do you want from me then?"

"Well to start, answer your emails. If you don't, I'll assume you're not taking your academic career very seriously."

"Is that it?"

"And transfer back into my class this semester."

"Fine."

"And one more thing, obviously I can't force you, but I really wish you would reconsider serving as my research assistant again this semester. We worked so well together and I have a lot of exciting projects coming up. I could use your help."

"Fine."

"That's not very enthusiastic. I only want your help if you *really* feel you can handle the workload. Do you *really* want to do it?" He asked with a smile.

"Yes."

"Yes to what?"

"Yes, I really want to be your research assistant."

"I'm so glad you reconsidered!" he clapped his hands together with triumph.

"Ok... can I go?"

"Certainly Julia, good luck with your semester."

She stood to leave and quickly moved to the door. "Wait!" he shouted. She meekly obeyed and turned to face him. He stood slowly and walked towards her until their bodies were inches away from one another. He lifted his hand softly and touched his palm to her cheek. She shivered at his touch and felt tears spring to her eyes. At that, he smiled and turned back to his desk, "Now you can go."

"You're going to be his research assistant?" Daniel gasped when Julia returned home and told him the news. She glanced miserably around their apartment in a sad attempt to avoid his stare. "I don't understand! You spent all break going on about how nice it was to be done. What the hell made you change your mind?"

"Bishop can be very persuasive," Julia said bitterly. "He really needs my help and says it's a *great* opportunity for my future."

Daniel didn't buy it, "There's something you're not telling me, Julia. I'm not stupid. I've tried to give you space about this, but I've had enough."

"What wouldn't I be telling you?" she met him with a challenging stare.

Daniel closed his eyes and rubbed the temples of his forehead in frustration. "Honestly, I'm just going to say it, I think Bishop is manipulating you. I'm not really sure how or why, but he makes me feel uncomfortable."

"Are you jealous? Seriously Daniel, the man is over fifty."

The thought of Bishop made Julia shudder, but she tried to hide her inadvertent reaction from Daniel. If he noticed something was wrong, he would intervene and Bishop would inevitably ruin her. She had been mulling over the terrifying possibilities all morning. "I don't like this, Julia," Daniel said at last.

"I know," she sighed, "but I'm just going to have to get through it."

FEBRUARY 2, 2016
Julia

To: *abishop@brooktown.academics.edu*
From: *jharrison@brooktown.edu*

Anthony,

I received your assignment, but I'm not sure I can finish it by the end of the week. The research is pretty dense, and a twenty page memo is going to take some time. I have a lot of reading in my other classes as well. Can I please have until next Wednesday to finish?

Thanks,
Julia

- - - - - - - - - - - - - - - - - -

To: *jharrison@brooktown.edu*
From: *abishop@brooktown.academics.edu*

Julia,

Please refer to me as Professor Bishop in our emails. I'm sorry, but I do need it by the end of the week. You made a commitment to be my research assistant, and I expect you to honor my deadlines. If it's too much work, of course you can quit, but I'd love to keep you on board.

Please bring the completed research to my office on Friday.

Thanks,
Professor Bishop

- - - - - - - - - - - - - - - - - -

To: abishop@brooktown.academics.edu
From: jharrison@brooktown.edu

Professor Bishop,

My apologies, I wouldn't want to be unprofessional. See you Friday.

-Julia

It was insurmountably difficult for Julia to concentrate in Professor Tryst's class. After tenaciously slaving through the night to finish Bishop's assignment, she had scarcely completed half of what she was expected to turn in the following day. Her workload had grown into a staggeringly unrealistic bundle, making it impossible to keep pace with the rest of her responsibilities. She felt herself growing weak with exhaustion, but stubbornly remained determined to stay afloat through the struggle.

In her most wearisome moments, she vaguely toyed with the idea of dropping out and leaving Brooktown completely, but the concept of letting her years of work go to waste felt inconceivable. Naturally, switching schools was also out of the question as it was a universal policy among all law schools not to accept third year transfers. She considered pursuing a different career entirely, but her crushing debt made the idea nearly impossible. With the amount of loans and interest she had incurred, if she dropped out now she was essentially guaranteed a life of financial ruin. She had a bachelor's degree in literature and most of her former work experience was in retail. In her current state, without an advanced degree, she would never obtain the salary she needed to make her costly loan payments.

She was again mulling over her these miserable options when Professor Tryst's voice snapped her back into reality. "Miss Harrison," she called, "can you please tell us the issue of the case?"

Julia sighed. "I don't know," she stated dully, "I didn't read it." An uneasy silence fell over the room as her peers turned their shocked faces in her direction. Even Tryst looked concerned at Julia's mishap.

"That's unacceptable, Julia. Your job as student is to read the cases and be prepared before the start of each class. If you didn't do that, there is no point in coming to class at all."

"I agree," Julia said stiffly as she tried to form a half-hearted apology. She looked up and saw Tryst's puzzled stare pointedly aimed in her direction, and for a moment sensed a layer of apologetic discomfort beneath Tryst's display of anger. Under normal circumstances Julia would have expected a downpour of fury and disappointment- and possibly a hint of delight considering her professor inarguably found pleasure in occasionally humiliating unprepared students- but today that wasn't the case. Tryst just turned her head and stared at Julia in a sad state of disbelief. Julia's eyes fell to the floor with despondency. She should have been embarrassed but her additional preoccupations were weighing on her so deeply that her brain couldn't muster any supplementary emotions.

"Ok Miss Harrison, I'm feeling generous. If you recite the facts of the following case, I'll allow you to stay." Tryst leaned forward with a heightened look of suspense.

Julia took a deep breath and answered slowly, "I didn't read that one either."

Kaitlyn Tryst shook her head in confusion. "If you're not prepared, you know the rules. You can't stay in class. It's not fair to those who have taken time to complete the assignment."

"Ok," Julia shrugged and stood to leave.

"Julia," Tryst called with desperation blatantly seeping into her voice. "I'm excusing you from class, but I'm not giving you permission to leave. Wait outside and come see me after lecture. Ok?"

Julia nodded before she sulked out the door. She stood in the hallway for about five seconds with the intention of staying as Tryst requested. She looked around the Brooktown common room, a place that had once been so cozy and secure, and felt as if it had been stripped of all its familiarities. Within moments of her wait, exhaustion overtook her and she collapsed into a callous defeat. She gathered her things and left the building without considering the consequences of disregarding Tryst's request. Suddenly everything apart from her conflict with Bishop seemed oddly insignificant.

May 21, 2016
Julia

Julia left the police station in a state of borderline hysteria. In a small panic, she immediately pulled out her phone and dialed Gabriella's number. "Listen," Julia said when she heard Gabriella's voice on the other end of the line, "I was just questioned by the police. You need to tell them about your relationship with Bishop. It's only a matter of time before they find out anyway. They already have suspicions."

"What did they say? What do they know?" Gabriella gasped in horror.

"Honestly, it's hard to make out what they know. I talked to this cop named Detective Weir. He's being really vague about it all, but he called me down to the station and asked me questions about you. He knows something was there, Gabby. He might not know the whole thing, but he's onto you. He specifically asked if I ever saw you pursue an inappropriate relationship with Bishop."

"But I don't understand how..."

"-Gabriella! Listen to me, the police aren't stupid. You wrote him letters, you sent him texts, you left him voicemails, and there might even be some of your DNA in his house from when you broke in. The fact that he ignored you is evidence enough of a motive. They could build a case off of that alone."

"How would they do that?"

"They're not stupid."

"This isn't even your problem, Julia."

Julia shook her head in a haze of frustration. She was trying to stay calm, but an inevitable state of frenzy was overtaking her conventional logic. "You don't understand, Gabriella. Please trust me on this, it's going to be better for you to come forward. The window of opportunity for me to help you is closing. "

There was silence for a couple of minutes as Gabriella thought this over. Finally she hesitantly conceded to the legitimacy of Julia's alarm. "Ok, but I want to talk in person. When and where can we meet?"

"That's too risky. They could be tailing you."

"But if they're going to find out anyway, why does it matter?"

"Fine," Julia sighed, "I have a plan."

"I've been going crazy, Julia," Gabriella moped several hours after their phone call. "I just want to die. It's the only way to get him out of me."

"You're not crazy Gabriella, we've talked about this. You have PTSD. The thought of him haunts me too, but he's dead now. You have to wrap your mind around that. Bishop *is* dead."

"Have you ever heard voices in your head before? Is that PTSD?"

"Honestly no," Julia sighed as she rubbed the temples of her forehead with her fingers, "but I also think you suffer from a mild case of schizophrenia, which is exacerbating your trauma."

"How do you know all this?"

"My mom was really sick for a long time, I know a lot about mental illness."

Gabriella's composure had obviously dismantled since their last visit, a month before Bishop's death. Although she was likely trying to hide it under an assortment of baggy clothes, Gabriella had noticeably gained a serious amount of weight, making her body look disproportionate and offbeat. She appeared to be overtly sleep-deprived with blood-shot eyes and thinning hair which was whisked into a greasy ponytail at the base of her neck. She barely resembled the bubbly, charming girl Julia had worked with as Bishop's research assistant.

Ashamed by her own inability to abstain from studying Gabriella's crumbling physical appearance, Julia stared down at her coffee in unsuccessful avoidance. She picked up a spoon and swirled around its contents as it inevitably grew cold in her neglect. She had barely eaten since Bishop's death, but coffee in particular had become distinctly unappetizing.

They met in a bakery near Anacostia, a neighborhood on the outskirts of the city, where they were less likely to be seen. Julia had instructed Gabriella to act as though she were taking the metro going North, but to switch directions when the doors started to close. This probably wouldn't be enough to shake someone if Gabriella was actually being followed, but she reasoned it was at least worth a shot.

"The bottom line," Julia stated calmly, "is that we both know you wouldn't kill yourself." She unintentionally let out a nervous gulp at the thought. In reality, Gabriella's sporadic behavior made it difficult to predict exactly what she would or wouldn't do.

"Why do you say that?"

"Because then he would win."

"I just keep thinking..." Gabriella began before obscurely trailing off without explanation. She often did this, sometimes for minutes at a time. Julia suspected these were mini episodes of dissociation, and tried to be patient even though these incidences were growing increasingly frustrating with the direness of their position. Julia understood Gabriella wasn't stable, but who could blame her? Julia didn't even try to comprehend what it would be like to live with the tragedies of Gabriella's life, especially compounded with what Bishop did to her last year.

They were unlikely partners, bonded in a hideous shared experience which resulted in a communal and unyielding hatred for Bishop. While their solidarity brought Gabriella a sense of comfort, it only made Julia feel weak and unappealing. Bishop had precisely selected each of them to victimize because of their flagrant vulnerabilities. He had watched Julia, analyzed her, and decided she was weak enough to exploit, just as he had done with Gabriella. It was a selfish notion to admit, but Julia resented the impression of Gabriella's company. Getting to know her now was like looking into a lucid mirror of her own shortcomings and inevitably reflecting on the mistake she had made in trusting Bishop at all.

Through her hidden animus, Julia took a deep breath and reminded herself that, despite their similarities, their differences were pervasive and unignorable. Julia knew these incongruities existed, even if Bishop hadn't initially picked up on their distinctions. She *was* stronger than Gabriella. This had become immediately apparent as the dynamic of their relationship naturally ran its course. Julia was clearly the more dominant personality of the two, and fell into an oddly maternal role as their lives grew entangled.

"Gabriella, the fact of the matter is that we both have to come forward with our stories. It's time. A man was murdered, and we're not going to fool anyone by hiding. We might both already be suspects."

"You mean *I* might already be suspect, you have an alibi. You have the *perfect* alibi."

Julia shook her head, "If you had just worked with me I would have made sure you had one too."

August 15, 2016
Gabriella

"He raped you?" Estes asked abruptly.

"I wouldn't call it rape," Gabriella answered with firm conviction. "We had sex, but I'm the one who initiated it."

"So you don't consider it rape if you initiated it? Even if you asked him to stop?"

"Well, I said yes initially. I even begged him for it at first. I was in love with him, and I think he was in love with me too. He just couldn't be with me because he was afraid he would lose his job."

Estes looked at her sadly and nodded his head, "That's rape, Gabriella. You don't have to believe me, but I won't call it anything else."

It was shocking to hear him voice such an uncompromising opinion. His detached style of therapy usually involved allowing Gabriella to form her own conclusions, prodding each of her notions with subtle analysis. Watching him take an objective stance on anything was unusual, but also a little comforting considering her position.

Regardless, labeling her encounter with Bishop as rape seemed like an unfair depiction of events. She had gone to Bishop willingly and asked for it repeatedly, even after he refused. She hated Bishop, but not because of what he had done to her that night in his office. She hated Bishop for his unwavering refusal to love her back. The rage she felt over his rejection still swelled inside her when she remembered how crushing it was to watch his interest in her promptly fade.

"Should you continue with the story?" Estes asked, returning to his usual removed voice.

Gabriella looked around the white, sterile room with discerning affliction. It was so cold and void of life that she almost felt inhuman in the barren environment. At least at Roberto's she had books and basic familiarities. Here, she had nothing but a stiff padded room and endless amounts of unwelcomed time. After enough time in this place, she was starting to feel as though she was slipping into a deranged version of herself and she almost wondered if she was in fact as crazy as they claimed. Absent mindedly, she rubbed her wrists, which were still swollen and scarred from the handcuffs.

Finally she looked up at Estes and nodded. "Things got a lot harder after that night..."

Gabriella spiraled into a state of delirium after the night in Bishop's office. She woke up the next morning battered with a shameful burden and tenaciously vowed to never see him again. This intimate promise immediately absolved itself and was abandoned completely within an hour of making. For months before the incident, her feelings for him had been her emotional benchmark. She replayed her fantasies again and again to fill the lonesome cracks of her day. Without this comfortable prospect, her mind was undeniably vacant and raw. She tried to fill the gap with justified vindication, but found the sentiment bitterly unsatisfying. Finally she abandoned her inhibitions and allowed herself to sink back into a bleak state of impossible longing. Eventually her stubborn obsession resurfaced with violent force.

She passionately yearned to see him again, childishly convincing herself that somehow they could shift back to their previous dynamic where he had generously spared her such tender acts of kindness. If she could only get him to acknowledge that he loved her just a little, surely everything else would fall into place. It would mean her grandmother was vastly defective in her judgment, and finally prove she was not a stupid whore like her mother. She imagined that underneath his reluctance, Bishop held a chivalrous virtue and perhaps could still love her in the proper setting. He wouldn't answer her incessant phone calls, so she wrote letters thoroughly explaining that she wasn't angry at all and just painfully missed his presence in her life.

After weeks of inflexible silence, her oppressive heartbreak became unbearable. She began pitifully lingering in the Brooktown parking lot every day, and waited in obscure corners of campus to watch him leave work. Although he normally traveled by car, one particular evening he took off walking at a confident pace. Breathlessly, she followed him through campus and into the bordering district. After miles on foot, they arrived at what she assumed was his home, a small two-story rowhouse just north of campus. After this discovery, she watched him from the street as well.

Looking back, she understood the evident delusions of these moments, but at the time the urge to see him was so overwhelming that she couldn't control her ludicrous compulsions. One night, on an impromptu impulse, she had even fallen asleep outside his house because she couldn't stand the thought of returning to her desolate apartment. Even existing in the unseen fringes of his disenchanted world was better than abandoning her habitual longings altogether. She woke up to the sound of his car the following morning, and watched him drive away as she sat on the stoop on the adjacent street.

After his car turned the corner disappeared completely, she calmly approached his home and meticulously studied the alluring outline of the building. After trying several entrances with strenuous defeat, she found a window unlocked in the back. She clambered through the opening and descended into his living room with a small thud as she hit the floor. After a moment of feverishly surveying the fine, expensive interior, she smiled to herself and paraded around his house like it was her own. Like a child, she imagined a world where she lived here as well, a thought she couldn't shake and helplessly indulged in for the remainder of the afternoon. To fulfill the fantasy she made herself at home, reading his books, eating his food, and finally taking a shower in the upstairs bathroom.

After spending all day in this state of bliss, she glanced at the clock and realized he would likely return within the hour. After weeks of watching him leave campus, she had instinctively memorized his rigid schedule. On Tuesdays, he would be home by eight. She realized it would be best to leave, but she couldn't bare the thought of her fantasy so bluntly absolving without an amiable ending. She told herself that if he just saw her again, maybe he would finally ask her to stay. After all, she had been able to persuade him to touch her in his office after he had initially refused.

In anticipation of his return, she climbed into his bed and wrapped herself in his thick mass of blankets. When she heard the door click open, she confidently called to him from upstairs. She heard him slowly ascend the steps and watched as he entered his bedroom with a painful look of discernable apprehension. Almost instantly with face lit up with a strident fury. "What the hell are you doing here?" He demanded, gasping in his own rage.

"I wanted to surprise you. I thought maybe if you saw..."

"Get the fuck out!" he screamed. He lunged and grabbed a handful of her hair as he dragged her out of bed. "If you ever break into my house again, I'll fucking kill you!"

Veins popped from his bloated forehead and neck as he shook with transparent madness. She laid on the floor bawling, too devastated to muster any additional reaction. Out of desperation, for a brief moment she tried changing tactics. "You know," she wailed in an odd outburst of anger, "you once told me that it was against the rules to sleep with a client. I could tell people what happened and get you into serious trouble."

He laughed at that, smugly shaking his head as if the idea of her threat was a joke in itself. "Are you kidding me? Do you know who I am? Who do you think they would believe? Me or a fucking crazy whore who broke into my house like a raging lunatic?"

Estes sighed as she finished the story, "Did you leave after that?"

"He kicked me out, literally," she whimpered. The story still brought her to tears. "Hurt isn't even the right way to describe what that night did to me. It *broke* me. I stopped feeling like a person. After that, all of my feelings for him turned from love to rage."

"When was the next time you tried to reach him?" Estes asked with a sympathetic nod.

Gabriella ignored his question as her mind inadvertently disconnected and aimlessly wondered. "My lawyer thinks I should take a plea deal," she explained dreamily. "What do you think?"

"I'm not here to give legal advice, Gabriella. I'm only here to assess your mental condition."

"I'm sure my lawyer thinks I'm a monster."

"Why do you say that?"

"Doesn't everyone? Why else would I need to plead guilty?"

"What's the plea exactly?"

"I was charged with first degree murder, but if I plead insanity, they can only charge me with voluntary manslaughter. That's only ten years in prison, less with good behavior. I guess it's not too bad, but if I plead insanity I have to admit I was unstable when I killed him, something about being incapable of forming intent."

"You talk like a lawyer," Estes pointed out, genuinely impressed with her knowledge of the case.

"You forget that I've been dealing with lawyers for a while now," Gabriella smiled weakly.

"*Did* you intend to murder him?" Estes asked calmly.

"Yes... I don't know. I wasn't me. I never stopped being afraid of everyone, including myself. I thought murdering him would make it stop."

"Would make what stop?"

"The cycle."

MARCH 1, 2016
Julia

Julia spent several months as Bishop's renewed research assistant. Their relationship was seeping with tension, but externally they had returned to an awkward state of cordiality. She stopped by his office every Friday to drop off her work, and apart from insisting that she call him Anthony, the two had effectively fallen back into a professional routine.

This might have brought her relief, had it not been for the fact that earlier that month she had bought a tape recorder and had since been carefully documenting their encounters. With the way he had acted before, she expected him to compulsively slip up with some kind of damaging statement within a few minutes of their next meeting, but the fickle change in his mood and recent dedication to a professional demeanor had rendered her tapes useless.

Her biggest problem now wasn't Bishop's civility, but the workload he was assigning on a weekly basis. His expectations had tripled since the beginning of the semester, and his insistence on a speedy turn-around was becoming unendurable. Julia was drowning under the the weight of the assignments, and had steadily fallen behind in her other classes. Growing desperate and manic with the burdensome duties, she suspected she would inevitably fail if she continued this pace of work. She begrudgingly made the decision to confront him.

"Here are the notes you asked for, and I marked the cases I thought were relevant," Julia announced, throwing a brief onto his desk as she entered Bishop's office for their weekly check-in.

"The cases you *thought* relevant?" he asked indignantly. He motioned her to have a seat as he slowly poured himself another cup of coffee.

"My mistake, I marked the relevant cases," she responded with sarcastic confidence.

"That's better, never say or do anything without conviction."

"Sure, Anthony."

"Great, well I'd love to go over this now, but I'm very busy today. I'll email you your next assignment tomorrow and I'll see you next week."

"I actually need to talk to you about that," she responded nervously.

"What do you mean?"

She let out a long, shaky breath, "The workload is too much. I can't do it all. I'm going to fail my other classes if I go on like this. I've neglected every other course trying to keep up with your assignments."

"You should have thought about that before you accepted the position as my research assistant."

"Yes, it was very foolish of me. I am a complete failure as a student, and an irresponsible person generally," she remarked bitingly under her breath. "Under the circumstances though, I think it would be best if you brought on another assistant or replaced me completely with someone more competent."

"You're at the top of your class, Julia. Do you really think anyone else is more competent than you?"

"Well then, maybe you should lower your expectations a little."

"Or maybe you should just take this more seriously."

"You're not listening, it is literally impossible for me to keep up. I'm not playing this fucking game, Anthony. No one could survive this workload and you know it. What exactly are you going to do to me if I refuse?"

He stared at her in silence as a satisfied smile crept across his face. He gave a small, dismissive shrug.

She continued in frustration. "Fine, I quit then. I can't do it all."

"Alright, I accept your resignation."

"Really?" She asked in disbelief as she stood to leave. "Just like that? You're going to let me walk away?"

"Well, that's an interesting thought, you haven't actually tried to walk away yet. Why don't you start walking out the door? Let's see what unfolds."

She held his eye contact, refusing to show any brief hint of intimidation. He confidently did the same. "You don't own me," she said, "you don't have any right to do this."

"You're adorable, Julia," he chuckled.

Would that be enough? She wondered, remembering the the tape recorder safely tucked away in her bag. Their conversation was unusual, but he hadn't explicitly crossed any lines. She decided to probe him further.

"You're truly disgusting, Professor Bishop."

"Well that's not a very nice thing to say, Julia. Also, we've been through this, I'd prefer it if you called me Anthony."

"Ok Anthony, here's the deal. I am going to walk out that door. I am going to live my life, and you are going to live yours. I won't tell anyone about what I heard, and you'll let me escape this. Deal?"

"I still don't know what you're referring to. You're a smart girl Julia, but sometimes you're so irrational it's hard to follow."

"My apologies, let me be more specific, I'm referring to the night you raped your client, Gabriella Rodriguez. The night I stood outside your office and heard her screaming for you to stop. The night you explicitly threatened me if I told anyone about it, and have since been ruthlessly using the information against me as if I'm the one who did something wrong."

For a strained, tense moment a harsh silence settled between them. He eyed her with mounting suspicion. "Give me your backpack, Julia," he demanded in a brisk, stern voice.

Her heart sank, "Why?"

"Why would it be a problem for you to give me your backpack?"

Without pause, in a swift motion she stood and tried to run to the door, but he met her halfway across the room and firmly pushed her against the wall. He put one hand over her mouth and grabbed her hair with the other. Tears uncontrollably rolled down her face as his hands moved to her neck and wrapped around her. She felt him shaking with rage as he pushed her deeper into the wall, smashing her face against the cold sheetrock.

"I'm going to let you go, and you're going to be quiet. Do you understand?"

She nodded and he released her with a final shove, immediately grabbing her backpack and turning it over. He emptied the contents of her bag onto his desk, allowing her things to spill chaotically over the surface. He picked up her tape recorder, and in one motion broke it in half and threw the pieces in her direction.

"You really do have a hard time behaving," he muttered without looking up. "You know," he continued, now back to his cold professional tone, "I've been thinking about this, and I believe the reason you're not getting your work done is because you're spending too much time with your boyfriend."

The words were callous and unimaginable, and the meaning behind them hit her so strongly that they might as well have been a punch. "No, no," she pleaded a little too quickly, "that's not it. I can get my work done. I'm sorry. I shouldn't have complained. Really, it's not a problem."

"I don't think that's the case. If you're going to continue as my research assistant, and I really insist that you do, I recommend that you break up with him. If you don't, I'll have to assume that you're not taking your academic career very seriously."

She tried to respond, but her head spun with shocking turmoil. She helplessly gasped for words, but could only muster a small, pathetic nod.

"I'll expect it done by next week," he said coldly, shoving her backpack into her arms. "Also," he warned, "if you ever try to record our conversation again, I promise you *will* regret it. If you don't believe it, ask Gabriella what happens when I'm angry."

Julia sourly walked home after her meeting with Bishop in a post-adrenaline haze. She shivered at a chilling gust of wind, and pulled her coat tightly around her. D.C. was notorious for its intensely frigid winters, but generally she didn't mind the cold. Today, though, the entire city felt gloomy, as if it too were in a painfully deep depression. She was struck with powerful waves of emptiness, and wallowed at the impending outcome of her bleak position. She wanted to cry, but she was too depleted from the events of the day.

When she got to their apartment, she stood outside for a while, holding onto the last few moments before her undamaged reality would shift and inevitably spiral. As she slipped inside, she was hit by a sharp wave of nausea, and for a moment she doubted her own strength to proceed. She studied their living room like she was seeing everything anew, allowing herself to indulge in the the memories of the space where she had built a life with Daniel.

"Hey!" he called at the sound of the front door closing behind her. He was cooking dinner and emerged from the kitchen carrying a spoon. "I need you to taste this sauce and tell me if it's too thick. I personally think it's perfect, but you know how I love confirmation..." his voice trailed off when he looked up and saw tears streaming down her face. "What's going on?" he asked with burning concern, dropping the spoon back onto the counter and instinctively reaching out to hold her.

She held up her hands to avoid his touch. "Daniel, we need to talk."

MARCH 5, 2016
Julia

To: jharrison@brooktown.edu
From: abishop@brooktown.academics.edu

Julia,

I'm overwhelmed with work on my recent case, so I am leaving school early today to catch up. Because I won't be in my office later, your usual method of research delivery is not an option. Please stop by my house to drop off your work. I live three blocks from campus, so I'm sure that won't be a problem.

Thank you,
Professor Bishop

- - - - - - - - - - - - - - - - - -

To: abishop@brooktown.academics.edu
From: jharrison@brooktown.edu

Anthony,

I'm very, very busy today. I can't make it to your house. My research really isn't urgent, can I just give you my work Monday? I also think I can easily email it to you- the information really doesn't requires a hardcopy. I'm attaching my research now, so I don't think any further action is necessary.

Thanks,
Julia

- - - - - - - - - - - - - - - - - -

To: jharrison@brooktown.edu
From: abishop@brooktown.academics.edu

Julia,

I'm afraid I'm still going to need you to drop by. After looking over your research, I have a couple of questions that would be better conveyed in person. I'm afraid time is of the essence. It won't take long.

Thanks,
Professor Bishop

Julia compulsively reread the harrowing string of emails until she had numbed to their chilling effect. Most of her emotions had been dulled anyway after weeks of restless anxiety and inescapable feelings of melancholy. With the growth of their tension, she had been suspecting a stipulation of this nature, but seeing the words flash on her laptop still shocked her into speechless discomfort. Their escalating interactions had more or less been leading up to this demand, and through her dismay she reminded herself that this could help solidify the plan she had been carefully crafting since their previous meeting.

Bishop strolled into the room and casually began setting up for class. For half a second, he looked up at her and smiled, as he often did before the start of lecture. She stared back blankly, trying to hide any external signs of her evident hostility. It was bad enough having to serve as his research assistant, but sitting through his lectures with superficial absorption had proved to be the most unbearable component of her semester. He toyed with her through invisibile aggression, continually asking for her opinions and forcing her to answer with artificial civility. He would smugly watch as she fumbled through her responses, shielding her hatred and leaving the rest of her classmates oblivious to the truth behind their dynamic.

Daniel entered the room and gradually made his way down the long steps towards the front of the lecture hall. Out of habit, for half a second he hesitated by Julia's seat before continuing to walk down the steep aisle. He settled in a chair near the front of the room on the opposite side of hall from Julia. She had foreseen this dramatic parade of their dissolution, but watching him publicly shun her hurt worse than she had anticipated.

Julia felt her classmates taking note of this behavior. Their seats weren't assigned, but Daniel and Julia had sat together in every class since their first day at Brooktown. She felt ripples of disbelief unfold around her as a number of small whispers and gasps panned across the room. She put her head on her desk in defeat and blinked back tears of humiliation. When class began, she half-heartedly opened her laptop and started jotting down fragments of the lecture.

Daniel made it halfway through the period, but when Bishop called on Julia, a look of disgust settled in his expression. Bitterly, he stood to leave and walked out of the room without explanation, his head hung low in shame. Nearly every single eye followed him with stares of both pity and shock. Julia glanced at Bishop, and saw a small, sadistic smirk unfold across his face.

MARCH 6, 2016
Julia

It could have been worse, Julia concluded as she awoke the following morning after visiting Bishop's home. She fumbled through the events of the previous evening, her mind still clogged and burdened with the repulsive memories. Her visit had started in a relatively cordial manner. She walked in, threw her research on his table, and then tried to leave before he could tell her to stop. For a moment, he acted as though he would permit such an exit, so Julia forcefully tried to stall.

"I broke up with him," she announced..

"Obviously," he mumbled, hardly glancing from his up from the papers strewn over his table.

"It was that obvious from class?"

"Well that and you changed your facebook status."

Julia paused, "You check my facebook?"

Bishop shrugged as if he was already bored of their conversation.

"Well," she announced, "I just thought you would want to hear it from me. You don't seem very pleased."

He looked at her with an emotionless expression. His ambivalence was almost worse than anger, and made her squirm with unease. "I told you to do it, so I knew you would. You don't get any credit for doing as you're told."

"Oh, I'm sorry, what exactly counts as credit then, Anthony?" She knew she was pushing him, but she needed more time.

"You're in a mood today," he said flatly. "Life as a single woman isn't going so well then?"

"Life is fine, Professor Bishop."

He looked at her sideways, trying to assess the motivation behind her provocations, "Are you trying to get a rise out of me? I'm tired Ms. Harrison, I'm not in the mood."

"Not in the mood to fuck with my life? I didn't know there were specific moods for that," she spat. That got his attention. At last she saw anger flood his eyes and noticed his fists clenching under the table.

"Did you buy another tape recorder?" he eyed her with suspicion. At that, Julia threw her bag on the table for him to examine.

"It could be on your body," he suggested.

"Even if I had one on me, you're not going to touch me."

He shook his head, and pushed the bag back towards her. "I could if I wanted to, but like I said I'm not in the mood."

She grew frustrated by his lack of engagement, and knew she had to escalate things further. "You know what I was thinking about today?" she asked cheerfully inching towards him with a smile, "Your reputation means a lot more to you than it does to me."

"You sure about that?" he responded flatly.

"Now that you mention it, I sure am. I'm pretty certain you would lose your job for harassing a student, don't you think? If you touch me at all, leave any bruises, or any other significant evidence that you hurt me, I think that would be enough for a full, very public investigation. Even if you did claim I was the monster, people would always wonder if under the surface you were actually the psycho. You would be ruined too. Plus, from what I hear you have a history with this kind of thing."

"Well it's a good thing I've never hurt you then."

"It is a good thing for a multitude of reasons, least of all being the fact that you could get fired. I'm just saying that I'm not the only one with their reputation on the line here."

"You're delusional."

"I don't think so, Bishop."

"There's one small flaw in your plan," he noted, "you can't practice law without being admitted to the ABA. I'm also fairly certain a law student would have a hard time getting barred after repeatedly harassing a professor in an inappropriate manner. Especially if I personally wrote a letter to the organization stating that, in my humble and well-respected opinion, my former student Julia Harrison is a very troubled young lady and is by no means fit to practice law. I might even talk about how she stalked me, tried to seduce me multiple times, and developed unrealistic expectations due to her emotional instability. I might mention the psychological state of your mother as well, which likely led to your downfall."

Julia had thought of this scenario many times, and had anticipated this kind of response. She actually understood that reporting Bishop wasn't a legitimate escape, but her intentions were to distract him in the moment rather than dissuade him entirely. She had to keep going to buy more time. Her threats didn't have to be perfect, just plausible enough to keep the argument going.

She looked him in the eye without backing down. "What do you want from me?"

"At the moment, I want you to shut up and leave," he mumbled through gritted teeth.

"You know what I fucking mean, Bishop. I'm not going to sit around wondering if you're going to do to me what you did you Gabriella. You're going to tell me your intentions now!"

Finally he laughed and stood in anger. "I don't have to tell you anything," he smirked and started moving towards her in a steady, rising rage. She backed herself against the wall. "This will go as far as I decide it to go," he continued. "How do you not understand that?"

Their bodies were now inches from each other, and she cowered at the sight of him so close. She closed her eyes and braced herself as he stood over her for a few moments. At last, though, his breathing began to slow. He put his palm up to her face and gently touched her lips with his finger. "You really are beautiful," he sighed and then briskly turned back towards his desk to continue working.

"By the way," he stated calmly, "if you did try and follow through with one of these outlandish threats, your legal career would be the least of your worries."

"What do you mean?" she squeaked.

"You're a smart girl, figure it out."

She wasn't sure if she had stalled long enough, but she couldn't take it any longer. The moment he stepped away from her, she had a deep and unyielding urge to run away. She shuffled to grab her bag and ran towards the door, tears again falling from her eyes.

Later that night as she laid in bed, miserably replaying the memory over and over again, trying to perfectly capture and hold each detail. She felt sick, but grateful she had escaped again unharmed. She turned to Daniel who was still asleep beside her and lightly kissed his lips. At least now she wasn't alone.

March 5, 2016
Daniel

Daniel purposefully chose a seat opposite of Julia, and could almost feel a puzzling wave spark through his classmates at their open display of estrangement. As he looked up at Bishop, his heart lurched in a blind fury and his head pounded at the sight of his professor's infuriatingly pompous expression. Julia had told him everything last night, and now the mere thought of Bishop made his blood boil with incessant rage. He kept his head down for the first portion of lecture, obsessively fixated on his target of the day.

Halfway through class, Daniel suddenly rose and stormed out of the room, just as they had prepared, and watched his classmates gawk with curiosity. While this outburst might appear brash, it certainly wouldn't come across as implausible. Surely anyone would be justifiably unstable after a breakup with a girl like Julia Harrison. After his exit, he quickly made his way to the third floor and scoured the halls for Bishop's office. In a wave of relief and curiosity, he found the heavy door unlocked. He glanced over his shoulder to ensure he was alone and hurriedly slipped inside. He checked his watch and realized he only had fifteen minutes until the end of Bishop's lecture. He frantically prayed they wouldn't let out early.

He began aimlessly probing through the dense expanse of Bishop's files, unsure exactly of his own endgame. It became immediately apparent as to why Bishop left his office unlocked, as all of his drawers were either locked, empty, or stuffed with discernibly harmless documents. He scanned the spread of papers sprawled across Bishop's desk, mostly consisting of mundane notes or cases. His eyes fell on a note from Julia, and for a moment he lingered at the sight of her handwriting. Anger swelled at the thought of the two of them alone in this space, but he forced himself to settle down and stay centered on the objective. *Not now*, he reminded himself, *if you want to help her you have to stay focused.*

He was on the verge of abandoning the prospect of finding anything of use, which wasn't altogether shocking considering the impossible circumstances of his mission. He wasn't even sure what he was looking for, and highly doubted Bishop would leave anything incriminating just lying around untethered. He checked the time, which was rapidly draining, and decided he would give himself two more minutes before heading out. He studied Bishop's shelves, which were filled with pictures of Bishop posing with celebrities and political figures, in a desperate attempt to evade the likely probability of leaving empty handed. Daniel rolled his eyes at Bishop's conceited display of prominent figures, and absent-mindedly picked up a picture of Bishop with a young Bill Clinton. In an unbelievable stroke of dumb luck, he discovered two small keys behind the photo.

He tried to open every lock in Bishop's office, and found that only one key fit into Bishop's bottom drawer, which housed a small bottle of scotch and two glasses. The other key didn't fit anywhere, even though it looked as though it belonged with a desk. Daniel studied it for a moment, before hastily sticking it into his pocket. He was running out of time and needed to make a quick exit before someone stumbled onto the third floor and found him inexplicably snooping through his professor's space. He did a quick scan to make sure everything was in place before quietly heading downstairs and exiting the building. He wouldn't classify the search as a monumental victory, but his humble find was better than nothing. At the very least it might give Julia a brief moment of modest relief which would make the entire ordeal worth the anxious struggle.

Julia and Daniel met during law school orientation. It wasn't exactly love at first sight, but rather a small spark of curiosity with a glaring attraction lurking through their interactions. Daniel was cripplingly shy, and rarely approached women, but when he saw her sitting alone on the back row, he summoned all of the courage he could muster to take the seat beside her. The most shocking aspect of their first encounter was that no one else had tried to snag this spot already. Julia had an infectious personality and was stunningly beautiful. Most people naturally gravitated towards her in a way that made Daniel marvel in admiration.

"I'm Julia," she smiled as he pulled out a chair.

"Daniel," he choked with a nervous grin. He tried to think of something interesting to spark a conversation but nothing in his mind seemed worthy of her attention. Finally, after frantically shuffling through his own muddled head, he inadvertently blurted out, "I was so nervous today I had to change my shirt three times... I sweat a lot when I'm nervous." For a moment she eyed him with obvious curiosity, and Daniel's heart sank with agonizing embarrassment. Then, in the most uncanny wave of relief, she started to giggle and touched his shoulder with a flirtatious smile.

"I know exactly what you mean! It's not even the first day of school and already I feel like I'm being judged. Maybe orientation is actually the first test."

"If that's the case, how do you think we're doing?"

"Probably not well. We're both sulking in the back of the room and apparently failed to arrive an hour early like the majority of our classmates."

"I thought sitting back here made us look cool."

"This is law school, no one is cool," she jested with a slight flip of her hair.

She was easy to talk to, somehow carrying the conversation while simultaneously asking him questions about his background. He suspected she might be flirting, but tried to refrain from assuming such intentions. Even if they had a small connection, he had never had much luck with girls and wouldn't know where to begin. Luckily, she was the one who took the lead.

"Let's go get lunch," she said casually after orientation had ended. At that, his heart skipped a beat, and he urgently led her to the nearest exit before their other classmates could sweep her away. People stared at her as they walked together towards the cafeteria in the center of campus, but she hardly seemed to notice. For whatever inexplicable reason, he had her full attention.

Within days of meeting, their lives became thoroughly integrated. It was strange how quickly their elementary spark melded into something deeper, but their chemistry was so innately transparent that neither party dared challenge the pace of their budding relationship. Daniel somewhat attributed their bond to the harsh environment thrust upon them in the first weeks of law school. Theoretically this should have been a burden on their courtship, but if anything it only secured their connection. Julia was the only thing that made Brooktown bearable.

When Daniel returned to the security of their apartment and triumphantly revealed Bishop's key, Julia did entertain a meager flash of pleasant relief, granting Daniel a short-lived moment of tenuous heroism. Her reprieve diminished within minutes though as she immediately commenced in outlining their next steps. He gravely squeezed her hands and articulated his fruitless concerns with the absurdity of her suggestions, but once she had settled on the most outrageous and treacherous plan, he knew it was hopeless to dissuade her stubborn ambitions. After an hour of debating the the details, he finally conceded to her fatal strategy.

"I still don't like this," he sighed as Julia began putting on her shoes to leave.

"It's the only thing we have, and I think it's worth a try. We have to do something," she responded in a dismissive tone as she planted a consolation kiss on his cheek.

"We don't even know if he has a desk in his home."

"Of course he does, and he has to be hiding something. Why else would he keep this key separate in his office?"

"Listen, I know you don't think anyone would believe you-"

"-I don't *think*? Daniel, I *know* no one would believe me-"

"-Let me finish, ok? Maybe there's another way out of this we haven't explored. I still think we should go to Dean Herrera."

"He'll ruin me, Daniel. I'll lose every single thing I've worked for. It'll follow me for the rest of my career."

He went over and grabbed her hand, stroking it gently as he tried to articulate his concern. "Julia, I know you think dropping out would be the end of the world," he said softly, "but some things are more important than this degree, your safety being one of them."

She closed her eyes and sighed. "Listen, you just found out that this is going on, I've been living with this for months. It's not just my loans... I've worked my whole life for this. I can't just give it up now, not yet at least."

He begrudgingly understood her dire synopsis. No one worked as hard as Julia, and giving up wasn't generally an option woven into her psyche. Any attempts to persuade her otherwise would be a painfully useless endeavor.

"I-I-I'm just afraid," he whispered. "What if he does try to hurt you tonight? What if I hear it from upstairs? I can't just sit by and let that happen, Julia."

"I know this is going to be hard to explain, but I'm positive he won't right now. It's still a game for him. If I keep playing, so will he."

"What if you're wrong?"

"Then I'm wrong, and you have to accept that you can't protect me."

"You know I wouldn't let that happen. I would kill him before I let him lay a finger on you."

Daniel watched Julia enter Bishop's home and gulped as she carefully left the door slightly ajar as they had planned. He followed her closely and readily slipped inside Bishop's house undetected. He heard Julia's voice from the opposite room as he crept through the foyer, and paused for a moment in an uneasy hesitation. He briskly surveyed the hallway, noticing the elaborate decadence and rich sophistication of Bishop's home. He had intuitively envisioned Bishop's dwelling as a barren and utilitarian space, and, for half a moment, marveled at the rich, intricate facets of the residence. In spite of himself, he was struck with curiosity about Bishop's cryptic layers.

He shook his head to snap back to reality and slowly crawled up the stairs in search of this coveted desk. He peered inside a few typical-looking bedrooms before he turned the corner and, to his relief, stumbled upon a luxuriously broad home office. It was a cavernous space with hundreds of text-books lining the shelves and various stacks of papers covering every surface. He quickly scanned the room for significant traces of secrecy, and settled on a large antique desk in the center. He slipped on a pair of gloves and held his breath as he took out the key and started inserting it into various locks. After several tries, his heart skipped when he at last heard the top drawer click open.

Initially, he thought the space was mostly filled with irrelevant documents- a deed to Bishop's house, tax returns, an old copy of a will- but underneath the mundane stack, he uncovered a suspicious box marked "personal." He lifted it from the drawer and inside found a number of files labeled with various female names. There must have been a total of fifty folders stuffed in the tiny box. He stalled when he saw one labeled "Julia," and flipped it open to find that Bishop had printed out every single email correspondence with her since last November. Daniel closed his eyes in momentary revulsion, but forced himself to suppress his anger and continued sifting through the files.

Next in the stack was a file labeled "Gabriella." He lightly skimmed her folder and saw a number of crumpled letters, but hurriedly set it to the side. He was growing concerned with the colossal number of files in front of him and the finite amount of time he had to secure some kind of proof. Strenuously, he scanned the tops of the documents and stopped when he saw one marked, "Melissa Antemie." The name struck him with a vague memory associated with Brian's story about Bishop's suspension. He mulled it over for a moment, and pulled out the file to study.

Suddenly, he heard Julia's raised voice from downstairs, and ultimately decided that his time had run out. He considered pirating the entire box from the office, but worried such an act would too quickly alert Bishop of their collusion. In a split-second decision, he grabbed the three files he had set aside- Julia's, Gabriella's, and Melissa's- and carefully returned the box to the bottom of Bishop's drawer. He locked up and attentively surveyed his surroundings to ensure his entry would go unnoticed.

As he exited the room and started making his way back to the foyer, he heard Julia and Bishop arguing below. He desperately longed to intervene, but instead helplessly waited halfway down Bishop's stairs, barely breathing as he grappled to understand the context of their argument. "You really are beautiful," he heard Bishop utter.

Rage shot through Daniel's body, and it took every ounce of his willpower not to run to her rescue. He realized then that he had never before wanted to hurt someone so badly. He was about to lose his composure completely, when Julia suddenly appeared from the next room. He watched as she skirted across the foyer in a shaky panic and exited out the front door. He fell back and took a few deep breaths to calm himself before he slowly he crept down the remainder of the stairs, praying Bishop would stay in the next room while he made his departure. Fortunately he did, and Daniel was able to successfully complete his full escape.

Julia was waiting for him at the end of the block, and instantaneously the couple embraced for a long moment of savoring relief. "Please tell me you found something," she said in a shaky voice.

"Maybe, but I can't tell what it means yet."

Tears began rolling down her face. "I was really scared, Daniel."

"I know," he said as he pulled her close, "but I would never let anything happen to you."

March 7, 2016
Julia

"Why does he keep these letters?" Julia asked with a distinct air of exhaustion the following morning. They sat on opposite sides of their kitchen table, delicately shuffling through each file Daniel had poached from Bishop's office.

"For the same reason he printed out your emails, I think he likes rereading them... which is actually pretty sick. I knew he was a creep when I saw that email he sent you last semester, but I never envisioned anything this bad."

"I still can't believe you went through my email," she rolled her eyes and shook her head with light chuckle.

"I haven't made it up to you yet by burglarizing our professor's home?"

"Fine, you're forgiven."

He couldn't help but give her a playful smile in spite of his weariness. "So," he continued as he scanned the array of documents, "these letters from Gabriella seem a little... heated."

"How so?"

"She's in love with him."

"What? You mean before he attacked her?"

"No, I mean now. Some of these are only from a couple of weeks ago."

"That doesn't make any sense. I heard Bishop with her in December. That was months ago."

"Are you sure it wasn't a... um... mutual encounter?"

"Daniel, I'm positive. If you could have heard the way she was crying-"

"-I believe you," he cut her off, and tried to dismiss the image. Every time the thought of Bishop and Gabriella entered his head, he couldn't help but think of Julia in the same position. He shuddered at the gruesome prospect.

"Maybe there is more to their relationship than I understood though," Julia admitted as she glanced over the letters. "Honestly Gabriella's always seemed just a little... off to me. She might be a tad crazy."

"Where does that leave us?" he asked.

"With a pretty unreliable witness..." she faded as they eyed each with noticeably sullied spirits. "I'm just saying that love letters from her won't prove anything, quite the opposite. So let's just move forward for now. Who's Melissa Antemie?"

"She must be a former client," Daniel answered. "She's talking about her case in these earlier letters."

Julia went over to her computer, and started typing the login information to her Lexlaw account, a database that kept a record of all legal proceedings.

"Don't do that!" Daniel yelled.

"What... why?" She asked with a startled jump.

"Lexlaw keeps a record of all our past searches," he said firmly, reaching for her laptop. They looked at each other for a lengthy, uncomfortable moment. For the first time they had inadvertently recognized the harsh, unavoidable truth: they didn't want to leave a trail of evidence connecting them to Bishop's history.

"I'm his research assistant though," Julia said slowly. "I could... I don't know, it just wouldn't seem that unusual for me to look up one of his past cases."

He shook his head, "Just use mine. I'm... well they're less likely to track mine if... if something were to happen to Bishop."

Julia gulped and considered his position before shaking her head. "No," she stated with finality, "we're going to use mine. I don't want you involved." Before waiting for his response she turned back to the laptop and typed *Antemie* into the search bar. "Alright," she responded after clicking through a few searches, "it's another immigration case. She was going to be deported, but the decision was overturned on appeal... and you'll never guess who her lawyer was... There's no other information though."

"Yeah... sounds like his type," Daniel sighed. "Let's keep looking through the letters then. Check these out." He slid a small stack of faded notes across the table.

Mr. Bishop,

I'm confused about last night. I know it was just a kiss, but you are my lawyer. It really doesn't feel right. While I appreciate all of the work you have done, I need to know that I can trust you. I won't be able to if you don't agree that last night was a mistake.

Sincerely,
Melissa Antemie

Mr. Bishop,

I don't know how to write this. You are my lawyer, and I respect all of the work you have put into my case. However, I think I should find another attorney to take this on. I am not interested in you. I have a boyfriend. Honestly, you're starting to scare me. Please leave me alone.

-Melissa Antemie

Mr. Bishop,

Please, I ask again that you just leave me alone. I know you I said you could continue as my lawyer, but only because you promised to stop. If I had known, I would have found someone else.

After last night, I don't think we should be alone together anymore.

-Melissa Antemie

- - - - - - - - - - - - - - - - - -

Mr. Bishop,

I am appreciative of what you did for me, and I understand that I will likely win my case because of your work, but after this is over, I want us to end our relationship on both a professional and personal level. I ask that you let this go in peace. I just want this to be done.

-Melissa

"Would these letters be enough proof?" Daniel asked.

Julia sighed and rubbed the temples of her forehead. "I don't know."

They stared at the stack in a still defeat. "Do you remember that story Brian told us about Bishop?" Daniel asked after a couple minutes had passed, "The one about him sleeping with his client and getting suspended?"

"Yeah... I do." The fond memory of their jovial exchange now felt like a different world from their dreary reality.

"I think her name was Melissa... And look, there's a return address," he noted. "We'll pay her a visit. We have to find Gabriella too. If you can all come forward together-"

"-Dean Herrera would probably believe it... he would be fired and I could stay."

For the first time since last semester, Julia's spirits lifted with a genuine feeling of hope. Daniel nodded and turned towards his laptop and began typing something into the search bar. "Julia," he interjected in a half panic, "Oh no..."

"What? What is it?"

"Melissa Antemie has been missing since 2013."

APRIL 2, 2016
Julia

Julia trudged through the populous blocks of Southeast D.C., rigorously attempting to pinpoint the return address listed on Gabriella's letters. Daniel had proposed they go together, but she vehemently insisted that he stay behind. She knew Gabriella was a little precarious, and worried Daniel's presence might scare her off before their conversation had a chance to unfold. The route on GoogleMaps led her to a rundown flat with faded chipped paint and an unstable door barely standing on its hinges. The place essentially looked abandoned, but she rang the bell twice before taking a step back to further survey the decrepit building. When there was no answer, she impatiently sat on the top step of the apartment and moped in a disgruntled state of impending anticipation.

For an hour she waited, laboriously mapping out a strategy of how to best unearth Gabriella's equivocations and prompt her to come forward with allegations against Bishop. She internally practiced her speech on repeat until at last she noticed a figure exit a bus at the corner and sluggishly head in Julia's direction. It took a moment to be sure, but she was struck with relief when she recognized Gabriella.

"Gabriella," Julia smiled zealously when the figure was several yards away.

"Hello... Julia?" Gabriella looked up, a little startled at the offbeat nature of this development. Gabriella had put on weight since their last meeting, and somehow looked damaged and more anxious than usual.

"It's really good to see you."

"My case is over," she responded flatly, already trying to maneuver her way around Julia to escape inside her apartment.

"This isn't about the case... there's something I need to talk to you about."

"Does he know?" Gabriella gasped.

"That I'm here? God no, he'd freak out if he knew I contacted you. He'd probably kill me," Julia blurted out impulsively. The words hung awkwardly in the space between them. "I just meant," Julia continued in a partial frenzy, "that I'm here on my own because we need to talk about some things that happened after your case."

"There is nothing to talk about," Gabriella stated as she dismissively pulled out her keys and began to make her way towards the door.

"Gabriella, whatever he's doing to you, I can help."

"He's not doing anything to me," she dropped her head like a mischievous child in the midst of a scolding, "that's the problem."

"Can you please let me in? I just want to talk to you."

Gabriella hesitated, but eventually nodded and allowed Julia to step inside. The interior of the apartment itself was even more rundown than the face of the building, probably one step from condemnation. The walls were barren and notably faded, with pieces of the ceiling sagging in a suspiciously threatening manner. The small room housed very few pieces of furniture, with the exception of a small mattress on the floor, an old table with one matching chair, and a crumbling bookshelf in the corner, which out of blind habit drew Julia's attention.

"You have a really nice book collection," Julia mused as she picked up an unfamiliar novel and turned it over to examine.

"Not really," Gabriella blushed. "I just don't have anything else to do so I read a lot."

Julia nodded and continued studying the shelf. "You have a lot of Hemingway. Honestly, I've never really liked him. He's too dry and I'm a fan of happy endings."

"I like him because his endings aren't happy."

"That's an interesting outlook, bleak but interesting," Julia pondered as she picked up another book to examine. "I read this one last year though and I loved it. It's a masterpiece, but sadly underrated."

"*Pillars of the Earth?*" Gabriella asked shyly, "You actually kind of remind me of Aliena."

"Why? Because we both have curly hair?"

"No, it's not that. She's just... strong. Even after really bad things happen to her."

A soft feeling of camaraderie settled between them as the two locked eyes and smiled. Julia turned back to the shelf and gently put the book back in its previous position. "I think reading is the thing I like best in the world. It got me through a lot when I was a kid.

"Me too."

"You know what the best part of it is?"

"What?"

"It's the one thing no one can take away from you. Once you've read a book, it's in your head forever."

Gabriella nodded thoughtfully, "I never thought about it like that, but I guess that's part of why I like reading too."

Julia could see Gabriella starting to relax and decided to push a little further, "Listen, we need to talk about why I'm here. Bishop is harassing me, I need to find a way to stop him."

"If he's harassing you, why can't you tell the police?"

"Because it's my word against his. I need proof. I need you."

"It's not like that with Bishop and me."

"What do you mean?"

"We were in love."

Julia sighed, "I know you think you were, but he's manipulative. You don't understand-"

"-Stop!" Gabriella said suddenly as she held up her hands, "Don't treat me like that. I'm not stupid. You never saw us together! How could you even know?"

"Gabriella, I heard you that night in his office. I was on campus and saw you walk in. I followed you. I heard you scream and tell him to stop. I was the one who knocked on the door."

Gabriella backed away in horror "You heard? Why didn't you come in and help me then?"

"I called the police!" Julia pleaded, "but... well, Bishop caught me half-way through the call. I'm so sorry. I panicked. I couldn't... I was afraid."

"You're a coward."

"I can't dispute that I was cowardly in that moment. I have to live with the fact I ran away, but now I'm trying to make it better. He's done this before to other women."

"Julia, you don't understand. It's not just that... I can't do it."

"What am I not understanding? Please, enlighten me."

"I need him."

"No you don't!"

"Yes... I do. I need him."

"Why?"

"I can't tell you..." Gabriella faded off.

Julia stood up and kicked the wall in frustration, "Damn it! If you won't do it for yourself, do it for me, or the next woman he'll do this to. Think of someone besides yourself."

"That's exactly what I'm doing."

Julia let herself calm down a little. It wasn't really fair to blame Gabriella. "Okay," she finally continued, "maybe you're really not going to change your mind, but I think you're a lot stronger than you realize." She scribbled down her number on a pad of paper and left it on the kitchen table. "I know with time you'll make the right decision."

April 2, 2016
Daniel

Daniel had an unusually difficult time finding the house listed on Melissa Antemie's return address in Virginia. After years of living in a packed city, the suburban outskirts felt abnormally scattered and foreign. He took the metro to Falls Church, and although it was only six stops from the city's edge, he marveled at the blatant discrepancies between this reticent town and D.C.'s steadily bustling environment. Over time he had grown to endure the sting of D.C.'s excessive intensity, but the past several months had brought him so much anxiety that he had grown new tiers of resentment. Falls Church suddenly felt effortless and secure, and he somehow envied the residents for their ability to escape the ongoing commotion.

After wandering through the unfamiliar roads for almost an hour, he at last found the house listed on Melissa's letter. He had essentially already labeled this endeavor a lost cause, but was obstinate in his resolution of tying up all loose ends of their amateaur investigation. It was a modest but charming, colonial-style home, which served as a strange backdrop against the unkept yard and garden. He knocked quietly three times before a middle-aged man met him at the door. "Hi… I don't know if you can help me," Daniel stuttered. "I was wondering if Melissa Antemie lives here… lived here."

The man was presumably attractive despite his greying hair and worn clothes, but his aging features held a bitter gaze of exhaustion and fragility. A skeptic look crossed the man's wrinkled face, and Daniel watched a pang of sadness flicker in his eyes at the sound of Melissa's name. "She hasn't lived here for years. Please go away." He moved to shut the door, but Daniel swiftly blocked the motion with his hands.

"Please," he pleaded, "I just need some information. Do you know a man named Anthony Bishop?"

The man halted in with sudden jerk of astonishment and cautiously let the door swing back open. He looked Daniel up and down with judgmental scrutiny, but slowly nodded and met his eyes with a somber curiosity. "How do you know Bishop?"

"I'm a student at Brooktown. He's my professor and my girlfriend's... well... he's been kind of a problem for her."

The man's head fell to the floor with a mournful sigh. "Ok... come on in," he said with a wistful shake of his head, as he led Daniel through a narrow hallway and into a small kitchen at the back of his house. "Have a seat," he pointed to a modest table in the corner. They settled on opposite ends and stared at each other for a few stiff seconds. "My name is Jared," the man finally said with a weak smile.

"So you knew Melissa?"

"I was her boyfriend. I'm the one who hired Bishop to represent her."

"What happened to her?"

"That depends on who you ask. I guess the official story is that she left town out of shame. Apparently she was so embarrassed after wrongly accusing Bishop of attacking her that she had to leave without saying goodbye."

"And the unofficial story?"

"I've been trying to put together the unofficial story for years. So tell me, what kind of problems are you having with Bishop?"

"He's been harassing my girlfriend, but in a way that's hard to prove. I actually tracked you down, hoping that maybe you would have some information about him or Melissa that might be useful."

"What do you want to know?"

"Everything, any information about him could be helpful."

"Well, he's a total creep. I thought he was the best guy to take on her case. Halfway through her representation though, she started acting weird. She kept insisting I go with her to their meetings, and her whole energy changed. I don't know... It's hard to explain... She just fell into a dark place. I could sense it, but I didn't know why."

Daniel gulped at the familiarity. "Did you ever find out what was happening?"

"She finally came clean and told me what was going on. He had been tormenting her for months. She wouldn't sleep with him, so he got really possessive and weird. Finally, I convinced her to come forward. I stupidly assumed they would disbar him over something like this. I thought if she just told the truth he would back down... or at least have some kind of consequence over it."

"Wasn't he suspended?"

"Sure, but he should have been fired. No one believed her, and they treated her like trash. Brooktown sure as hell didn't want word getting out that their prized professor was a psycho degenerate, so they essentially gave him a slap on the wrist."

"I don't understand."

"It was his word against hers. That's bad enough, but to make matters worse, halfway through the investigation she drastically changed her story, even to me. She started saying it was her fault, that she misinterpreted things, and that he really didn't deserve to be punished for anything."

"Weren't you mad at her for lying?"

"Melissa had never lied before, it just wasn't in her nature. I asked her so many times to tell me what was really going on, but she would just shake her head. She was terrified. He did something to her after she came forward, I'm sure of it. It had to have been something that scared her into compliance, but she never told me what it was."

"That's horrible."

"What's horrible was that the day after her testimony at Brooktown, she disappeared. I came home to find a note that said she was embarrassed for lying and decided to leave town. It was bullshit. She wouldn't have just left me like that."

"How can you be sure though?"

"Because I knew her! I know her! She was the love of my life. Whatever Bishop did was the one thing she couldn't trust me with, so I know it had to have been bad. Does that make sense?"

Daniel sighed, "Yes it does, unfortunately. So you think Bishop had something to do with her disappearance?"

"Somehow, someway I think he was involved. Obviously, that's a hard thing to convince anyone else of though. I went to the police, and they told me they couldn't investigate a hunch and a wild theory. I know how it sounds, but I'm positive about this. He did something to her."

"Do you think he killed her?"

"It's possible. Honestly, I don't know what he's capable of. If I were you though, I would tell your girlfriend to get out now."

April 2, 2016
Julia

"I hope you had better luck with Melissa," Julia called out to Daniel with heavy dissatisfaction as she entered their apartment and energetically thrust her bag onto the floor. To her disappointment, his comforting response failed to echo back, and for a moment she sulked in the lonely stillness that overwhelmed the apartment in his unwelcomed absence. In her state of debilitation, she turned the corner and headed to their bedroom with the intention of collapsing for a few hours out of exhaustion. As she moved through the subsequent room, she abruptly froze when she unexpectedly spotted an alarming figure from the corner of her eye. Almost instinctively, she felt Bishop's presence before she turned to see him calmly sitting at her table.

"Hello, Julia," he announced coolly as he folded his hands on the table and looked up at her with a serene expression.

Julia's heart sank in paralyzing fear as she grappled with this startling development and noticed he was wearing thick leather gloves. "What do you want, Bishop?" she gasped through strained breaths of air. For a moment, she thought she might faint as her knees locked amidst her staggering anxiety.

In a crushing wave of horror, she watched him slowly rise from the table, and, without breaking his harsh eye contact, step towards her. In a brief moment of desperate lucidity, she lept towards the door in a poorly executed struggle to escape. He immediately lunged after her, knocking her to the ground with a heavy and painful thud. She started to cry and senselessly tried to fight back, but he overpowered her within seconds as he pinned her arms to the floor and let his mouth curve into sadistic smile.

"You're not going to run," he revealed in a decidedly confident voice. "I'm going to let you up, and we're going to have a little chat." She nodded in an almost hysteric state as tears streamed from her face and fell to the floor. He pulled her up, grabbing her by the shoulder and trusting her down onto a chair. He sat across the table, blocking her path to the door, which she eyed with defenseless longing.

"So," he said calmly, "Why have you been missing meetings?"

"I... I... I'm so sorry."

"That's not an answer."

"I've been busy..."

"You see," he interjected, "I have a theory about that. I believe you're skipping meetings because you didn't actually break up with your boyfriend, as you were told to do. After seeing this cozy shared apartment of yours, where you both obviously reside, I would conclude that my theory has been confirmed."

Julia couldn't speak, and instead started sobbing in a painful flood of fear. "Are you going to kill me?" she gasped. The words felt thick and abnormally gruesome as they strenuously left her mouth.

"I'm not going to kill you, Julia. That would ruin all the fun. I might kill him, though," he stated casually with a small shrug of his shoulders. She shook her head and he continued. "Oh, you don't believe me? Watch what happens if you push me further. I'll have you know that I really don't like sharing." He turned his head for half a second and Julia saw a number of veins noticeably popping out of his neck as his fist clenched with apparent fury. "That's not why I'm here though. You see, I want to talk to you about your future. What do you plan on doing after graduation?"

Julia shook her head with a blank expression, "I-I don't know."

Bishop suddenly pounded a fist on the table causing her to jump with surprise, "That's bullshit! A bright student like you, surely you have some vision. I assume you've even settled on a firm."

She stared at him in misery and shook her head. "Please... I just-"

"-No?" he finally spoke with a tiny hint of a smile surfacing in the corners of his mouth. "Well then I'd like to offer you job, Miss Harrison."

"I-I-I can't..."

"Nonsense. I'd like to hire you as my, full-time, post-graduate research assistant. We work so well together, it only makes sense. I'll only hire you if you really want it though..."

Julia let out another small sob and turned her eyes to the floor. All she could do was shake her head in a despondent unease. "Please... I just want this to end."

"I'm offering you a job, Julia. Why wouldn't you take this opportunity?"

She finally looked up in a powerless haze and met his eyes for a moment before begrudgingly giving a small nod of her head.

"Is that a yes, Julia? Speak up."

"Yes," she squeaked.

"Wonderful! I can't wait to continue our work together. Oh yes," he paused for a brief moment as he fished around in his bag, "I almost forgot to show you these." He held up the stack of folders Daniel had commandeered from the break in, and threw them onto the table. "I noticed someone had haphazardly shuffled through my things. I wasn't sure it was you until I found these in your apartment!" His voice was furious now, dripping with unhinged rage. Julia gaped at him helplessly and tried to form words to explain. "I... well..." she involuntarily trailed off with a feeble whimper.

He stood from the table in one fluid motion and moved towards her. "What do you have to say for yourself then?" Without waiting for a response, he violently grabbed the back of her chair, twisting it to face him so that they were now inches away from each other. "Don't you ever go through my things again!"

She lurched in a fruitless attempt to get away, but he instantaneously grabbed her neck and pushed her back onto the chair. He tightened his grip until she couldn't breathe.

"Please!" she gasped, as her body convulsed and tears incidentally flooded her eyes. Her vision started to blur as she strained for a gulp of air. After a few seconds of struggle, he released her with a final jolt and stepped back to stare at her with solemn revulsion. She fell from her chair at his discharge and inadvertently collapsed onto the floor. She vigorously rubbed her neck in unsteady relief. "You will learn to do as you're told, Julia," he said with a twisted, half-smile. "You'll learn or you'll be very, very sorry."

He clutched the folders and stuck them back in his bag before quickly turning to leave. "I'll see you in class, Miss Harrison."

"Please tell me you found something at Melissa's place," Julia whimpered softly as she rubbed her bruised neck. Daniel tenderly stroked her hair and tightly wrapped his arms around her. He had been stubbornly glued to her side for most of the evening after coming home and finding her in a state of devastating turmoil. She stammered to recount the story through a muddled sea of discomposure, but when she finally told him that Bishop had been inside their apartment, it took hours for Julia to talk him down from his unruly exasperation. At the sight of her swollen neck, he had incessantly paced up and down the hallway and mumbled to himself for a brief period of uncontrollable frenzy, trembling in his own maddening resentment. Finally he had calmed at the sight of her tears and resolutely settled beside her.

"Let's not talk about that right now," he insisted.

"I want to, though. I have to know."

"So... I'm assuming it didn't go well with Gabriella then?" he asked.

"Yeah, you could say that. She's crazy, Daniel."

"Elaborate, please."

"She thinks she's in love with Bishop. She kept saying that she *needed* him over and over. She's not going to help us. She just wants to protect him. Anyway, please tell me some good news. Did you find Melissa?"

"No," Daniel sighed, "I found the address on her letters, but she hasn't lived there in years."

"Fuck!" Julia shot with a frustrated pound of her fist. "You didn't find anything at all?"

"Well yeah... I found her boyfriend, Jared. He was the one who reported her missing three years ago. After she testified against Bishop, she disappeared. Jared thinks Bishop had something to do with it."

"What do you mean?"

"I mean that Bishop might have played a role in her disappearance. I'm not sure what that role would entail. That's the only speculation we have."

Julia reflected on this new information for a few moments as she absent-mindedly pulled at the ends of her hair. "Do you think Bishop was a suspect after she disappeared?"

"Probably not, honestly. It's not like it was a murder case. Jared said the police acted like he was crazy when he told them Bishop was involved."

"Do *you* think he could have murdered her?"

He gulped, "The thought crossed my mind, and I think that's a factor we need to consider."

"Why do you say that?"

"Because it's not too late to stop this now. I think we should both drop out and run away. He could have killed you today."

Tears welled up in her eyes. "Is that what you want? To just give up?"

"Julia, please be reasonable. If something happened to you... I just... I can't imagine life without you."

"I know, but I just... I can't give up. I can't let him win."

He huffed at her stubborn disposition. "Fine, but if we're staying, we have to elicit some form of outside help. Who do we know? Who can we trust? Surely there's someone."

"I don't know. Everyone just seems so enamored with him. It's like he can do no wrong."

"Have you ever heard anyone say *anything* bad about him?"

"Not really. Wait... actually," she paused for a moment in thought. "Professor Tryst once said something."

"Tryst? Why Tryst?"

"She pulled me aside when I started working as Bishop's research partner. She seemed worried about me."

"Why didn't you tell me this before?"

"Honestly, I forgot about it until now. I just thought she was being kind of weird, but she legitimately did seem concerned. Maybe she knows something about him that can help."

"What could she possibly have on him that we don't? Wouldn't she have already come forward?"

"I don't know. It's probably a lost cause, but at least it's an opening."

"Ok," Daniel sighed, "it's a start."

August 15, 2016
Gabriella

"I'd like to talk about your suicide attempt," Estes approached the subject with considerate discretion.

"What about it?" Gabriella shrugged as she took a sip of water and laid back in her padded chair.

"I want to know why you did it, and if you still want to now?"

"Why would I want to now?"

"Well, to begin, you're about to go on trial for first degree murder."

"I'm aware," she huffed impatiently. "We can talk about why I killed him, but I don't want to talk about my attempt."

"It's important Gabriella, why did you do it?"

"Because I was pregnant."

Gabriella decided to kill herself with unquestionable resolve the day she heard Anthony Bishop was dead. Every morning after receiving the news, she would adamantly promise herself that on this day, she would finally unearth some paltry semblance of a stable backbone and undergo her ultimate responsibility, a task which was growing more vital with each transient day. However, when it came time to initiate her own demise, panic would invariably overwhelm her frail intentions. She would line up the pills she had been hoarding for months, before intuitively remembering the harrowing baby steadily growing inside of her body. Her hesitations would perpetually overpower her objectives, and she would inevitably allow herself just one more fleeting day of life.

Despite this bothersome delay, one evening in late July, she felt her child vigorously kicking from inside her swollen belly, and sensed the clear urgency of her dwindling time. She was almost eight months pregnant and knew she had to complete the task before she went into labor or else risk bringing a tiny, unwelcomed piece of Anthony Bishop into the already merciless world. Allowing his baby to survive would be a sin too atrocious to stomach.

The thought of pregnancy crossed her mind mere weeks after her grievous night with Bishop in December, but in her denial, she ignored the earliest prominent signs. She credulously speculated that her physical warnings were imagined, and dismissed the idea as an added delusion. Roberto had habitually supplied her birth control while she was working, and after years of having a contraception served every morning with her breakfast, she had never really considered pregnancy as a legitimate possibility. However, after a few months of suppressing such groundless uncertainty, her body's abnormal symptoms refused to yield, and her new reality became an unavoidable truth.

Upon this grim realization, in an ambitious emotional blunder, she had somehow convinced herself that Bishop would rescue her from the misfortunes she was bound to endure. Financial security was a discernible factor in this developing fantasy, but her longings mostly stemmed from the recognition that her baby would undeniably need a father. Her life had crumbled in the absence of her parents, and she refused to force a child to live out a similarly tragic story. Even if she couldn't force Bishop to reciprocate her love, she had naively believed he would somehow come to embrace their relationship and devote himself to a child on his own terms.

However, when she disclosed the actuality of her situation to Bishop, he remained stubborn in his firm abandonment. Her pleas for his assistance went unanswered, which had initially spurred her need to incessantly stalk him until he conceded to his obligations. When he found her in his house, she had cried "I'm pregnant" over and over again, but he hadn't even acknowledged her galling proclamation. Before he threw her out, he grabbed her hair and stated with cold simplicity "You're a liar," as he kicked her down the front steps. After that incident, the thought of suicide had pervasively plagued her consciousness with unyielding strain. Finally, upon hearing of his death and accepting the dissolution of her senseless longings, she made the ultimate decision to end her life.

When the time finally came, she summoned the last of her broken will-power, went to her small kitchen table, and lined up the pills she had been me-ticulously stockpiling since winter. She poured herself a lavish glass of scotch, the same brand she drank with Bishop in his office, and began examining the array of medication. After reaching her awaited verdict, there was very little hesitation as she grabbed the pills by the handful and tenaciously stuck them into her mouth and obstinately swallowed. She downed her scotch at the end, and cringed as the remaining pills and alcohol slid down her throat with thick discomfort. The pain seemed entirely insignificant in the face of its temporary nature.

Her head began to spin as her consciousness slid into a series of discern-ible flashes. One moment she was at her table... then she was on the floor... in the next moment she was holding a phone... she thought she heard "hello?" on the other end and tried to respond... but in another flash she was lying on her bed. She melted into an obscure haze and gravely realized that she was now likely down to her last fading moments.

She speculated at the strangely ordinary nature of her dying thoughts. She had inadvertently assumed that she would somehow acquire some piece of untold wisdom upon facing her own mortality, but instead her brain only noticed trivial aspects of her familiar surroundings, like the way her blanket was uncomfortably scratchy against her back or the small cracks that envel-oped her crumbing ceiling. For a moment, she thought of her grandmother, but quickly dismissed the biting memory. She wouldn't waste her final mo-ments on that woman.

Who do I want to think of as I die? Gabriella solemnly considered as her vision began to blur. She thought of revisiting a beloved character from one of her treasured novels, but it felt like a striking mistake to dwell on a fictional cast in the last few moments of her worldly reality. She wanted to think of a real, audaciously strong person who had plainly impressed on her a sense of comfort in a tangible way. *Oh yes,* she thought at last with a soothing realiza-tion, *Julia.*

Gabriella had been enchanted with Julia's allure since their first meeting in Bishop's office. She was the authentic manifestation of every literary heroine Gabriella had idolized. Julia was Hermione Granger, Jane Eyre, Elizabeth Bennet, Arya Stark, and Katniss Everdeen all rolled into one mesmerizingly competent person. "Julia," she said out loud as her head began to swirl. Adrenaline was coursing through her veins now and she felt her body quietly giving into the drugs. "Julia, do you think I could have been like you? Maybe if everything was different?"

"Gabriella," she heard Julia's voice reply. It couldn't have been real, but the sound was a welcomed comfort to her failing senses. "Gabriella" the voice said again. It was so clear, she thought for a moment that she must already be dead.

"Julia," she said again as her eyes strained to flutter open one last time.

"I'm here, Gabriella," the voice replied, "Open your eyes! Look at me!"

"Tell Julia... you have to tell Julia-"

"Gabriella, wake up! It's me! I'm here with you. I'm Julia. You called me. I already called 9-11. Please, stay with me... Oh my god, are you pregnant?"

She felt Julia's touch on her stomach. Was she really here or was this some kind of cruel hallucination emanating from the pills? Julia couldn't be in her apartment. Surely she was dreaming.

"Tell Julia," she said, "that she's Aliena of Shiring. Just like *Pillars of the Earth*."

"You're not making sense, Gabriella! Stay with me!" she heard Julia cry.

"Yes... you're Aliena. You'll beat him in the end."

"Stop it! Please stay awake! You have to for your baby."

October 1, 2012
Melissa

Melissa was vanquished with startling grief as she abruptly left Brooktown after her testimony. She was a notoriously terrible liar, but convincing the ethics board of Bishop's innocent nature and the banality of their relationship proved to be a surprisingly easy task. Within minutes of taking the stand, nearly every juror had graciously welcomed the falsified account which painted her as an unstable, pathological stalker. In actuality, she found Bishop unbearably repulsive, but her story had been commandeered by the staggering weight of his sobering threats. Now he pulled her strings like a feeble puppet, shaping her account to mirror his own.

One of the professors from the disciplinary hearing, Kaitlyn Tryst, had followed her out of the building and sat with Melissa as she impatiently waited for her bus. The sincerity of Kaitlyn's concern wasn't necessarily dismissed, but the substance of their conversation was tragically too late to have any positive effect. Bishop had already infiltrated every aspect of her freedom, and Melissa's fatal decision was set in motion. She left their encounter without wavering in her course.

Melissa marveled at Brooktown's exquisitely charming campus, as her bus pulled away from the scene. Within moments of her departure, her phone rang with an unknown number flashing across the screen. Of course, she instinctively knew it was Bishop from one of his prepaid phones. That was the only way he cautiously contacted her, always careful not to leave any incriminating traces she could point to as proof of his continuous onslaught of incessant invasion. For the first time since deferring to his control, she clicked off her phone without answering and stuffed it into her bag with a smile. It felt surreal not to jump at his attention, and she was suddenly struck with a renewed sense of refreshing immunity.

It took nearly an hour of restless travel to get to Falls Church by bus, but she still had plenty of time to prepare before Jared would return from his job in the city. Her heart weighed heavy with the towering burden of leaving him, but her departure was a calculated decision, fixated on ensuring his safety. After she came forward with allegations against Bishop, he had shifted his sobering threats from her to Jared, promising to kill her precious boyfriend if her accusations continued. She agreed to back off and testify to his version of events, but even after the performance she gave at the hearing, she knew it wouldn't be enough to appease his unrelenting malice. He was losing patience with her noncompliance, and had become obsessed with control. Consequently, she had firmly resolved to remove herself completely from the equation.

She wrote Jared a deliberately uncomplicated note, and carefully placed it on their kitchen table. She unequivocally declared that she was leaving due to her crushing shame, an astounding hardship which was empathetically her burden to carry. She specifically indicated that he shouldn't expend any energy in trying and find her, and that all efforts would inevitably lead to his disappointment. She packed a bag, but only to make her story plausible. It felt strange to bundle and remove the few intimate belongings she owned for such trivial appearances. As she wadded up the last of her clothes and stuffed them into an old bag, the reality of her plan finally ripened and hardened into fact. The once treasured momentums in their apartment started to seem oddly unfamiliar and morbid. She could already feel herself detaching with a natural tranquility as she finished her preparations. With one final sweep through her former home, she gave an earnest nod and turned to leave without a hint of reluctance.

From Union Station, she bought a bus ticket to West Virginia. The journey would take most of the night, but the route would drop her in a fundamentally remote and desolate area. She needed to find a place that was entirely secluded and unexpected so that no one would find her body for a lengthy amount of time. The thought of her abandoned, mangled self brought her a pang of discomfort, but this was unquestionably the only viable solution to her dilemma. Bishop would undoubtedly go mad at the news of her disappearance and the sudden loss of his critical control. She mulled over his imminent anger with heartening satisfaction. He might have succeeded in severing her life from Jared's, but to Bishop's dismay, at least she wouldn't be owned.

Counting down the withering hours of her life felt strange and almost dreamlike as she settled into a peaceful haze. Her busride, which normally would have made her sick as they twisted up the crooked mountain paths, only left her with a harmonious feeling of gentle relief. The sun was slowly rising as they pulled into the edge of the uninhabited wooded area she had chosen for her departure, and she smiled at the dazzling colors which struck her as particularly beautiful on her final morning. When the the bus driver announced their arrival at her stop, she grabbed her backpack and rose with a genuine sense of soft abatement. She graciously thanked her driver for such a pleasant trip who tipped his hat as she disembarked.

She stood at the base of the mountain and surveyed her surroundings with a feeling that bordered on amusement. Immediately, she started her ascend to the top. For a moment, she imagined what Jared would say if he saw her in this scene, and immediately sought to dismiss the thought. Before Jared met her, he had always been content with a fruitful and steady life. This was the only way to return him to his natural state of simplicity.

After hours of hiking, she at last reached a sufficiently high and isolated cliff. She screamed a few times to ensure its seclusion, and nodded decidedly when she received no response. In a swift and natural motion, she threw her bag off the cliff and watched it spiral down, flying through the air before at last hitting the bottom with a satisfying burst. For one last moment, she glanced around and allowed herself a brief pause to admire everything beautiful about the site. In a final inescapable and thrilling feat, she hurled herself from the edge.

May 5, 2016
Daniel

"My God," Brian gasped in shock, "You look terrible, man."

"I've had a lot on my mind," Daniel replied miserably as he took off his glasses to rub his eyes. Brian joined Daniel who was sitting on the ground in the Brooktown common room and let his back rest against the wall. They were waiting for Bishop's class to begin.

"A lot on your mind, huh? You mean besides the breakup? What's going on?"

Daniel sighed. He desperately wanted to sit Brian down and pour out the heartbreaking events of the past several months in a generously long and tragic conversation. He longed to share his burden with someone on the outside, detached from the whirlwind with Julia, but he knew such a disclosure was impossibly too risky.

Tension with Bishop had steadily grown into a constant and rigid unease. Julia had been avoiding their meetings for two weeks now, regularly making excuses and deliberately canceling at the last minute. His impatience was blatantly intensifying with each of her evasions. When she broke off their meeting again last night, he didn't bother responding. His bitter silence was almost worse than extraneous resentment.

"Seriously Daniel, I'm worried about you," Brian continued, "I haven't seen you in months, you look awful, and I don't understand why you can't just talk about what's wrong. I know you're bummed about the breakup, but at some point you need to move on."

"I'm not even upset about that anymore, okay?" Daniel snapped with an impatient moan, immediately regretting his outburst.

"So what is it then?"

"I don't want to talk about it."

Brian shot him a hurtful, powerless glance. "Okay... I guess I'll let you work shit out then. I just... miss seeing you around."

Daniel didn't respond, but gave a slight, pathetic nod of understanding. He grabbed his bag from the floor and sulked into class in a miserable state of desolation. He was nearing his breaking point. He probably already would have gone crazy with resentment, but he had to stay strong for Julia. When Bishop entered the room and casually began lecture, Daniel turned red with anger and clinched his fist beneath the table. He was shaking with uncontrollable animosity and allowed his brain to fantasize about how satisfying it would feel to watch Bishop's demise, no matter how outlandish this delusion was to entertain.

"Miss Harrison," Bishop called to Julia's row, "what is the issue in this case?"

"Um... I think it's whether a landlord can discriminate based on religion when deciding whether to rent to a tenant," Julia answered softly.

"You think?" Bishop spat with a harsh roll of his eyes.

"No, I don't think-"

"-That's not how you make an argument, Miss Harrison. You're supposed to state your answer with confidence. Now, what did you think of the footnote on page 782?"

"The footnote?"

"Yes, the footnote. I assigned that page as part of the reading. If you didn't read it, you clearly didn't complete the assignment."

"I'm sorry, then I didn't complete the assignment," Julia replied, her voice cracking with embarrassment as her cheeks flushed red.

"What about the footnote on 824?"

"I didn't read any of the footnotes, sir, I apologize."

"You're a third year law student, Miss Harrison. Do you just think you can now ignore all of your responsibilities? I will fail third years if they are unprepared. I will give you a zero if you refuse to read the assigned pages!" He was yelling now, startling everyone in the room, including Julia who looked as though she might cry. "Your ineptitude is holding up my entire lecture, and

I'm tired of this smug attitude you seem to have adopted. Do you no longer feel it's necessary to do your work?

"I-I-I'll do my work from now on, I promise."

"Damn right you will, or you will not pass this class and you will not graduate."

Daniel stared at Julia as she nodded her head and turned her eyes to the floor. His sweet, confident, brilliant girlfriend looked suddenly devastated and utterly broken. A tear rolled down her cheek as she halfheartedly fumbled through her casebook to unearth some impossible answer to temporarily satisfy his anger.

"And I'll tell you something else," Bishop continued, "If you ever-"

"-Enough!" Daniel yelled as he pounded a fist on his desk. He was standing now, dumbfounded by his own brash reaction. The entire room eyed him with intensified fear and intrigue. Bishop studied him closely, clearly stunned by this unanticipated outburst. For the first time all semester, Daniel was suddenly confident and unwavering in what he needed to do. He dismissed the consequences of his fortuitous rebellion and gathered his things without explanation. He moved towards Julia's desk and plopped down in the seat beside her. Her jaw fell open in a nervous state of admiration and relief, as he grabbed her hand on top of the desk so that their professor could see the full extent of their reunion.

Bishop stared at them in seething disapproval, but Daniel only shrugged and turned to kiss Julia on the cheek. "I'm sorry for that interruption, Anthony... I mean Professor Bishop," Daniel said with a sarcastic smile. "Please, continue when you're ready."

Daniel waited for Brian later that evening at a dark bar on H Street. It was a quiet establishment with only a handful of decaying tables and a few dark booths in the corner. He sipped his beer with a complacent smile as he again remembered the satisfyingly helpless look on Bishop's face when he grabbed Julia's hand. All day he had been replaying the incident with an ecstatic sense of celebratory relief. Part of him was undeniably terrified, but he couldn't help but delight in Bishop's rapid and vigorous deflation of power.

"Hey," Brian smiled nervously as he collapsed into the bench across from Daniel, "What's going on?"

"Not too much, I guess."

"Really? That's shocking considering you've apparently completely lost your fucking mind."

"Why do you say that?"

"Oh, I don't know. You allegedly broke up with Julia, you stopped calling me back, you just picked a fight with your favorite professor, and now you're calling me and saying you desperately need a favor? What the hell has been going on? Are you and Julia back together then?"

"Ok... I see why you're confused."

"Yeah, no shit-"

"-But there are some things I can't explain right now. I just need you to trust me for just a little longer while I sort some stuff out.

Brian closed his eyes and gave his head a sharp nod. "What do you need?"

"Do you remember in college when I sat with you through your withdrawals?"

"I certainly haven't forgotten."

"Well you told me then that if I ever really needed you the way you needed me, you'd be there for me."

"Of course, Daniel. Just tell me what's going on."

"I need your help with something, but for now we have been keep it a secret from Julia."

"Ok... What is it? Why can't we tell Julia?"

"I want to throw her a surprise party... to celebrate our engagement."

June 20, 2016
Detective Weir

To: jharrison@brooktown.edu
From: abishop@brooktown.academics.edu

Julia,

After your outburst today in class, I really insist you come to my office today so we can work out exactly what happened. I trust that you'll take this matter seriously and respond before you damage our professional relationship. Please get back to me, immediately.

Sincerely,
Professor Bishop

- - - - - - - - - - - - - - - - - -

To: abishop@brooktown.academics.edu
From: jharrison@brooktown.edu

Dear Anthony,

No.

-Julia

"Was that their last correspondence?" Stilwell, Detective Weir's partner, asked as he scanned the email again with hardening suspicion.

"Yep." Weir Responded, "It was sent on the day her boyfriend made that scene in class. All of their emails just seem... off. Not incriminating, but strange. I can't put my finger on it."

"I'd say the nature of their relationship seems pretty questionable. Surely something was going on."

"She has an alibi," Weir stated with a small shrug as he looked over his own report for the tenth time that hour.

"It's too perfect though. You said so yourself. It's rehearsed."

Weir let out a long, helpless breath and shook his head in a disgruntled state of annoyance as Stillwell exited his office. It was true. The perfection of Julia's story, in itself, raised a series of suspicious red flags, but not a single person had voiced an imposing concern about her stainless character. Her reputation around Brooktown was almost as flawlessly crafted as her unblemished alibi, as she was reportedly one of the most well-liked students on campus. The picture of her relationship with Bishop was doubtlessly incomplete, but developing her story was like absurdly chasing a vapid shadow. Weir shuffled through the file again in a half-hearted attempt to grasp one more piece of the strangely calculated events of the day.

Bishop was last seen on the morning of May 15, casually walking into Brooktown Law. Six people had noticed him arriving and greeted him as he sauntered to his office on the third floor. There were no reports of unusual or noticeably abnormal behavior, but it was a memorable morning as the graduation ceremony was scheduled to take place later on campus within hours of his arrival.

In studying Bishop, Weir quickly learned that he was a creature of meticulous habit who customarily kept a stringent routine. He arrived at Brooktown each morning at seven, went to the third floor lounge to make coffee, and then always retired to his office for a couple hours of research before his morning lectures began. He kept a special coffee brew in the lounge, and would fill a thermos with a mix at the start each morning to sip on throughout the day. At some point in the 24-hour period before his murder, someone had added cyanide into Bishop's coffee grounds.

As Brooktown's star professor, Bishop was naturally scheduled to speak at the law school's graduation. Initially, no one thought much of his tardiness, but five minutes before the ceremony was scheduled to begin, Dean Herrera sent Professor Bodell to fetch their resident celebrity. In her statement to Weir, Herrera had said that she was "frustrated but not surprised" as Bishop often became consumed by his work and was notoriously late to significant events. At 10:04 a.m., Professor Bodell found Bishop dead in his office, just about the time that Julia Harrison was standing up to deliver her commencement speech.

The tricky thing about the murder was that over a hundred people at some point had entered the lounge during the 24-hour period before his death. It became crowded at various times throughout the day, but there were an insurmountable number of moments when someone could have slipped in alone and added the poison without being detected. Professors generally used the lounge in the morning to relax, students used the lounge in the afternoon for tutoring sessions and article reviews, and the janitorial staff had access to the lounge in the evening. Weir had tried to narrow down a list of suspects who had access, but ultimately his list was over a hundred people long and, without a security camera, it was impossible to firmly pin down anyone on the scene.

It was no secret that Bishop had a significant number of enemies. As a radical left-wing advocate, he habitually received various death threats throughout his life. However, in the months leading up to his death, Weir couldn't identify a single threat that looked particularly serious or unusually gruesome. Even if he had, someone certainly would have noticed an outsider entering Brooktown, loitering around the third floor lounge. It seemed far more likely that the culprit either worked or attended school on campus.

Weir learned quickly that Bishop didn't have any family or close friends. The only student who had any sort of relationship with him outside of his professional capacity was Julia Harrison, his former research assistant. Through his interviews with various staff and students, Weir learned how indisputably adored Julia was by her peers. It came as no surprise when she was voted by her classmates to speak at graduation. Some students did report a few minor changes in Julia's behavior in the months leading up to Bishop's death, but they felt extraordinarily mundane in the face of a murder charge. Allegedly there was an outburst in class between Bishop and Julia's boyfriend a week before their graduation, but nothing about the event was serious enough to adamantly pursue.

The day before Bishop's murder, her boyfriend had taken Julia on a trip to New York to celebrate the end of law school. They had carefully documented the day with a string of pictures on social media. That evening, he proposed in a crowded restaurant, an event which was witnessed by over thirty people and was immediately documented with a picture on Facebook showing the New York skyline in the background.

They returned to D.C. later that day, where Julia was welcomed with a surprise party, planned by Daniel and attended by over fifty of their fellow classmates. Apparently the party had been orchestrated with help from Daniel's former roommate, Brian. When Weir had asked Brian why he would go to such lengths to plan an elaborate event of this nature, Brian shrugged and stated, "You don't understand Julia. She's one of the most well-liked people I've ever met. I'd do anything for her, all of us would."

There were pictures of Julia and Daniel at the party all over social media, posted by dozens of various people. It had lasted nearly all night, and Brian explained that a handful of students were too intoxicated to drive so he offered them a place to sleep on his living room floor. Naturally, Julia and Daniel also chose to stay the night. It would have been nearly impossible for either one to have snuck out of the apartment without being seen by a single one of the other guests. There was even a picture of Daniel and Julia passed out on Brian's couch, holding each other after the party had ended.

The next morning, Julia woke up at Brian's house and encouraged a group of five friends to go get breakfast. She arrived at Brooktown with ten other people around nine and spent the next hour taking photos around campus with her friends in their caps and gowns before making their way to the ceremony. Julia started her speech right at ten. Meaning, not a single minute of her day before Bishop's death was unaccounted for.

Weir had requested a video of the speech, claiming it was an essential part of the investigation so that he could piece together the entire spectrum of the day. In reality though, he was just curious about Julia Harrison and wanted to see the way she conducted herself during the ceremony. He wasn't sure what he had been looking for. Strange behavior wouldn't have been out of the ordinary for young girl giving a speech to hundreds of people. On the video though, she had walked up to the podium calmly and smiled with an easy charm. She spoke without so much as a quiver in her voice. Something about her speech struck Weir as odd, but there wasn't a single tangible indication of her guilt. Ultimately Weir admitted that there was nothing alarming about her account of the day or Julia's behavior during the hours preceding Bishop's death.

The only part of the video that seemed at all abnormal was Daniel as he walked across the stage to receive his diploma. He was shaking so hard, he could barely reach for Dean Herrera's hand, and he even looked a little sick. However, from interviewing his classmates, Weir got the impression that Daniel was very shy and hated being in the spotlight, so this behavior wasn't necessarily remarkable for him either. Despite the fact that Weir couldn't find fault in either party's demeanor, he couldn't shake the feeling that somehow these two were involved in Bishop's death. Eventually, he did find minor evidence to corroborate his hunch.

When they searched Bishop's home, three sets of fingerprints had been found throughout his house. One of course had belonged to Bishop, but another belonged to Gabriella Rodriguez. They also found a drawer filled with suspicious letters from over fifty women, with correspondence from both Gabriella and Julia in the file. Each note that they found seemed more troubling than the next. Gabriella had clearly developed an unhealthy attachment to Bishop, while Julia's emails were cold and riddled with troubling undertones. The more he read the emails, the more he decided that Bishop's dark side went much deeper than his reputation insinuated.

Obviously, the letters he found most troubling were the ones from Melissa Antemie, who had been reported as a missing person several years earlier. Her case had never been seriously investigated, but her boyfriend at the time, Jared, had adamantly claimed Bishop had something to do with her disappearance. Months before she went missing, Melissa had come forward with allegations of inappropriate advances by Bishop, but his punishment for this had been minimum as the ethics committee assigned to his hearing had seemed eager to clear his name of all wrongdoing. The consequences were so insignificant that they hardly gave Bishop an obvious motive to cause her harm. However, the letters they found in Bishop's home suggested otherwise. She was apparently afraid.

One of the most worrisome aspects of the case, also uncovered in the search, was the fact that the last set of fingerprints they found in Bishop's home belonged to Julia. This was one of the few pieces of tangible evidence that indicated there was more to Julia and Bishop's past than she was letting on. However, Weir knew he didn't have enough to bring charges, he barely had enough to justify an interrogation. Besides, did he even want to? He couldn't decide if he suspected Julia because his gut was instinctively leading him in the right direction, or if he was making a grossly unfair judgment about her character. Perhaps her secretive nature about the case could be attributed to a darker side to her relationship with Bishop. It wouldn't have been the first time a professional in academia had engaged in inappropriate relations with a student, and all signs suggested that Bishop had a pattern of such behavior.

There was also the issue of Gabriella. She had a troubled past, and her letters indicated some level of obsession with Bishop. When Stilwell had gone to interview Gabriella, she suspiciously couldn't remember where she was the day of Bishop's murder. However, the thought of her involvement with his death felt undeniably out of place. She might have been obsessive, but she wasn't calculated.

"Weir," Stilwell blurted out as he entered his partner's office without waiting for an invitation, "we better get down to the hospital."

"Why?"

"Gabriella Rodriguez just tried to kill herself."

"What? When did this happen?"

"Looks like they brought her in a couple of hours ago," Stilwell answered an eager shakiness in his voice.

"Is she going to be ok?"

"They're not sure yet... but you'll never believe who found her. Julia Harrison."

June 21, 2016
Gabriella

Gabriella had been awake for about an hour, but she stubbornly kept her eyes tightly shut and sulked in the irritation of her disastrous failure. She lay awkwardly on an inflexible mattress, swaddled in the deep resentment of her defeat, and marveled at how her unwarranted existence now seemed devastating and misguided. When she finally did allow her eyes to flutter open, she was faced with a bleak and sterile hospital room which reminded her of the somber walls which outlined Roberto's house in Virginia. She curiously scanned her surroundings, and let her gaze to settle on Julia who was patiently watching her from the corner. She glanced around a little longer and saw a man hunched over in a small chair outside her room. Instinctively, she sensed he was waiting for her.

"Why is he out there?" Gabriella asked Julia, pointing to the man outside.

"He has to guard your room in case you get violent. They do it for every patient they think is a suicide risk, especially on the first day," Julia answered. "It's just a precaution to ensure you don't try and hurt yourself again."

"So it's only been a day," Gabriella shook her head. "How did you find me?"

"You called me," Julia answered with a curious look.

"Really?"

"You seriously don't remember?"

Gabriella shook her head.

"Yeah, I could barely hear you, but I knew something was wrong," Julia sighed and pointed to Gabriella's belly, still swollen and full with a child. "Is it Bishops?

"Yeah..."

"Oh Gabby, why didn't you tell me? This... complicates things."

"Complicates things how?"

"If I had known, I would have found you a lawyer a long time ago. They're going to think you killed him. This gives you a motive."

"Oh... well I won't be needing a lawyer."

"They don't have enough evidence to charge you with anything, but they'll probably want to get a statement. You really, really should have told them right away. Regardless though, this alone isn't enough to send you to prison. Is that why you tried to kill yourself? You thought you might be a suspect?"

"You don't understand," Gabriella shook her head. "That's not why I did it."

Julia let out a long, frustrated breath, "Why then, Gabriella? I just want to help you. We survived him together. How can you give up now?"

"I gave up a long time ago, Julia. I tried to kill myself because I didn't want to have his baby."

"You know, your child is going to be ok. I talked to your doctors earlier. You might have done some damage, and they're not sure of the extent, but for now it looks like your baby is going to make it. I don't think I was supposed to tell you that yet, but I'm tired of secrets between us."

Gabriella absent-mindedly rubbed her stomach and mulled over this news. "Why did they even tell you all that?"

Julia shrugged and revealed a tiny smile, "I can be persuasive."

Gabriella glanced out the window and let her eyes gloss over with tears. "My baby's name is Jude. I didn't kill him?"

"No, Gabriella. He's surprisingly healthy. He's a fighter, just like you."

"I want to talk to a doctor about him. I want to hear everything they know."

"I'll try to grab someone," Julia smiled as she turned to walk out the door. She returned within minutes with a triumphant look suddenly plastered on her face. "A doctor will come in soon to tell you this, but Jude is still in good condition. They're a little hesitant to burden you with the full extent because they're afraid you're not stable. If you ever want to see Jude and be his mother, you have to convince them that you're ok. You have to let them know that you'll never try to kill yourself again, and that you're capable of taking care of another human being."

"I understand," Gabriella nodded.

"Listen, I want to stay, but I have to go meet Daniel. I'll come visit you again tomorrow. Will you be ok?"

"Yes," she answered with a weak smile. Julia grabbed her hand and rubbed it gently. "You got engaged?" Gabriella asked as she felt a ring through Julia's grip.

"Yeah, last month before graduation. The timing was a little strange," Julia laughed, "but I guess in a way it was also perfect."

"I'm happy for you, Julia," Gabriella gave a genuine smile. "I really am. You deserve it all. You're so strong."

"Just like you," Julia leaned down to kiss her cheek. "I can't wait to meet your son."

"Hey Julia?"

"Yeah?" she glanced up with an innocent smile as she reached to grab her bag from the floor.

"Did you kill Anthony Bishop?"

Julia froze for a moment with a paralyzed look of honest confusion before returning to the side of Gabriella's bed. "No, Gabriella, I didn't kill him." Her voice was unwavering and confident in its resolution, leaving Gabriella a little disappointed in its definitiveness.

"Oh... well if you had, I just would have said thanks."

July 29, 2016
Gabriella

Gabriella was entering her tenth hour of unbearable labor. The pain was excruciating but the window for an epidural had long passed. "Keep pushing," echoed Doctor Tucker, trying to hide the fatigue seeping into his tone.

She sighed and laid back in exhaustion. "I can't do this," she pleaded, "I need a break."

"You're almost there," he urged again behind a hint of masked anxiety. She was smaller than most of his patients, and initially he had considered a C-section, but now the process of vaginal birth was far enough along that he wanted to remain on course. "I promise," he continued, "the worst is over. I see your baby's head."

Gabriella didn't believe him, but she obstinately kept pushing anyway. She was dripping in sweat which made the coarse hospital sheets stick to her back, and she felt strands of her knotted hair scratch against her neck when she tried to rest her head. Several nurses had wiped her forehead with a damp towel, but that did little to relieve the rest of her exhausted body which was now shaking in agony. In her misery, she inadvertently thought of Bishop and wanted to cry in his absence. Despite her "progress" in grasping the honest nature of their shallow relations, her volatile feelings for him still teetered between hostility and longing.

"One more big push," Tucker announced with a patient smile.

"I'm telling you I can't do it!" she moaned, "I'm out of energy. I feel dizzy."

"That's normal," he assured her, but he looked a little bothered by her grave reaction to the pain. "Tanya!" he snapped as he turned to a nurse behind him, "get her some water." Tanya quickly obeyed and held a straw out to the side of Gabriella's mouth. She greedily gulped it down, but only felt worse as the liquid slid down her throat and hit her knotted stomach like a rock. "Be careful," her doctor ordered. "If you drink too fast, you'll make it worse."

"How much longer? Please don't lie to me," Gabriella mumbled as she once again let herself collapse back onto the bed in her exhaustion. She shamelessly yearned to have Julia sitting beside her. Something about Julia's presence made Gabriella feel stronger.

"I promise we're minutes away if you keep pushing," he responded with a restored level of sincerity. She could sense this answer was at least half genuine, which gave her enough motivation to push a little longer. She had denied the inevitable arrival of this moment for most of her pregnancy, and had never fully reflected on the amount of pain she would experience during labor. Unlike most mothers who underwent months of physical and emotional preparation, she had barely considered the complexities of the birthing process. She had spent the majority of her pregnancy planning her suicide rather than her labor.

When her water finally did break, she was still in the psychiatric ward of the hospital, undergoing painstaking monitoring subsequent to her suicide attempt. Instead of reporting the pain immediately, she had absentmindedly dialed Bishop's number to hear his distant voice on his answering machine.

After several hours of rising agony, the reality of Jude's arrival sunk in. At first she contemplated trying to escape from the hospital to give birth back at her apartment. However, when the waves of pain continued to grow steadily worse, she unwittingly let out a groan in front of the nurse on duty who immediately called for a doctor. By the time they transferred her to the maternity ward, Doctor Tucker told her that an epidural was out of the realm of possibilities. The fear of fatal complications crept into her mind as the strain on her belly steadily increased. However, as it turns out, the amount of excruciating pain she was experiencing was at least somewhat normal according to the medical experts around her, it was just far more terrible than she had anticipated.

"One more!" Tucker urged, "Gabriella you have to keep going."

She screamed and grabbed the bed to push harder, suddenly spinning with a renewed sense of determination. At last, she heard a baby cry and felt a solid wave of both emotional and physical relief. She had the urge to fall asleep immediately, but Tanya quickly placed the child in Gabriella's arms. She was suddenly overwhelmed with an unexpected feeling of tranquility and began to cry tears of joy.

"He's perfect," Tanya smiled, "worth the pain?"

"I'm still deciding," Gabriella joked, but she then knew that he would have been worth even more. For a brief moment the memory of his conception infiltrated her mind in a flash, but she firmly pushed the image out of her mind. "Yes," she said as she cradled her baby, "it was all worth it for you."

"You did a good job," Tucker smiled, "he's a beautiful boy."

"I have the birth certificate ready," Tanya smiled. "What's the baby's name?"

"Jude," Gabriella said confidently, "Jude Bishop."

"Who's the father?" Tanya asked.

"That doesn't matter," Gabriella answered with a dismissive wave of her hand. However, as soon as the words escaped her mouth, she suddenly felt as though they were a lie. Again, the memory of Jude's conception snapped into her brain, and this time she let it linger and roll around in her mind. After a moment of allowing her emotions to swelter, she again looked at her perfect baby. This time she met the figure she was holding with a wave of rage.

Tanya nodded and carefully took Jude from Gabriella's arms. "What are you doing?" Gabriella gasped in a sudden panic.

Tanya shot a nervous glance at Doctor Tucker who calmly sat at the edge of her bed. "You've done great this past month, but we have to make sure you're completely ready before we allow you to keep him."

Tears immediately sprang to Gabriella's eyes. "Do you have children?" She asked. Doctor Tucker nodded and let her continue. "Listen, I know I'm not in a good place, but I'm still his mother. I desperately need this." After a few moments of contemplation, he nodded to Tanya, who promptly went to fetch Jude from the corner. Gabriella reached out and took the baby in her arms, freely allowing a stream of tears to roll down her sweaty cheeks.

"I know," Tucker replied, "I felt that way when I first held mine too."

A few minutes passed before Tanya gently informed Gabriella that she had to give back the baby so they could both get some sleep. "Please don't," Gabriella cried, "Just let me hold him a little while longer. I just want a few more minutes. Can I just have some alone with him?"

Doctor Tucker hesitated but finally gave a small, nervous nod. "I'll let you have just a few minutes, but then he has to go to the nursery. It's not just for your sake. He was a little early and still needs some extra care."

"I just need a minute," Gabriella answered as Tanya and Doctor Tucker slowly turned to leave.

She stared at Jude and cried harder in the face of her overwhelming failure. She couldn't believe she had allowed him to come into this world, this cruel and cold world. This poor, perfect baby had no idea of the painful life that lay ahead. She instinctively understood how unfit she was as a mother.

Again, she looked down at her baby- her poor, perfect baby- and for the first time saw that his eyes were the same color as Bishop's. She froze at the sight as anger pulsed through her body. Those eyes, the same color as the ones who had laughed at her as she cried and screamed. The same ones that were filled with fury when he found her in his bed and called her a whore. The eyes of the man who had given her a chance at a new life, only to ruin it. She didn't love Bishop, she hated him. She understood that now, and suddenly she was the one who began to laugh uncontrollably.

She continued laughing as she reached for her pillow and held it over Jude. She continued laughing as the nurse came in and screamed, desperately grabbing the baby from her and feeling for a pulse. She continued laughing until a team rushed in and held her to the bed. She laughed as they poured sedative into her veins and as she slowly drifted into a state of unconsciousness.

When she woke, she was groggy and weak. She didn't exactly remember what happened, but a strange feeling of satisfaction still lingered in her memory. She tried to sit up and realized she had been tied to her bed. She looked outside and saw that there was a different man guarding her now, a police officer. Within minutes a second officer also walked up and the first stood to leave.

"Sorry I'm late," the second officer said. "I know you've been on this shift a long time."

"It's fine, she's just been sleeping."

"I don't even know the assignment. Is she dangerous?"

"Very, but we have to wait until she's a little stronger before we can actually arrest her."

"What is she being charged with?"

"The murder of Jude Bishop, her baby."

July 29, 2016
Julia

Weir called Julia to tell her about the death of Gabriella's son. Stunned and dizzy with guilt, Julia cried helplessly on the other end of the line. "Where is she?"

"In advanced psychiatric care," Weir answered briskly.

"I can't believe she did that. It doesn't make any sense."

"Really? I thought you would understand more than anyone why she went crazy after her issues with Bishop."

"What's that supposed to mean?" Julia asked indignantly.

"Why do you think she called you when she tried to kill herself?" Weir responded, abruptly changing the subject with a unsophisticated fumbling of his words.

"I don't think she had anyone else to call."

"Your number was written down on a piece of paper on her kitchen table. It looks like your handwriting. Did you ever go visit her?"

"Am I being interrogated?"

"Not right now, but I think it's time for you to come down again to the station and discuss a couple of gaps in this case."

"I didn't do anything wrong," Julia pleaded, her heart sinking in an anxious frenzy.

"I still think it's a good idea for you to come down."

"Ok," she finally agreed, "but I'm bringing a lawyer."

"I would expect nothing less." At that, he let out a quick huff of breath, and bitterly hung up the phone without a goodbye.

Within moments of their interaction, Julia called Professor Tryst. "Hello?" Kaitlyn answered.

"Gabriella Rodriguez apparently smothered her own baby," Julia said in a panic. "She was babbling about killing the last piece of Bishop when they found her. I think Detective Weir believes Gabriella and I are both somehow involved in Bishop's murder. Gabriella has a motive now: Bishop's scorned ex-lover who he abandoned during pregnancy, and somehow they've connected her to me!"

"Slow down," Kaitlyn assured her, "you're innocent."

"I know that, but this doesn't look good! I need an attorney. I need a really, really good criminal defense attorney to get me out of this."

"I'll take care of that," Tryst announced coolly. "Just tell me when and where he needs to meet you."

Julia hung up the phone and headed to her bedroom where Daniel was lying on their bed. She fell into the space beside him and instinctively grabbed for his hand.

"I heard what you were saying on the phone," he said gently. "You're not going to jail, Julia. We're innocent."

"I'm still so scared though. This doesn't look good. There's a lot connecting me to him... and to Gabriella for that matter who has apparently completely gone mad."

"All you have to do is tell the truth... well maybe leave out a few details, but we have an alibi. They can't charge us."

"I still can't believe she killed Bishop."

"We don't know that for sure."

"You don't think it's suspicious that right after I told her about this, Bishop winds up dead? She even made sure we had a perfect alibi." Julia shook her head in disbelief.

"Of course it's suspicious, but we still don't know for sure. I personally don't want to know, ever."

"So you don't think we should ever ask her?"

"Honestly Julia, I think some things are better left unsaid."

"Do you feel guilty?"

"I'm not sure," Daniel sighed. "It's not like we had any idea what Professor Tryst was planning."

"I guess you're right. I just wish we had helped Gabriella too."

APRIL 29, 2016
Kaitlyn

Kaitlyn's office suited her personality. It was cold and bare, with nothing on the walls but a diploma and a single picture of her sister. She had no children, which most didn't find particularly shocking; she was brilliant, but nothing about her signaled a strong maternal instinct. Julia Harrison now sat in front of her with a look of exhaustion and defeat.

"Good afternoon Julia," Kaitlyn began, "what can I do for you?"

"I don't really know how to begin, but I know I need help. Earlier in the year, you told me you were afraid for me to work with Bishop. You said if I had problems to come to you, and that's what I'm here for." After a long deep sigh, Julia plunged into the story, disclosing every horrible detail she had kept tucked away for months.

Kaitlyn let out a long breath, "I've been expecting this."

"There's no way you knew the full extent of it," Julia shook her head.

"That's true, but I also probably know a few stories you're not aware of either."

"So it has happened before?"

"I've never been able to prove it, but yes. I've tried to get him fired, but he's tenured and very well-respected. I need definitive proof. I'm assuming you don't have proof?"

"Why do you say that?"

"You wouldn't be here if you did, and I don't just mean here in my office. If you had proof, I would be worried about your safety. I was on the disciplinary board after Melissa Antemie came forward. I watched her testify in front of Bishop. I believed her, but I could also see that there was something much darker in her testimony. I tried to tell her this, but she disappeared the moment I felt like we were reaching a breakthrough."

"Do you know what happened to her?"

Kaitlyn sighed, "Sadly, no. I spoke to her the day before she was reported missing. She was terrified."

"We talked to her boyfriend. He thinks Bishop had something to do with it."

"I assumed it was something like that," Kaitlyn nodded calmly.

Julia looked shocked at Kaitlyn's lack of surprise. She could see it made Julia feel a little uneasy. "Has anyone else apart from you expressed concern about him?" Julia asked.

Kaitlyn nodded, "You'd be surprised how many people actually hate him below the surface, Julia. He has a lot of enemies, and very few close friends. In fact, I don't know anyone he's close to. However, no one has ever come forward with anything particularly incriminating."

"So what are our options?"

"You could drop out and move away," Kaitlyn suggested, "but that doesn't exactly solve the problem. You would give up your law degree, he would likely find you eventually, and he would go on doing this to his next victim."

During her time as head of Brooktown's criminal justice clinic, one case always stood out to her. A young girl named Madison, who had been brutally beaten over the course of several months. When she reached out to the Brooktown clinic, Kaitlyn immediately agreed to take her case. However, when her boyfriend Jayden found out about her hiring a lawyer, he immediately found her and beat her again until she died of internal trauma.

In the weeks after Madison's death, the only thing that brought Kaitlyn comfort was knowing that Jayden had been arrested and charged with the murder of her former client. If everything else in this world was chaos, at least Kaitlyn could rely on the justice system to run its course and ensure that Jayden would be sent away for life. She followed the case closely, checking in with the prosecutor about once a week and offering her expertise when she had something significant to contribute to the setup of the case. Weeks before the start of Jayden's trial, the head prosecutor of the case, Stephen Goldberg, called her into his office to discuss their progress. Kaitlyn gathered the notes she had been meticulously keeping about the trial strategy and went to meet him, almost giddy with anticipation for the prosecution to begin.

"Here's what I'm thinking," Kaitlyn announced as she swung open the door of his office and immediately pulled out her notes, "the witness list is lacking-"

"-I'm going to cut you off for just a moment, Kait," Goldberg interjected. "I have something to tell you that I think is a good decision. I'm hoping you'll see it that way too."

"Ok..."

"We've decided to offer him a plea."

Kait stared at him in disbelief. "A-a *plea*?" she asked slowly without attempting to hide the disgust in her voice.

"Now, I know you were looking forward to a trial, and this might not be your ideal outcome, but-"

"-Not my ideal outcome? Are you kidding me?"

"Kaitlyn, you know as well as I do how hard a conviction is going to be in this case."

"What are you talking about? It's a slam dunk!"

"We really don't know that. Our only witness passed away."

Kaitlyn let out a small moan of frustration, "What are the terms of the plea? Manslaughter?"

Goldberg shook his head. "Assault."

"What? He'll never even serve time! At most he'll get one year of probation!"

"I'm sorry, Kaitlyn. My hands are tied."

Any shred of dignity Kaitlyn saw in the legal system was squashed that day. Although externally she rarely let it show, all of her hope of finding justice for victims like Madison had been thoroughly extinguished by the experience.

"I could come forward. If you backed me up, wouldn't that be enough?" Julia asked.

"Honestly, probably not. I've seen cases like this before, they never end well," Kaitlyn took a deep breath. "Also you're overlooking something very important."

"You think he'll ruin both of us."

"He does have a lot of power. A lot of people would believe him. Even if both of us came forward, things would get messy. What we need is proof."

"How do I get that?"

"We have to find a way to provoke him, and document his reaction."

Julia let out a long, nervous breath, "I'm afraid if I provoke him, he's going to hurt me though. He's already furious with me. I've been avoiding him for several weeks now."

"Can you do it from afar? We have to make him angry enough to ensure that he'll react, but also make sure you're safe."

"He does check my facebook. That's how he keeps tabs on what I'm doing. I could post something that I think would provoke a reaction, but I don't know how often he goes online. It might fall on deaf ears."

Kaitlyn sat back and contemplated their situation for a couple minutes until confidently looking at Julia with a smile. "I know what we have to do now. First, like you said, we need to make him mad. The first step should be in person though. Make it obvious that you and Daniel have gotten back together somehow. Throw it in front of his face, preferably in some setting like his classroom where he can't react without everyone noticing. If you do something like that, he's more likely to compulsively check your facebook."

"Ok... then what?"

"Next, you'll go somewhere safe, New York City seems appropriate. You'll do something to make him angry, *really* angry, and post about it over and over again on your facebook."

"What should I do?"

"I would tell Daniel to propose."

Julia nodded, "that's pretty brilliant, actually. It would certainly make him mad."

"You'll do it the day before graduation. After that, come back and have a party with a multitude of your friends to celebrate. Make sure it's planned, have someone like that vile friend Daniel seems to love so much, Brian, throw it for you. Tell him it's a surprise so no one talks about it before, just to make sure Bishop doesn't know where you'll be. The most important thing is that you're not alone. Once this starts, I'm afraid Bishop will try and hurt you. Promise me you won't be alone for a second, not even a single moment after you start posting pictures of your trip."

"I promise."

"You'll ask to speak to him in his office after the ceremony. I'll bring Dean Herrera. We'll be waiting outside. The moment he starts to act inappropriate, we'll catch him in the act."

"You think that will work? I've tried to record him before. He's smart, he'll know what we're doing."

"I think if you make him mad enough, he won't be able to help himself. The most important thing is that you leave the day before, document absolutely everything, and make sure you're never alone. I'll take care of the rest."

July 30, 2016
Roth

When Roth walked into the station, Kaitlyn and Julia were sitting outside Detective Weir's office. After so many years of practicing criminal law Roth rarely got intimidated by interrogations, but today's meeting held exceptionally high stakes.

"Hello Julia," he smiled. "I've heard a great deal about you. Like I discussed with Kaitlyn, I'll be taking your case pro-bono."

Julia shook her head in confusion, "Why would you do that?"

"Your professor and I are old friends. She actually used to work with me before she abandoned the trade for academia. She said you might need a good defense attorney."

Julia opened her mouth as if to ask another question, but before she could speak, Detective Weir walked out and eyed the three with a suspicious glare. "Who is this?" He asked in frustration, pointing to Roth.

"Her lawyer," Kaitlyn responded cooly.

"I thought you were her lawyer?"

"I haven't practiced in years, so I thought I'd call my old friend, David Roth. You might have heard of him, he's pretty well-known in the world of criminal law."

"Did you really think that was necessary?"

Kaitlyn shrugged, "I think a good defense attorney is always a good idea even when it's not necessary."

"It's nice to meet you," Weir stated in a cold, brash voice. "Professor Tryst, you can wait outside then. The two of you should follow me," he motioned for Julia and Roth to come forward, and led them to a small interrogation room near the back of station.

"I'm going to be straight with you Julia," Weir said at last after the three had settled into uncomfortable seats in a small, sterile room. "We found three sets of fingerprints in Bishop's home- they belonged to Bishop, Gabriella Rodriguez, and you."

"I was his research assistant," Julia answered with minor hesitation. "A couple of times he asked me to drop off my work at his home.."

"That would explain the fingerprints... but not the nature of your emails."

"What exactly are you asking my client?" Roth interjected.

"I'm asking her about the true nature of their relationship?" Weir stated almost sarcastically. "I think that's a fair enough question."

"Go ahead and answer, Julia," Roth nodded.

"Ok," Julia said, "one night Bishop and I got into a fight while I was dropping off my research. He pushed me against the wall."

"Why didn't you report it?" Weir replied.

"I was afraid of him. At the time he was being very controlling, and I feared if I came forward he would get violent. Plus, I didn't think anyone would believe me. Surely you understand how I was intimidated."

"What do you mean *controlling*?" Weir asked with a genuine flicker of concern.

"It never got too bad, but a couple of times I thought he was hitting on me. Eventually it escalated, and when I confronted him in his home, he attacked me. After that, he backed off though. That's really the end of the story."

"Were you angry with him?"

"Don't answer that," Roth said sternly.

"Why can't she answer that?" Weir threw up his hands.

Roth stared at him without responding. "Fine," Weir continued after a moment, "Julia, when you say Bishop was hitting on you, did the two of you ever engage in inappropriate relations?"

"No," Julia sighed, "But he tried."

"What do you mean?"

"Nothing ever happened, but he made suggestions."

"How... how long did this go on? Did you tell anyone?"

"I told my fiancé- my boyfriend at the time. We tried to find a way to stop him, but there were no good options. I came very close to dropping out."

"But lucky for you, Bishop disappeared, right?"

"Don't answer that," Roth snapped again.

"Fine," Weir let out another frustrated sigh. "I want to know more about the trip to New York you took before graduation."

"Yes," Julia smiled, "that was Daniel's idea. He's wonderful, isn't he? That was the weekend he proposed."

"Sure, but why did you go the day before?"

"Graduation felt like a new phase in life, he said he didn't want to spend a single day of that new phase without promising to marry me. Ask him, I'm sure he'll say the same thing."

"Yes, I'm sure he will," Weir remarked with a bitter smile.

"Detective Weir," Roth interrupted, "do you have a single piece of evidence that connects my client to this crime?"

"I can't disclose that either way."

"Well, considering my client is here voluntarily, I will assume you don't have enough for an arrest or a charge. You don't even have a warrant to search her home- which I'm certain would be a fruitless effort even if you did. You're grasping at straws instead of trying to find the true murderer. This poor girl is a victim of an older superior making inappropriate passes and physically attacking her in his home. Now, as Miss Harrison's attorney, I have to say that I feel your entire investigation is completely void of all merit. If you find any evidence that directly connects her to the crime, we can arrange a chat then. In the meantime, I'm sure you can agree that this girl has been through enough and deserves a little peace."

Weir leaned back in his chair and closed his eyes. He was silent for a long time, before he finally nodded. "You can go Julia, I appreciate your cooperation."

Julia was shaking as they exited the police station. "You did well," Roth told her in a way that felt almost paternal.

"I didn't kill him," she responded and scanned his face to gauge his belief.

"I believe you," he said sincerely and put a hand on her shoulder. He looked up to see a young man around her age approaching them cautiously.

"That's my fiancé," Julia nodded in his direction. "I'm sure he wants to take me home."

"Go home then," Roth smiled. "It's over, Julia. I know how these investigations go. If he gives you any more trouble, you can call me, but I guarantee he sees this as a dead end."

"I don't know how to thank you," she mumbled as she let her head hang to the floor.

"No need." Roth stated as Daniel approached her and gently wrapped an arm around Julia's waist. After a brief introduction between the two men, Daniel thanked Roth for everything and promised to make sure Julia got home and found a way to relax. After they walked away, Roth turned to leave and saw Kaitlyn sitting in her car across the lot. She swiftly motioned for him to join. As he got in and they drove off together, for a while they sat in eerily calm silence.

"Cyanide, huh?" Roth finally said at last, stroking his beard in contemplation.

Kaitlyn shot him a tired, irritated glance. "What about it?"

"Nothing," he shrugged with false innocence. "I just think it's an odd coincidence."

"Again, I'm sure I don't know what you mean."

"Almost two decades ago you defended John Rowland, who happened to pull off the almost-perfect murder. I'm not sure if you remember, but he used cyanide when he allegedly killed Gregory Jansen."

"I haven't forgotten." For a moment they returned to a state of silence before Kaitlyn finally continued. "Bishop would have killed her, David," she finally said softly. "There was no other way to stop him. She would have disappeared before she even got the chance to testify."

Roth nodded patiently. "I've done this work a long time now, Kait. I've seen cold-blooded killers and those who act in defense of others. I know the difference between the two... If someone in your position killed Anthony Bishop, I'd say they were in the latter category."

"I don't feel sorry for him," she said at last.

"Neither do I. I can't say you did the right thing, but I can say that I don't begrudge you," he said as she flashed a weak smile. He continued, "Can I ask you something though? Everyone knew who he was, but no one knew him personally. What was he really like? Who was Anthony Bishop?"

Kaitlyn thought about this for a long time, "I have no idea."

A Note From the Author

The few people who I let read this book before publication all asked me if Julia was based on my own personality. I can say completely and unequivocally, no. Although I do see glimpses of myself in the character, both good and bad, Julia and I drastically differ. Ironically, she is also possibly my least favorite imagined character, which I guess says a lot about the complications of my own personal perception.

A far more difficult question for me to answer is if Anthony Bishop is based off of a real set of incidences or a specific authority figure. The truth is that I do see bits of Bishop's personality in certain men from my past, always those who have been my superiors. I've obviously never been a suspect in a murder case or experienced the depths of harassment my fictional characters endured, but like most professional women I have had issues with multiple male bosses and a few inappropriate moments with former educators.

If Bishop sheds light on any dark part of society, I hope it's that the feelings of helplessness sexual harassment instills go beyond what I suspect most of my harassers imagined. What might seem like an innocent comment or invitation, could spiral into something much darker if said to a person who is not in a position of power.

Finally, I want to acknowledge the fact that a blatant theme in my book is that the legal system has inherent flaws, particularly for women and especially women of color. Although Julia faced a series of injustices with no legitimate legal recourse, Gabriella's journey obviously took a much harsher turn. This was intentional. I do not owe my readers a happy ending for Gabriella when so many victims of the justice system do not get one for themselves. I based this decision on the realities I have seen during my time in the legal profession, and especially as an immigration attorney where I work with a population I feel is most vulnerable to falling through the cracks of justice.

All that is to say that ultimately I do respect my profession, my colleagues, and the vast majority of superiors I have had in the past. I owe my mentors in this field not only my success in the legal profession, but also the very contents of this book.

ACKNOWLEDGEMENTS

I have to first say a very special thank you to my best friend and first editor, Michelle. You were the first person to read this book and tell me it would be published someday. You are the other half of my brain.

I want to thank Monte, Lauren, and Tate Slatton. The three of you mean the world to me. Always remember there was nothing worth sharing like the love that let us share our name.

To Austin, you are the love of my life. I cannot thank you enough for how you stood by me during the tumultuous writing process and always believed in me when I didn't believe in myself.

To my family, no matter where I go or what I do, my heart is always in Texas with you. A special thanks to my grandparents who I'm sure will place this book on their mantelpiece and speak of its brilliance to all who enter their home.

To my former classmates at Pepperdine Law, Section B. Please read this book while getting "nice and amiable" with a glass of wine. Total world domination, right?

To my best friends, many of whom I used for names of my characters, I deeply appreciate how supportive you have been of my writing. I love you all like family.

To all of my amazing teachers, professors, and mentors. All of my successes are yours as well.

To every victim of sexual harassment, I wrote this book for you. I hope you find peace and empowerment. If that doesn't work, I highly recommend writing a murder mystery novel, I've personally found it to be quite cathartic.

55013136R00135

Made in the USA
San Bernardino, CA
27 October 2017